AUTHOR	CLASS	M
BANNISTER, D	F	G
TITLE Hard walls of ego	No	
	02438411	

Lancashire County Council

This book should be returned on or before the latest date shown above to the library from which it was borrowed.
LIBRARY HEADQUARTERS
143, CORPORATION ST. PRESTON PR1 2TB

HARD WALLS OF EGO

Love is something far more than desire for sexual intercourse; it is the principal means of escape from the loneliness which afflicts most men and women throughout the greater part of their lives. There is a deep-seated fear, in most people, of the cold world and the possible cruelty of the herd; there is a longing for affection, which is often concealed by roughness, boorishness or a bullying manner in men, and by nagging and scolding in women. Passionate mutual love while it lasts puts an end to this feeling; it breaks down the hard walls of the ego . . .

Marriage and Morals
Bertrand Russell

HARD WALLS OF EGO

Don Bannister

Secker & Warburg
London

To Sharon Ruth Jackson
without walls

The quotation from *Marriage and Morals* by Bertrand Russell is
reproduced by kind permission of Unwin Hyman Ltd.

First published in England 1987 by
Martin Secker & Warburg Limited
54 Poland Street, London W1V 3DF

British Library Cataloguing in Publication Data
Bannister, Don
  Hard walls of ego.
  I. Title
  823'.914[F]   PR6052.A495

  ISBN 0 436 03277 5

Set in 11/12pt Linotron Ehrhardt by
Hewer Text Composition Services, Edinburgh
Printed and bound in Great Britain by
Billing & Sons Ltd, Worcester

The road dipped and ended abruptly, the tarmac fading into an unkempt cinder path. As Joe slouched down the slope to the little wooden bridge that spanned the wet ditch at the bottom, he gazed up at the terrace of six houses jutting out on the spur of the hill and thought again that it all looked like a half-finished stage set or some sort of abandoned corporation enterprise: a road that gave up short of an isolated row of houses, only two of them lived in, no bus service, no shop, no street lamps, no road signs, one scruffy hawthorn, silhouetted on the skyline, marking the end of the terrace.

Lengthening his stride, he began to climb up the stony hillside, wondering what the plan had been, back at the turn of the century, when the houses were built. There were no farms nearby, no workplaces nearer than Scarby, three miles away. Maybe the vision had been of a big community, complete in itself, houses, shops, pub, factories, village hall, maybe a quarry. Something new to put on the map. Then they built a tiny bit of an alley and the idea died, they never even carried the road all the way to the houses. So it stood there being called Hannover Street. Now there was a daft name. Breathing heavily up the last few yards, he turned to his customary game of thinking up new titles for the terrace. Should have called it *Tinpot Street. Nowt Much Lane. Back of Beyond Street. Toddy Little Avenue*, that would suit it. Again he reflected that the rent must be about the cheapest in the land and the council had never even tried to sell these gaunt brick hulks to their tenants. Strange they had run electricity out to them. That must have been costly, with only tiny returns.

He nodded as he passed his neighbour's front window and Nelly Hurst, who was sewing in the last of the evening light, waved a hand at him. He kicked open the weak catch on his front door and inevitably thought that at least you never had the bother of locking up in Hannover Street. It would be a real hungry burglar who came all the way out here to rob him or Nelly and Albert Hurst. Hanging his raincoat on one of the hooks at the bottom of the stairs, he shuffled sideways through the brightly coloured bead curtains, left there by some previous tenant, into the living room. He congratulated himself on having troubled to lay the fire before he left home that morning, lit it, draped his jacket across the back of an armchair and went through into the kitchen to fill and switch on his electric kettle. Out in the back yard, he shivered in the cool damp air of the early spring evening. Shuffling into the gloom of the coalhouse he swore as he stumbled against the wheelbarrow he used to fetch the sacks the coal merchants left for him, up on the road. He half-filled a bucket with slack, topped it with big lumps and carried it back into the house.

He made his mug of tea and stood at the kitchen window, watching thin, smoky spirals of rain cloud moving in across the valley. Soon the first drops splattered against the window followed by drumming on the slates and hissing and gurgling as water poured down eaves and gutters. He said aloud 'Good night to be indoors' and remembered an argument he used to have with his mother when he was a child. When it rained heavily she used to say 'God help sailors on a night like this' and he used to dispute with her and say it was worse for tramps because they were out in the open and sailors could shelter inside their ships. He recalled lying in bed at night, trying to imagine what it was like to be a tramp, sleeping under a hedge, with rain soaking into you.

He pondered and decided that the meal he had eaten at the cafe in Scarby had not been enough. He made himself a thick round of bread and cheese, larding it with piccalilli. Munching it as he went upstairs, he stared at the two one-gallon jars of home-made wine in the airing cupboard. He concluded that fermentation was finished and brought them down to the kitchen,

2

one tucked under each arm, the remains of the sandwich clenched between his teeth. He switched on the light, poured himself a second mug of tea, finished the sandwich and set to work sterilising bottles and decanting the wine into them.

In an hour he had fourteen bottles of assorted sizes stored in the wire racks that hung from hooks on the kitchen wall, his gallon jars were rinsed and put away, the kitchen and living room cleaned and tidied. Settling a lump of coal onto the fire and banking it with slack, he searched for his *Radio Times* and *TV Times*, failed to find them and remembered that he had lent them to his neighbours. He listened to the rain swishing down in the darkness outside, decided against going next door and settled for switching from channel to channel on his television set. After a few minutes he switched the set off and sprawled in his armchair, legs thrust out in front of him, contemplating the fire, till he fell asleep.

A crack of thunder woke him and he stood, stretched and yawned, put more coal on the fire and shuffled to the window to watch the sheet lightning playing brilliantly across the horizon. Restlessly, he prowled around the room, straightening pictures, winding the mantelpiece clock, fetching water for a dusty vine that straggled out of a pot on the window sill. He studied the titles of the books on the shelf above the settee, took down an old copy of *Whitaker's Almanack* and found the turned corner of the page that marked where he had got to on his last reading.

Beginning with centenaries falling due in nineteen-seventy-three, he moved on to periods of British architecture, wondering how they could be so precisely dated, tried to memorise nautical measures and was pleased to learn that the nautical mile was the rounded length of a minute of arc of a great circle of the earth and not the arbitrary whim of sailormen spurning the land mile. He noted bank holidays across the world, skimmed through the national values of global trade but studied carefully different items imported and exported by Great Britain. He spent a little time on car production figures and wondered why a page of conversion tables for weights and measures came in the middle of information about activity levels at the world's airports. He spent a long time considering railway accident statistics and railway fares, before moving on to details of the principal shipping lines.

An hour later he was studying a comparison of Canadian total population figures and the membership figures given for each religious grouping. Reaching a pencil stub from the mantelpiece he totted the figures on the page margin and discovered that there was not a single atheist or agnostic in the whole of Canada in nineteen-sixty-one. He was deep into Eskimo population trends when the knocking on his front door separated itself, in his mind, from the clatter of the rain. He looked at the mantelpiece clock which showed just after ten, shrugged his shoulders and, carrying his book with his thumb keeping his place, he went to the door.

The woman, standing huddled in the rain, clutching a briefcase and a big torch to her chest, was short, with strings of jet black hair hanging lankly from under a soaked headscarf. She leaned forward into the dim light of the doorway, half-closing her eyes against the strike of the rain, and spoke with an American accent.

'Mister Joseph Telford.'

'I'm Joe Telford.'

'My name is Janis Bragg. I'm from the university and I'm writing a thesis on the syndicalist tradition in Britain.'

'What bloody syndicalist tradition.'

'Well. The Guild Socialists.'

'Pie in the sky mob, them.'

The woman shook her head, scattering raindrops. She spoke hesitantly.

'Not just them. You wrote about it. I've read them. Your pamphlets.'

'You must like ancient history.'

She sighed. Joe looked over her shoulder into the darkness and said 'How did you get here.'

'By car. It took hours to find. I had to leave it up on the road. And it took me a long time to get up the hill. The road just seems to come to a stop.'

'It does.'

She rubbed her nose fiercely with the back of her wrist and said 'You're not on the phone.'

'I know I'm not on the phone.'

'I'd have rung you. To check about coming. If you'd been on the phone.'

4

He turned down the page corner of his almanac and said 'You'd better come in.'

She stood in the middle of the room, looking vaguely about her. The warmth of the room brought on a fit of shivering. Joe pulled the briefcase and the torch out of her arms and put them on a small corner table. Looking her up and down he said 'You're soaked.'

'I know that.'

'You'd best get your wet things off.'

She tugged at her headscarf and gave it to him. He squeezed it into a ball over the fire, making the coals hiss, and draped it from the mantelpiece, weighting the edge with a chipped china statue of a boy with a bicycle. She peeled off the coat which was clinging wetly to her and he hung it across the hooks at the bottom of the stairs. She leaned forward awkwardly, tugging the damp fabric of her skirt outwards. He folded his arms and chewed his bottom lip. 'I've got a dressing gown someplace. I don't wear them miself but somebody give me this. A long time ago. It's up to you. Would you like to borrow it.'

'That would be a great boon, Mister Telford.'

He fetched the dressing gown from the shelf above the airing cupboard and she grinned at the deep, red-splashed, mauve colour of the towelling with its broad scimitar shaped sash. As she put on the dressing gown and slipped off her skirt, Joe busied himself checking the drying of the headscarf. She passed the skirt to him and he held it out in front of the fire. She waited for a moment before saying 'Perhaps a hanger.'

'A hanger.'

'A coathanger.'

Joe fetched a wire coathanger from the wardrobe in his bedroom and hooked the skirt onto the frame of a picture of the Scarborough lifeboat that hung in the recess next to the fireplace. Janis Bragg was half-lying in the armchair, her legs straight out, shoes off, warming her feet. He muttered 'You could do with a bit more heat' and rummaged behind the sideboard, disentangling a battered, two-bar electric fire from underneath a typewriter. Plugging it in, he looked down at her.

'You all right now.'

'Fine.'

'Would you like something to drink. Warm you up.'

5

'Please.'

'Tea or coffee.'

'I like English tea.'

He raised his eyebrows.

'It'll more likely be Indian but I'll get you some.'

While the kettle was boiling he leaned on the jamb of the living room door.

'Milk and sugar.'

'Milk, no sugar.'

'How did you find me. I mean where I lived.'

She rubbed at her hair with the collar of the dressing gown.

'I went to talk to Peter Gow about the old National Guilds League and he told me he still writes to you. Says you don't often write back.'

'Sentimental bugger.'

'I thought he was a fine old man.'

'Spent his life trying to persuade the postal workers' union to fight for workers' control. That's what you call a lost cause.'

'Why don't you write back.'

'He keeps nagging on at me to join him in some crusade or other. There's nothing you can say.'

'He has quite an admiration for you.'

'What did you say your name was.'

'Janis Bragg. Way back I'm supposed to be related to Braxton Bragg.'

'And who was he when he was at home.'

'He was a Confederate General in the Civil War.'

'Was he any good.'

'Not very. Somebody said he could snatch defeat from the jaws of victory.'

'Doesn't sound much cop.'

'Can't choose your relatives.'

He came across, built up the fire and moved back to the door.

'I'm not related to Tommy Telford.'

'Who was he.'

'You've not heard of Tommy Telford.'

'No. Sorry.'

'About the best canal and aqueduct builder we ever had. You can see his work all over the place.'

6

'I must look out for it.'

'He didn't die happy though. At least I reckon not.'

'Why so.'

'Well, when he built the Shropshire Union he put in this long, high earth bank to carry the canal over this dip in the contours and it would never stand up. Four or five times it collapsed and let the canal water run away and he had to go back and build it up over again. Then on his death bed they came to tell him it had fallen down again.'

'That's god awful.'

'I don't suppose it made him laugh a lot. After he was dead I think Cubbitt fixed it up and it stayed all right.'

He went back into the kitchen, brewed up the tea and returned with two mugs. Handing her one, he pulled the corner of the settee towards the fire and stretched out on it.

'So. You're writin' this thesis about old time syndicalism in Britain.'

'I am.'

'For the university.'

'It's my PhD thesis. I'm a lecturer in the Department of Political Science.'

'Are you now.'

He sipped at his tea, holding his mug up to look at the picture of a steam locomotive on the side.

'What sort of song you singin' then. How fascinating that some quaint old workers had this strange idea they should control their own industries.'

She sat forward in her chair and spoke sharply.

'No way. I have an overt commitment to the syndicalist ideal and I make no bones about it. I don't believe in phoney objectivity. I state my political position at the beginning of the thesis.'

He nodded his head slowly backwards and forwards.

'Do you now. Support the syndicalist ideal. Fancy that. I take it to mean you think the workers should be politely consulted from time to time, so long as they don't get ideas above their station and really try to decide something. Usual liberal patter about profit sharing. Industrial democracy as a bit of icing on the managerial cake, so to speak. I suppose it could be coming back into fashion.'

7

She flushed, stuttered and shouted at him, her mug shaking so that tea splashed onto his trousers.

'You patronising bastard. Just where do you get off telling me what I believe in. You know damn all about what I believe in. You know nothing about me. You arrogant son of a bitch.'

She was out of breath for a moment then added 'Who the hell are you to pass judgement anyway.' Joe patted his knee where the tea had splashed, held his arm out and said 'Hoddup a minute.'

She started to shout 'I'll say what I damn well like' and he raised his hand again, like a child wanting to speak in class.

'Listen. If you'll steady on a bit I was goin' to apologise. I had no right to say that. It's just that I've got this big fat gob. Mi Dad always said I had. It was an ignorant thing to say.'

She sat stiffly upright for a moment, glaring at him, before leaning back in the chair and muttering 'Well all right.'

'I'm sorry. I think I might have got a bit jealous.'

He plucked at his trouser knee and she said 'I'm sorry about the tea.'

'No, I asked for that. I shouldn't have been sarcastic.'

After a pause he said 'Let's start again. How did you come to be interested in syndicalism in the first place.'

She put her mug down on the iron fender and rubbed the palms of her hands along the upholstered arms of the chair.

'It started way back but I got to wanting to write about it after I did my Master's on the IWW. The Industrial Workers of the World.'

He cocked his head on one side and she said 'I'm sorry. I guess you know what the IWW is.'

'Just about. So you told the tale of the Wobblies.'

'Yup.'

'Another glorious band of no-hopers.'

'A lot more than that.'

He grunted and said 'I suppose they were. That it.' He pointed to the briefcase.

'How did you know.'

'Can I have a look at it.'

'Surely.'

He opened the briefcase, fetched out the heavy, black-bound manuscript and went back to his settee, opening it at the title page.

'University of West Virginia. Up in the Blue Ridge Mountains then.'

8

'Near. Have you been there.'

'No. It was just the song.'

She looked puzzled.

'Laurel an' Hardy sing it, with Chill Wills.'

He sang falsetto 'In the Blue Ridge Mountains of Virginia, on the trail of the lonesome pine.'

'Oh.'

'Don't fret about it.'

He settled to scanning the thesis, reading some sections slowly, sometimes flicking through runs of pages. Janis Bragg stared into the fire and after a while closed her eyes and let her head lean against the backrest. The rasping ticking of the metal alarm clock on the mantelpiece seemed to become louder while the sound of the rain softened to a sibilant murmur.

After a long silence Joe said 'When you talk about the IWW spreading abroad you don't mention the Australian mob, in Sydney.'

She blinked, put her hand to her forehead and said 'There's a special section on them, in the appendix. I think it's numbered four.'

'Ah. I haven't got to the appendix yet.'

He dumped more coal on the fire, poked it into life so that the room became more oven-like and went back to the thesis. Occasionally, he would shake or nod his head or stare for a while towards the window. The pages swished as he flicked them over and the binding slithered on his lap as he hauled it about to get at the references in the back.

'All this detail on how they used the law to chop up the Wobblies, nineteen-nineteen on. How did you get hold of that.'

She spoke hoarsely.

'I travelled around and dug into local court records, jail entries, state and local police files, Espionage and Sedition Act prosecutions. That sort of thing.'

'You really toiled at it.'

'I did.'

'Shows how they really murdered the poor buggers.'

A few minutes later he muttered 'All this stuff on the Colorado copper mine disputes, I never came across any of that before' but she made no comment.

9

Much later, he thumbed back several pages and said 'This analysis of why the Wobblies hated the guts of the Communist Party. You've got the American scene sorted out clearly but you could show as well it's a kind of historical inevitability. Like the old Stalinists used to say. Ideological opposites. If you look at the struggles between the anarcho-syndicalists and the communists in Spain, Civil War time . . . .' He looked up and saw that she was asleep, jaw dropped, shoulders hunched forward. He studied her for a long time before leaning across and touching her arm. She woke suddenly, shuddering. Yawning and still shaking, she mumbled 'I'm sorry. I sorta fell asleep.'

He marked his page in the thesis, put it back on top of the briefcase and stood looking down at her.

'You sound a bit croaky.'

'I do feel a bit washed out.'

'It'd be a mess goin' back down that muddy hill in the dark.'

'I guess so.'

He looked out of the window.

'And it's still raining.'

'There's that too.'

He put one hand on the mantelpiece clock and waved the other.

'Being as it's late you could stay the night if you wanted. Please yourself.'

She grinned and bobbed her head.

'As we-all say in the Blue Ridge Mountains, that's mighty hospitable of you, neighbour.'

'Aye. Well. You can sleep in my bed and I'll kip down here.'

'That seems unfair.'

'I often sleep down here. When I'm too idle to go up to bed.'

She stood and hugged the dressing gown to her. He waved his hand towards the stairway.

'You go on up. The bathroom's at the top of the stairs. I'll bring you some hot milk in a minute. An' there's a sort of electric overblanket thing on the bed. You switch that on and it'll warm you up.'

'Great.'

'You want anything to eat.'

'No thanks. Thanks a lot.'

She lingered by the bead curtains, looking towards him.

10

He paused at the kitchen door.

'Come on, girl.'

She frowned.

'I'm not a girl. I'm a woman.'

He scratched his head.

'How old are you.'

'Twenty-eight.'

'An' I'm marching on towards sixty. So as far as I'm concerned you're a girl.'

'No.'

'All right, go to bed, woman.'

She scrubbed her teeth with her finger then examined the sparse array of toothpaste, soap, shampoo and thick bleach in the bathroom before peering into the box room at the shadowy piles of books, pamphlets, files and untidy bundles of newspapers dimly outlined by the sixty-watt bulb on the landing. She stifled a sneeze brought on by the acrid smell of dust.

Sitting up in the centre of the double bed, still wrapped in the dressing gown, she listened to the faint sounds of Joe moving about in the kitchen below and surveyed the bedroom. The porridge wallpaper was overlaid with posters of political meetings and campaigns, mostly dating back to the late forties and fifties, interspersed with large portraits of Buster Keaton, Gandhi, Kropotkin, Jaques Tati, Koestler, Proudhon, Orage, Tolstoy and some others she failed to recognise. The back of the door had a long quotation from Winstanley's *Law of Freedom in a Platform* sellotaped to it and there was a tattered, old, embroidered trade-union banner stretched across the corner by the window. She observed that the posters were faded and many were peeling away from the walls. She murmured 'More your museum than your campaign headquarters.'

He came in with two glasses of milk, handed one to her and sat on the edge of the bed. She sipped at it and sucked her lips.

'There's something in this.'

'Whisky. Just a spot. Medicinal.'

'Are you being medicated too.'

'Just to keep you company.'

They sat in silence for a while. As she started to ask him about the posters and photographs, he cut in and said 'That's one hell of a fine thesis.'

'You really think so.'

'I do that. There are bits I could squabble with but taken by and large you've done the old Wobblies proud.'

She smiled and said 'I'm glad you think so. I got very attached.'

'I could tell you were a bit in love with 'em.'

'They're all long dead and gone and I never knew them in their time. Just piles of musty old documents. Old letters. And a lot of 'em were casual labourers. You could hardly read what they wrote. And way-out old pamphlets saying they were going to put the working class in possession of the world. Great phrase that. In possession of the world. I felt so close to them, I cried about them being wiped out.'

Joe took her glass.

'They were a rough tough lot of old buggers but I reckon they would have appreciated your tears.'

She smiled and squared her shoulders.

'Right. Now when you sleep in a guy's bed you can't really go on calling him Mister. So what do I call you.'

'Joe.'

'Not Joseph.'

'My parents only called me Joseph when I was in trouble and I was goin' to get thumped, so it always has a funny sound to me.'

'Joe then.'

'And you.'

'Jan or Janis. I don't mind.'

He moved to the door and put his hand on the light switch.

'You can sleep in, in the morning. You never know, you might get breakfast in bed.'

'Thank you, Joe.'

'Goodnight, Jan.'

He switched the light out and padded softly away down the stairs. She punched the pillows into a cradle shape and burrowed down into the bed.

She woke to bright sunlight slashing into the room and the sound of a quavering tenor from downstairs. It was lalling its way through a song that puzzled her till she caught the words 'Carry

Me Back to Old Virginny' and smiled. Propping herself against the wooden headboard, she stared through the small, dusty window at ragged moorland, before sliding out of bed and wincing across the cold linoleum to the bathroom. The sound of running water in lavatory and washbasin brought Joe's voice booming from the bottom of the stairs.

'When you're washed, get back into bed and look queenly and I'll bring you some breakfast.'

She snorted assent through cupped hands full of water.

A quarter of an hour later, he sidled into the bedroom, balancing a tray with a mug of tea, two boiled eggs, cutlery, toast and marmalade in one hand, her skirt, swinging on its hanger, in the other. He handed her the tray, hung the skirt on the picture rail and sat on the end of the bed. She made sounds of pleasure and said 'Sure is a luxury establishment. And thanks for the serenade.'

He fumbled in his shirt breast pocket and produced a salt cellar.

'I forgot this. In case you want it.'

He put it on the tray and blinked as she sharply decapitated the eggs.

'So you heard me chanting did you. I popped in a couple of times earlier on but you were well away.'

Jan dabbed a soldier of toast at the yolk running down the side of the egg cup.

'It's a real comfy bed.'

Joe pointed to the pot of marmalade.

'That's Cooper's Oxford marmalade. I generally get the cheapest in anything but not in marmalade. Cheap marmalade's poor stuff.'

'I'll bet this is delicious.'

'Mark you, it's not an English company any more.'

'What isn't.'

'Cooper's. The marmalade.'

'Ah. I see.'

He got up from the bed, stretched and walked across to the window. Peering out, he said 'Grand day, making up for last night.' Turning round, he sat on the wooden sill and watched her as she zealously ate her way through the eggs.

'I finished your thesis.'

13

She looked up from the tray.

'Do you still think it's all right. Like you said last night.'

'It's grand.'

He crossed one ankle over the other and folded his arms.

'I was tickled by the bit at the end where you quoted old Clough's poem about "say not the struggle naught availeth". With the Wobblies coming mostly from the West it finishes up nicely with that bit about "but westward, look, the land is bright".'

'It seemed to fit.'

'Did you know Churchill used that same idea during the war.'

She shook her head.

'It was one of his speeches, either just after America had come into the war or gev us fifty duff destroyers or something like that. Anyway he quotes Clough's poem and it let him finish up thundering "but westward, look, the land is bright". Good morale-boosting stuff.'

'I'm surprised you're a fan of Churchill's.'

Joe grimaced.

'He never did owt I much liked but when it came to rhetoric he was bloody magnificent.'

Jan sucked marmalade off her fingers.

'Putting that poem in the thesis pushed my supervisor close to cardiac arrest. He wasn't into poetry. He said it made overt the partisan nature of my ideological stance and showed my blatant uncontrolled bias. He said he wouldn't allow me to present the thesis with that kind of thing in it.'

'What did you say.'

'I said that if he didn't allow me to present I would tell his wife about his blatant uncontrolled bias towards getting into the pants of his lady students.'

'And that changed his ideological stance.'

'Sure did.'

Jan put the tray on the rickety bamboo table by the side of the bed, sank back and said 'I shall recommend this eatery to all my friends.'

Joe strolled round the room and tacked back a couple of posters that were drooping.

'Ever tried to get it published. The thesis.'

'I guess I thought about it. You're bound to. But it's not exactly a

14

fashionable area academically and it's sure as hell not popular with the general public.'

'You don't know that. You're taking it for granted. Why don't you tackle Spear Press. They're based in Manchester. The bloke that runs it is called Neil. Michael Neil. Used to be an old mate of mine. Say I recommended you to him. Say I think it's right up his alley.'

'You really think I should try.'

'Wouldn't tell you to if I didn't think so.'

She chewed her lip.

'OK, I'll give it a try.'

'Of course, even if he fancies publishing it, he'll want you to take out some of the pompous bits.'

Jan looked startled.

'What the hell do you mean. Pompous bits.'

Joe picked up the tray.

'Keep your hair on. Mostly the writing's fine but here and there you've got bits where you start tripping over your vocabulary.'

'Such as what.'

'Well, you've got a sentence near the start where you say summat like the IWW was a nexus of interaction between laminates of socio-economic alienation. Which means, as far as I can gather, that the Wobblies were a collection of assorted bums.'

She frowned.

'Did I really say that.'

'I may have missed out a few syllables but it's near enough that.'

Jan looked downcast.

'Christ. That is nasty.'

'It's nowhere near as bad as some American stuff I've read. Generally, Yank writing tries to make everything sound like some bullshitacious technical manual.'

He moved to the door with the tray.

'Now if you can bear to part from your bed, get dressed and come on down. I've got some stuff I want to go over with you.'

'What sort of stuff.'

'Well pieces that I wrote and some other bits to do with your new thesis, the syndicalist effort.'

Jan bounced up and down in the bed.

'Great. That's what I came for. Last night.'

15

'I gathered that. So shift yourself.'

Downstairs, she found Joe sitting at a window table spread with papers and two fresh mugs of tea, chewing on a pencil and staring out at a patch of weed-grown garden, surrounded by the low brick wall, that fronted the house. He said reflectively 'There's some potatoes in that lot but they got lost.'

Jan sat down opposite him, sipped at her tea and spoke in a bright commanding voice.

'Right. Let's get this show on the road.'

Joe wagged a finger at her.

'Have you looked at the time, young Bragg.'

She glanced at her wristwatch and squawked 'Holy cow, it's nearly midday.'

'Aye. And while you've been doing your Sleeping Beauty act, I've been sorting things out and putting the world to rights. So pay heed.'

Jan sat up straight.

'I took a liberty and looked at the notes in your briefcase. The outline of your syndicalism thesis. If you don't mind.'

'No siree.'

He jabbed at one of the piles of writing paper with his pencil.

'Now here's what I've done. I've been through your references and these are ones I can think of that you don't seem to have come across. At least they're not in your notes. As far as I can see.'

She looked intently at the sheets, running her finger down the list and muttering 'They are new to me. Hell, have I missed all this lot.'

'Not to fret. It's mostly just background stuff. A lot of it's not really talking about workers' control as such but it brings it in from one angle or the other. But there are one or two you want to take particular note of. Like this one.'

He pointed to the top of the first page.

'It's a pamphlet by the Rhondda Miners' Federation, 1913, called *The Miners' Next Step*. Now that's a beauty. It seems to have come right out of the blue but it doesn't hedge at all. It's one of the few bits of straight syndicalist argument you'll find from a British trade union.'

He pointed half-way down the page.

'And I am surprised you've missed out *Jack's As Good As His Master*, that's a nice oldie and goldie. And you've got all that wishy

16

washy co-ownership maundering and you've missed out the London League for Workers' Control writing, after the last war. I've listed them at the back.'

Jan flicked through the pages.

'Tell me more.'

'No, I shall have to be quick, love. You academic types are all holidays I know but this wage slave makes a few extra bob on a Saturday, toiling at Mester Gomersal's betting shop. And I'm going to be late as it is.'

Jan took a pencil from him and began to underline some of the references.

'Where is this betting shop.'

'Scarby.'

'Then I could drive you there, save time. That's if my car hasn't been stolen or fallen down a mud hole.'

'That'd be all right. Give us time to spare.'

'You're on. Now what's this pile.'

'Well you seem to have got pretty nearly everything I ever wrote but there is one or two things you've not listed so presumably you haven't got 'em. The top one is a duplicated effort and it was never printed.'

Jan seized the document and began to thumb through it.

Joe wriggled in his chair and rubbed his lower back with both hands.

'It's not a bad effort. I tried to analyse out all the different kinds of decision that have to be made in an industrial set-up. Then I analysed, for each kind of decision, what characteristics it had in terms of timing, information needed, so on and so forth. I tried to think of some arrangement you could have in a workers' co-operative that would be able to deal with that kind of decision. OK.'

'Fine. You did something like that in that book chapter you wrote on decentralised decision making.'

'Yes but this is more worked out. It's a bit of a dot and comma effort.'

'And what's this.'

'That's copies of letters between me and Peter Gow and Ray Pickering and a couple of other blokes. We had a sort of corresponding circle about industrial democracy. The idea was

17

each letter was to comment on all the other letters and we were going to try and make 'em into a book, eventually. That never happened but there's some interesting bits of argument in the letters.'

Jan fingered the pile of manuscript lovingly and as Joe explained the content of the rest of the papers, she began to scribble notes on top of his notes.

As Jan drove sedately down the narrow main street of Scarby, Joe looked at his watch.

'We've got time for a quick drink and a sandwich. Before I have to get to Gomersal's. If you like.'

'I like.'

'Take the next left, left again and park at the back of the Malt Shovel.'

She followed his instructions and they entered the saloon bar of the pub by the back door. Only one customer sat amongst the mass of heavy wooden tables with iron-pillared legs, scattered higgledy-piggledy through the long bar-room. He nodded and said 'Joe' and Joe nodded and said 'Harry', as he led Jan in and seated her on one of the long benches that ran under the leaded front windows.

'What'll you have.'

Jan gazed at the bar, framed by its heavy, carved wooden canopy, and smiled at the fat barman who was watching her while he polished the shining brass handles of the beer pumps.

'I'll have a glass of white wine and a meat sandwich. Beef if they've got it. Otherwise ham or whatever.'

'Pickle.'

'No thanks.'

Joe went to the bar and ordered. The barman leaned confidentially towards him as he drew a pint of bitter.

'That's a neat lass you've got there, Joe Telford.'

Joe looked back at Jan.

'You could say that.'

'How does a feller like you come to pick up a lass like that.'

'I didn't pick her up. She just wandered in out of the rain.'

'I'll bet.'

The barman poured a glass of white wine and busied himself with the sandwiches, looking at Jan's reflection in the deep mirror that ran the length of the bar.

'A reight dinky little lass.'

Joe dug a handful of coins and notes from his trouser pocket and sorted them out on the bar. The barman clattered plates.

'She a relative of yours, maybe.'

'Not that I know of.'

'Then how come she's going about with a sour old bugger like you.'

Joe sipped at his beer.

'I've got hidden charms.'

'Soddin' well hidden.'

Joe paid for the sandwiches and drinks and carried the whole lot precariously back to the table. Jan sipped at her wine.

'What were you two saying about me.'

He opened the sandwiches to check which had the pickle.

'Think well of yoursen, don't you. What makes you think we were talking about you.'

'The way you both kept looking at me.'

'Sharp.'

He took a large bite of his sandwich and washed it down with a gulp of beer. Jan nibbled at the stringy beef and said 'Well.'

'He said you were a reight dinky little lass.'

She pursed her lips.

'I'm not sure whether to take that as a compliment or a rotten sexist remark.'

'It's both.'

'I'm not so sure about that.'

'You are a reight dinky little lass but then you're a lot else besides.'

She pulled a stool towards her and put her feet up on it.

'What's the old word you use in these parts, when you're attracted to somebody.'

'What word's that.'

'Fancy. That's it. Do you fancy me.'

Joe looked at the ceiling in an exaggeratedly thoughtful manner and said 'Just a bit.'

Jan raised her glass in a toast to the barman who was still staring at her and he bowed and smiled.

'What do you do in the week, when you're not working at the betting shop.'

Joe carefully slid the piece of tough beef from between his two slices of bread, so as not to disturb the pickle, and chewed on the meatless sandwich.

'When I'm not working for Mester Gomersal the bookmaker, I work for Mester Pritchard the timber merchant. I do his stock records for 'im. Drive the van a bit, delivering orders. Oddjob man, really.'

'Not exactly mad with ambition are you.'

'Not so's you'd notice.'

They finished their snack in a companionable silence and Joe led the way back to the car. He stood awkwardly, the skirt of his raincoat hoisted up by his hands which were thrust into his trouser pockets. He looked at the sky for a moment and started to say 'Well I have enjoyed your visit' when she interrupted him and asked if she could have a look at the betting shop. He leaned against the car and kicked at pebbles.

'There's not a lot to look at. Just a betting shop.'

Slowly and deliberately she blinked her eyelashes at him and murmured, in an affected, husky voice, 'Please, Joe.'

He shrugged his shoulders.

'It's a scruffy hole.'

They walked side by side along the High Street, Jan looking up at him as she asked questions.

'Can I make a bet.'

'That's supposed to be the general idea. In a betting shop.'

'What do I bet on.'

'Flat racing or sticks, at the moment.'

'And how do I do that.'

Joe shook his head in disbelief.

'Have you never made a bet before.'

'I just say what horse I want to win.'

'Well that's one way to do it. Miself, I generally bet doubles or cross bets. When I bet at all.'

'What's a double.'

'It's a double. You bet on two horses in two races and if the first one wins your winnings go on to your selection for the next race.'

'That sounds too complex. I just want to bet on one horse at a time to win one race.'

He opened the door in a shop front which had its windows painted with horse and greyhound racing scenes and ushered her in. She gazed round intently at the few men, mostly elderly, who stood against the walls, leaning on a shelf that ran nearly all the way round the room, bent over newspapers, scrawling on them. She looked up at the fly-speckled fluorescent tubes and down at the unswept floor, littered with pieces of paper, at the plump woman sitting under a blackboard behind a grill at the far side of the room, knitting. She whispered 'You don't seem to do a lot of business.'

'We do the big stuff privately, in the back room, where I work. Out here's just for tupenny ha'penny punters like you, to have their little flutter.'

Still keeping her voice low she said 'How do I know what to bet on.'

He led her to the shelf, pulled a newspaper across and pointed to the top left-hand side of the page and looked at the big clock at the back of the room.

'Right. Your next race is two-fifteen, Doncaster. There's your card. You just take your pick.'

Jan gazed hopelessly at the newspaper.

'What does it all mean.'

Joe sniffed.

'By 'eck. Two university degrees and you can't read a race card. The big black letters tell you the name of the horse, left-hand side of that is its form in its last six races, right-hand side you've got bloodline, you've got trainer, you've got the weight it's carrying, you've got the jockey and down here you've got the odds.'

'Which one do you think will win.'

'You'll only blame me if you lose your money.'

'No, I promise I won't.'

'God's honour.'

'Sure.'

Joe scratched his chin and made humming sounds.

'You could try Sailor Boy. He likes soft going, it's about the right distance. He's won on this course before.'

'And how do I make a bet.'

He took her arm, led her across to the woman behind the grill and said 'Milly, this is Janis Bragg. She's yer total innocent about horse racing, so can you guide her on how to throw her money away.'

The woman smiled and leaned forward.

'Course, love. What you fancy.'

Joe patted Jan's shoulder and as he lifted the flap in the counter to go through into the back room, he said 'I'll come back in a bit. See how you're getting on.'

He came back into the front part of the shop, half an hour later, to find Jan surrounded by a small group of men, all of whom were giving her competing advice. He listened to the confident voices asserting that this horse had never been fetched such a long way for nothing, while that horse was a sure thing now they had got it up to the right distance, while the other was carrying so much extra weight there was no way it could win. Jan was looking eagerly from one man to the other, questioning them, cross-referring their arguments, scribbling furiously on the race card. Joe grinned to himself and went back into the rear office. When he came out later, everyone was listening to the race commentary coming over the tannoy, the men looking down at the floor, Jan staring up at the loudspeaker as if she could see the race being run across its woven canvas front. Turning, as the winner was announced, she saw Joe watching her. She pulled down the corners of her mouth and hunched her shoulders. He raised his eyebrows and said 'More of the family fortune gone down the drain.'

'It's exciting though. Even losing. It's the commitment.'

'How much you lost.'

'Three pounds each on four races. Only twelve pounds.'

'So far.'

She held the paper out to him and said 'What do you pick for the three-thirty at Cheltenham.'

He waved the paper away.

'I'm not going to be held responsible.'

'In that case I shall consult my racing advisers. What are you doing in the back anyway.'

22

'Mmm, a bit of this and a bit of that. Laying off at the moment.'
'What's laying off.'
'Well, when we get a bet that would be a bit heavy for us to pay out on, we don't risk it. We lay it off with a bigger bookie. Or turf accountant as our Mester Gomersal says.'
'Well you go and lay off and I'll show you how to beat this racket.'

It was some time later, as Joe was bundling up betting slips with elastic bands, that he heard Jan yell against a background of cheering. He went out to find her being backpatted and handshaken by the men around her. She faced him, her eyes shining.
'Three pounds on Merry Minstrel at one hundred to eight, Mister high an' mighty bookmaker. How much do I get.'
'Thirty-seven pounds fifty plus your stake money back.'
She raised a clenched fist.
'Told you I could beat this racket.'
'How much did you lose beforehand.'
'Fifteen pounds.'
'Fair enough.'
She pushed him to one side, away from the little group around her, and said hurriedly 'Look. Considering I got this money here, won it, well, anyhow it's spare. I'd like to splash it. Kind of a celebration.'
'Mmm.'
'How about letting me treat you to dinner. Tonight. You know, somewhere good. Posh. A slap-up meal.'
'Not fish and chips.'
'Assuredly not fish and chips.'
He looked at his feet and after a few seconds Jan began again.
'It's really to thank you. I owe you something for all the help you've given me, with the thesis. All the references. This is just to say thank-you. I'd really appreciate the chance. How about it.'
He poked at his ear and said 'I shan't be finished here until sixish.'
'Well I'll go for a stroll round downtown Scarby, have a cup of tea and so on and I'll come back and pick you up around six.'
'I suppose since you've robbed mi boss of his ill-gotten gains, it's fair enough to have it your treat.'
'Exactly.'
'There is a big hotel up on the moor road. They do a good meal.'

'See you at six then.'

Jan punched his shoulder lightly and went over to the counter to collect her winnings. Joe lifted the counter flap and as he went through to the back office one of the older men leaned across and said 'She's all right, that one, Joe.' Joe murmured 'Seems to be the general opinion.'

The elderly waiter, with the shiny bald head, scribbled in his pad as Joe worked his way down the menu.

'A Mulligatawny and pâté for starters. Sole for both of us. Then we'll have the sorbets, one lemon, one orange. Valencia duck for me and Coq au Vin for my partner.'

He looked up at Jan.

'The house white's a Sauvignon. OK.'

'Fine.'

'A carafe of the house white and thank-you kindly.'

'And a glass of iced water, please.'

The waiter collected the menu cards, jerked into a tiny bow and trotted off to the kitchen. Jan picked at a bread roll from the basket and said 'You really enjoyed choosing your meal.'

'You reckoned I'd order roast beef, two veg and roly poly pudding.'

'Not exactly. Well, sort of.'

'Too many years hanging about on the fringe of the middle class.'

'You should try iced water. Clears the palate and it's healthy.'

'Never.'

'Why not.'

'We English don't trust ice. Not since the *Titanic*.'

Jan poked her middle finger at him and looked round the restaurant, at the checkered tablecloths, the cane-backed chairs, the tricolour flag over the big wall map of the wine regions of France and the rows of reproductions of Impressionist paintings. She listened to the trickle of accordian music being piped into the room and said 'They seem set on doing the French bit.'

'The bloke that owns it is your genuine Frog.'

They sat watching the bracken-covered moorland softening its

24

colours in the fading light and only when the wine and the first course had been brought did Joe take up his questioning.

'You never told me how you got started on all this. Crusading for the downtrodden masses and such.'

Jan prettied a tiny square of toast with pâté.

'Well it started because my family are rich. Loaded. Filthy stinking rich, you'd call it.'

'Doesn't usually have that effect.'

'Maybe I'm a contrary bitch. We owned some coal mining interests. Among other things. In West Virginia. So, come adolescence, I used to go up there to see where the money was coming from. It's a real grim place. A lot of the mines are open cast and they've mauled hell out of the countryside. When I got into communication with the people, I found the mining companies had mauled hell out of them too. Even in this day and age, if they get a union man who gives too much trouble, they negotiate him with a baseball bat. And if he still doesn't see reason, some company goon might just try and change his mind with a shotgun.'

She pointed to his plate with a knife full of pâté and said 'How's the soup.'

'Good.'

'Can I taste it.'

Joe leaned across and fed her a spoonful of the soup.

She grimaced and said 'It's peppery.'

'What did your parents think of you hobnobbing with the hoi polloi.'

'They didn't know for a long time. I knew if I started arguing with them, while I was still trying to work things out, groping for new ideas, there'd be endless rows. I'd get confused and paint myself into a corner. So I kept quiet about what I was thinking and reading and who I was talking to, for a long time. Till I'd put my act together. With no outside interference.'

Joe dropped his spoon into his emptied soup bowl.

'You were uncommon wise. It's like Durante says.'

'Durante.'

'Schnozzle Durante.'

'Says what.'

Joe spoke with a comical American accent.

'Everybody wants to get in on the act.'

'I never heard that.'

Joe shook his head, sadly.

'You were saying.'

'Then I met this old guy who'd been with the Wobblies, back in the early days. I'd bring him a bottle of Jack Daniels and we'd sit out on his porch and he'd tell me how they fought the company police in Arizona and what sort of leader Bill Heywood was, what their dreams were. All sorts of things.'

She paused and pondered.

'I always used to worry about that porch. It creaked all the time. You kept thinking it was going to collapse and dump you all the way down the hillside. He had a funny cracked voice and he used to sing hobo songs. His favourite was "Big Rock Candy Mountain". You know it.'

Joe smiled.

'I know that one. It got to be something of a pop song over here back in the fifties. Burl Ives used to sing it, when he was popular.'

'I used to love that line about the hobo's idea of paradise.'

She declaimed.

'Where all the cops have wooden legs and the dogs have rubber teeth.'

She refilled their glasses, raised hers and said 'Here's to fine dreams.'

Joe clinked his glass against hers.

'His name was Sealy. Hector Otis Sealy. He was a lovely dried up, scrawny little bastard. He died on Christmas Day, just before I came over here. To this country. His lungs were all choked up. He showed me some of the early writings and letters and he helped me meet one or two old timers from the IWW. That got me started. I knew when I got to college and graduate school, I was going to write about them.'

The waiter, who was hovering behind them in the nearly empty restaurant, cleared the dishes. Joe flapped at crumbs with his serviette and grumbled, when the sole was served, about what a daft invention fish knives were.

'What did your family say when they finally discovered you'd gone astray.'

'It was funny that. There was no big row or anything, when I started coming out with ideas about workers' rights and revolution and such. At first I thought my parents were being sympathetic and understanding. It took me a while to figure they didn't really understand what I was saying. They thought it was some kind of hobby I'd taken up. It didn't matter how I expressed it. They heard me as saying I was interested in all this, like I was interested in history or pottery or something. And when I got to graduate school to write a thesis on it, that seemed to prove they were right and it was just a kind of academic hobby. I mean my father was a lot more upset when I used to say Nixon was a liar and a cheat. To him, that was real political talk, real opposition to the establishment. He thought when I talked about workers' control of industry it was a sort of fairy story I was interested in.'

'Could have a point there.'

For the rest of the sole and through the sorbet they talked about Jan's father's political outlook, Joe taking a defensive stance on her father's behalf and arguing that maybe Dad was tolerant as well as ignorant. When the main course arrived they fussed over and talked about the food, before Joe returned to his questioning.

'How come you didn't carry on at an American university. When you finished your thesis on the IWW. Why come over here.'

'Because I wanted to do my PhD on the syndicalist tradition in Britain.'

'Seems logical. More or less.'

She fiddled with her chicken, chopping it up and transferring her fork to her right hand. After a long pause she said 'No, that's a lie. I didn't decide to do a thesis on the British syndicalist tradition till quite a while after I came over here.'

'So why did you come here. Real reason.'

'Deep down.'

'Deep down.'

She refilled their wine glasses, drank and said sharply 'Personal reasons.'

'Ah.'

'What do you mean ah.'

'Just ah.'

She looked at him, speculatively.

'If you must know, I was in pursuit of a man.'

She watched his face as he put on an absurdly innocent, enquiring expression.

'He was Sociology Lecturer at West Virginia State. He had a beard and soulful eyes and he cried about the essentially tragic nature of the human condition. He wrote poems asking you to go to bed with him.'

Joe murmured 'Don't see how you could resist a bloke like that.'

'I was truly smitten. He came to England to do some documentary research at the British Museum. I followed him over here and so on and so forth.'

'So forth.'

'I bullied my way into his house and we lived together and there was lots of passion and lots of poems till I discovered he wasn't very interesting.'

'A fatal flaw.'

'He used to take me to German lieder concerts. You into German lieder.'

'Not since Hitler. I haven't kept up with 'em.'

'Shut up.'

'Yes, ma'am.'

'In fairness, I don't think he found me very interesting either. So, one way or another, it died the death. I suppose it sort of dwindled. In the end there was just ceremonial screwing and doing the domestics and listening to him recite his poems. And that didn't seem to be enough, somehow. So, one morning, I left the regulation note propped up on the mantelshelf and walked out. Anyway, by then I'd come to like living over here so I decided to see if I could stay on. I dropped lucky and got this lecturing post at your local university. That was three years ago. And here I am.'

Joe tore up a roll and mopped at his sauce.

'What happened to the fond and doting.'

'Fond and doting.'

'Parents, the wealthy parents.'

'Well, they're still wealthy and every summer they come over here for a while and rent a stately home and have me to live with them for a few weeks and spoil me. They think I'm a little tetched but there is a snob value in being an academic and I am their only child. If I get too bolshie, Pop just points out that when they die

28

they'll leave all their money to me and I'll be so wealthy my radical friends won't even talk to me.'

They debated a while whether radical friends would ever see their way clear to forgiving anybody enormous wealth or, if you wanted to give it away, who would be the most troublemaking recipients. Jan suddenly pointed an accusing fork at him and said 'I notice we're digging into me, what about you.'

'What about me.'

'Well everything. How were you brought up, why are you doing what you do, what do you intend to do in the future. Everything.'

'That's all dull stuff.'

'And that's a cop-out.'

'Could be.'

'All right, if you're going to be evasive at least answer me one thing.'

'Like.'

She pointed a fork at him.

'You used to be the inspiration man in the Tenaby Producer Co-operative. Way back, when everybody thought it was the model for a really fine democratic collective, and other set-ups were copying its constitution and so on, it collapsed. I never found anything you ever wrote about it or why it collapsed. So what happened.'

He sipped his wine, screwed up his face and clapped his hands vaguely together.

'It was a fucking shambles.'

He looked out of the window into the darkness.

'Not at first though. We had a fairish economic base. That kind of light engineering is somehow flexible, you can compete with the big buggers on small runs and one-off stuff, you can switch to new products fairly easily. We were under-capitalised, like you'd expect, but we had enough to get set up. And the thing really worked, politically. It was your gen-u-ine democracy. The constitution was a practical sort of job, even if the writing was a bit flowery. You read it.'

Jan nodded.

'It let us elect people into chairman-type roles so they could take fast decisions, if necessary. And the collective would back them up. And if the chairman type kept making decisions no bugger

29

liked, they kicked the character out and put somebody else in. We had some pretty good conference-type arrangements for long-term policy decisions. There was a nice feel to the place. A lot of humour. It didn't get as heavy as most political efforts do. We were pretty good on training each other too. I was taught to work a capstan lathe, believe it or not.'

His voice dropped and he seemed to be talking half to himself. 'Quite summat, showed the bastards who were always whining that there has to be a boss, that we were more efficient than they were and we were democratic at the same time. And it polished the old ego, being a kind of show place.'

He hunched down in his chair and stared out of the window again.

'So what went wrong.'

He roused himself and sliced the remains of his duck.

'Well at the root of it all was being a bit of a commune and a collective at the same time. A lot of the people who worked in the co-operative lived together in a commune set-up. The usual thing. Sharing their money, dividing up all the domestic chores, organising a crèche, having meetings to sort out problems. And they recruited pretty well. So that there was always this big overlap between the workers in the co-op and the commune attached to it.'

Jan leaned forward and said 'Sounds like a good idea.'

'It was too ambitious, at least I think it was. You see we were always getting a kind of louse-up between commune and collective. The people in the commune lived in each other's pockets, so if there was any trouble between them, it immediately spilled over into the factory and vice versa. All sorts of things. Say you got two blokes screwed up about the same woman. Pun intended. The next thing you got was all kinds of rows in the works committees, which were really echoes of the commune foul-up. I'm sure when we got arguments inside the co-op they were made more fierce because we were too close, personally.'

He jabbed vaguely at the carcass of his duck before pushing his plate aside.

'Either the commune or the collective might have worked but having them together meant we were like a big family. We were living like a family, with all the sorts of stresses you get, but we

30

weren't a family. So we didn't have the kind of tolerance you have in a real family. Anyway it died.'

He flicked a thumb and middle finger at his wine glass and it rang like a bell.

'There were other things, financial pressures, a hell of a lot of hassle from the Tory borough council about planning permissions and so on. But I still think it was too ambitious. It grew too fast and it tried to be too much a complete revolution in one go.'

'That's a shame.'

'It was a crying shame.'

Jan leaned back as the waiter collected the dishes and took them away. She poured the last of the wine and said 'Were you one of the two blokes who got screwed up about the same woman.'

Joe stared at her and said 'You cheeky bugger.'

Jan giggled and said 'Were you.'

'I might have been. Water long gone under the bridge.'

The waiter came back, hauling a sweet trolley behind him. They bowed to look at the lower levels of the trolley and enquired and debated their way into figs for Joe and chocolate gâteau for Jan. Spooning cream over the gâteau she asked him why he had never written about what went wrong with the Tenaby co-operative.

'I didn't write anything about anything after that. You can get fed up of writing stuff nobody reads. I've done a lot of that.'

'Was it after Tenaby you came up here.'

'Not long after.'

Joe hacked the stalk ends off his figs and laid them in a line on the side plate.

'I meant to tell you, there could be a big hole in your thesis. Judging by the outline anyway.'

'What big hole.'

'You're not setting the whole thing in its political scenery. Not enough, anyway.'

Jan swallowed a large mouthful of gâteau and said 'Give me a for instance.'

'Straight Labour Party politics. How thickies like Ernie Bevin stamped all over any syndicalism in the Labour Party. He got it into his thick head that if the workers had any responsibility for controlling industry it would put 'em at a disadvantage when it came to wage bargaining. That's the sort of treacle the poor old English syndicalist had to swim in.'

Jan raised a spoonful of gâteau in salute to him and said 'Thank you kindly, Mister Teacher, sir.' Joe shrugged his shoulders.

'There's no need to be sarky. I was only trying to help.'

Jan knocked herself on the head.

'Sorry Joe. I appreciate what you're saying and I will bear it in mind. Did you come up here as a kind of retreat.'

Joe sucked on a fig.

'A bit. Would you like coffee.'

'Fine. And since I'm paying for it I'll have a liqueur as well, I'll have a Drambuie. You have something with your coffee.'

Joe flagged for the waiter and ordered the coffee, a Drambuie and a Remy Martin. As he watched Jan painstakingly clear her plate of the last shreds of gâteau he said 'Brandy's like marmalade.'

'I'd never noticed that.'

'No, I don't mean it's like marmalade. I mean it's like marmalade because if you get the cheap end, you've got rubbish and it's only worth having if you buy expensive.'

'I'll make a note of that.'

Over drinks Jan tried to draw him out about some of the meetings and campaigns blazoned on the posters in his bedroom but he dismissed the topic and asked her about her teaching work at the university.

The waiter looked quizzically at Joe when Jan paid the bill and Joe winked knowingly at him. As they groped their way through the darkened car park, she slipped her arm into his and said 'Don't get nervous, Joe, but here's where I suggest I see you home.'

Joe replied in a girlish falsetto.

'I'll tell the vicar.'

He answered himself in a deep bass.

'I am the vicar. The whip, the whip.'

Then falsetto.

'No. Anything but that.'

Then bass.

'Anything.'

Then falsetto.

'The whip, the whip.'

Jan giggled and asked what it was all about. Joe said it was ancient rubbish.

Jan let the car roll to a stop at the end of the tarmac, so that they looked across the little valley, at the lights of Joe's neighbour's house, up on the far hillside. She switched off the engine, stretched and said 'That was a fine meal and a fine day.' Joe said 'It was a reight grand day,' leaned towards her and before she quite realised what he was doing, he had shaken her hand and was getting out of the car. He bowed to window height and said 'It'll be a grand thesis and I'll be sure to watch out for it, to read, when it's finished.'

She scrambled out of the driver's side door and looked at him across the roof of the car. She said 'You've helped a lot.' He moved back a little and said 'It's been a real pleasure. Well, I'll bid you goodnight then.' She hesitated and spoke, in a rather loud, jokey voice 'But the night is young, sir.'

Joe put his hands in his pockets and moved onto the pathway. 'Aye, but tomorrow's a crack of dawn job for me.'

He moved backwards, a few steps, down the path.

'I always go to see my old man on a Sunday. He's in a sort of old folks' home place and it's a hell of a long trek from here.'

Jan quietened her voice.

'It's just . . . It's just that there's a lot more questions I wanted to ask you. About the thesis, about your own pamphlets. What you think now.'

Joe half-turned away and said 'It's kind of you but I wouldn't attach too much importance to 'em. You push ahead the way you've got things laid out and you'll do fine.'

She shouted 'Goodnight' and got back into the car, slamming the door. Joe said 'Goodnight' and walked away down the slope. He crossed the plank bridge, turned and stood, looking back up the hill. The car was still at the top, its headlamps striking across the valley, like two small searchlights. After several minutes, he murmured to himself 'There are some would say you are a stupid bugger.'

He walked back across the plank bridge and started up the slope. Half-way up, he heard the engine revving noisily followed by a grating of gears. He saw the headlamps go backwards in a half-circle, so that the red tail lights came into sight, then moved away and disappeared over the crown of the hill.

He stood for a while, murmured 'Could be all for the best' and turned back down the slope. As he climbed up the hill on the far side, he started to sing, softly.

> *Allelujah, I'm a bum,*
> *Allelujah, bum again,*
> *Allelujah, gimme a handout.*

Jan propped herself on her elbow and looked intently at the face of the man sleeping beside her. She tried to decide what it was she disliked about it. It was too rounded, she thought, too smooth, the lips were too fleshy, the dimple in the chin too cute, the skin too pink and shiny, the eyelashes too lush, the eyebrows sparse and an unattractive sandy colour, the ears stunted and all the features set in a self-satisfied pose. Even sleeping it looked pleased with itself. She concluded that if a frog were turned into a prince and it only half-worked, he would look like this. Leaning forward, she sniffed at his hair and reflected that she had not liked the smell from the moment they got into bed. A greasy sort of smell. His breath bubbled and he rolled heavily towards her. Hastily, she slipped from under the bedclothes and stepped backwards. He sighed, extended his arms and sprawled onto her side of the bed. She wrinkled her nose.

Tiptoeing to the wardrobe she shrugged into a housecoat and slippers and went lightly down the broad wooden staircase to the big lounge and through into the kitchen. She put a kettle on, poured muesli into a bowl and slopped milk over it. For a few moments she drummed her nails on the lid of the kettle, then went to the front door and opened it to fetch the newspaper off the porch. She knelt for a while, peering out at the open-plan estate with its neat, modest trees and geometric flower patches, noting that the men must have gone off to work because there were few cars about, but it was too early for the women to come out shopping. Back in the kitchen she scanned the headlines till the water boiled, made coffee and carried cup, bowl and spoon to a wicker table and chair, placed against French windows, looking out onto a trim shrubbery.

She had finished her breakfast and was reading the newspaper

34

when the man came downstairs. Wearing only his bright blue underpants, he stood on the bottom step, gripping the ceiling boards above him and leaning forward, so that his stomach muscles flexed. He smiled brightly.

'Top of the morning, honey lamb, honey chile, honeysuckle rose.'

Jan turned the page of the newspaper and patted it flat.

'Morning.'

'Reached for you an' found I was cuddling a pillow.'

He folded his arms and stretched up onto the balls of his feet.

'Sleep well, Janis.'

'Fairish.'

He scratched at his black, wiry chest hair.

'Any chance of sustenance for a hard-working young feller. Been a long night.'

She spoke without looking at him.

'You can try the kitchen. Get what you want.'

'Ah. Self-service. Right.'

He strode to the kitchen and while she searched out a pen and made a half-hearted try at the crossword, she heard him clinking plates, tinkling a spoon on china, flicking the toaster on, running the tap, sawing bread, thudding cupboard doors and humming snatches of 'Onward Christian Soldiers'. He came out, after a few minutes, with toast, sliced apple, cheese and coffee and took the seat across from her. He crunched, smiled, sipped at his coffee and said 'That was a bloody marvellous night, Janis. It really was. Fabulous.'

'You think so.'

'I really, really do. Don't you.'

Jan abandoned the crossword and turned to the financial page.

'In fairness, it had its moments.'

He grinned.

'Long, lasting, lovely moments, luv. We really hung on, round the corners, down the dip and over the top. Never-ending, suddenly ended, as old Papa Hemingway used to say.'

Jan fixed her eyes on the paper and the man munched loudly on pieces of apple.

'It was great the way we woke up in the middle of the night and started all over again. Like old Donne said, licence my roving hands and let them go et cetera.'

'Yes. Well there's no need to smack your lips quite so loudly.'
He frowned and mumbled through a mouthful of toast.

'I'm not smacking my lips. And you've changed your tune. You were crooning with delight when it came down to it. Eager wasn't the word.'

She shouted 'Goddammit. Stop your bloody adolescent drooling about it.' He stood up and pushed his chair back, spraying crumbs.

'I'm not drooling. I just think if we enjoyed ourselves in bed then we ought to be able to talk about it. It's not some dark satanic secret, for God's sake.'

Jan tugged at her hair.

'All right. All right. I'm sorry I shouted. Now why don't you just get dressed and we'll part company. That way we won't get to spitting.'

The young man put his hands on his hips, elbows pointing outwards.

'I don't want to part company.'

'Hard luck. Or as we Americans say, tough titty.'

He gazed blankly at her, then smiled, nervously.

'Please, Janis. I'm sorry if I shocked you. I didn't mean to. Look, why don't we go back to bed. Have a good, long cuddle. Settle it there. Seriously.'

Jan shouted again.

'Jesus, you really don't understand, do you. For Christ's sake get dressed.'

He shouted back 'All right, if that's the way you want it' and tried to stamp upstairs but failed because of his bare feet. As he dressed, he peered over the top stair rail and called down.

'Any damn way, young lady. Who picked who up at Tony's party. And who chatted who up. And who was being lovey-dovey and chewing my ear. And just who suggested we come back to your place.'

'I did.'

'Well then.'

'Well then what.'

'First you come on strong and practically rape me. Now you go all frosty and want to kick me out. It makes no sense.'

36

He paused and said 'You hear me.'
'Yes.'
'And don't say it's because you didn't enjoy being fucked either, because I know you did.'
'I never said I didn't.'
'Well then.'
'Stop saying well then.'
She heard him swear about losing his shoes and the scraping sound of the bed being pulled to one side. He appeared again at the stair rail.
'You've been dead against me from the word go this morning. Sour as hell. Haven't you.'
'Yes.'
'Spoiling for a fight.'
'Yes.'
'Why.'
'I don't know why.'
'You must know why.'
'Yes, I do know why.'
'Then why.'
'Ah shit.'
She clasped her hands on top of her head.
'It's like they say in the old movies. If you don't know I can't explain it to you.'

 He came downstairs clutching his jacket and stood in front of her. He spoke quickly.
'Janis. Why don't we meet again and talk about it. When we've had a chance to cool off. See how we feel. Meet on neutral ground.'
'No.'
'Seriously. We deserve another chance. I really didn't mean to imply it was just a one-night stand. It's not like that. I've wanted to get to know you for the longest time. Honestly.'
Jan glared at him.
'Look, Mister. Being as you're such a star of the English department you should know that poem by Millay, even if she was American.'
'What you talking about.'
'See in this poem, the guy has screwed her and she liked it but she

37

tells him not to make a big deal out of it. She winds up, and I quote,

> *. . . let me make it plain:*
> *I find this frenzy insufficient reason*
> *For conversation when we meet again.*

Get it.'

He said 'Very well,' struggled into his jacket, walked to the door and slammed through it, shouting 'Get stuffed.' She shouted 'Not by you, I won't.' She listened to the sound of his car being driven away, gazed upwards and said, loudly but calmly, 'You are an unfair bitch.'

She cleared the pots, made more coffee and took it, with a tin of biscuits, back to the wicker table. A long time later the phone trilled. She guessed it was the young man so she sat still, counting. It trilled thirty-eight times before it stopped, convincing her that it was the young man.

A while later she searched out a notebook, fetched a copy of Cole's *Studies in Class Structure* from the bookcase and began to leaf slowly through it, making occasional notes. For nearly an hour she worked on the book before giving up and staring out at the shrubbery, occasionally glancing at the phone. Finally, she marked her place in the book and stood up to take it back to its shelf. Balancing it on her head, she swayed across the room, left hand on hip, right hand floating airily, crooning 'I yam an English lady, I yam, I yam.' Putting the book away, she turned, looked at the phone again and murmured 'Faint heart ne'er won.' She picked the phone up and dialled directory enquiries and asked for the number of Pritchard's, timber merchants, of Scarby.

Joe stood in the doorway of the sawmill, squinting his eyes against the sawdust swirling round him. He pointed his clipboard at the man in front of him and tapped him on the chest with it. 'I'll bet it's the same in every soddin' timber yard in the country. You stroll about like gormless kids, handing out bits of wood and tekkin' bits in, an' stackin' it anywhere and never a sign of a chit about what's sold or bought. And you flamin' well expect me to keep a stock record. You've no idea.'

The man fumbled in his overalls and brought out a grimy sweet bag.

'Have a toffee.'

38

'You'll not sweeten me with toffees.'

He took one and tapped the man's chest with his clipboard again. 'Well, what about this vanishing pine, Henry. According to my records, I should be knee deep in pine and there's not enough round 'ere for a box o' matches.'

The man unwrapped a toffee for himself.

'I'll bet that was Percy Fenton wantin' the hardboard.'

'What's he got to do with it.'

'I told him he wanted pine.'

'His docket says he took hardboard.'

'He was better off with pine. For what he wanted it for.'

'But the docket says hardboard.'

'That's not strictly true to life. It says what he came in for.'

'You dozy bugger. That must be why I've got a load of hardboard I shouldn't have.'

'You see. It's simple when you think about it.'

Joe had begun to explain the nonsense this made of invoicing when a voice from the window of the clinker-block office building shouted that he was wanted on the phone. He jabbed his clipboard at the man and said 'Stay put, you soft bugger. I'll be back.'

He disentangled the phone, which hung by its cord down behind the radiator and said 'Telford.' A voice said 'Who' and Joe mumbled 'Just a minute,' spat the toffee out of his mouth into the waste paper basket and said 'Telford.'

'Joe Telford.'

'Aye.'

'Remember me. It's a few weeks since we met.'

'Course I remember you, Jan. You're not easily forgotten.'

'Glad to hear that. How are you.'

'Fair to middling. How about you.'

'So so.'

'How's the thesis goin'.'

'Not bad. Slow but sure.'

'That's the stuff.'

'How's Mester Gomersal's betting shop.'

'Still making money.'

She paused, cleared her throat and said 'I've something to ask you.'

'Yes.'
'You can say no if you want to. Naturally. It's just a thought.'
'What is.'
'You'll probably say no.'
'I might.'
'It's hardly your cup of tea.'
'Very likely not.'
'I won't mind if you're not willing. I'm asking on the off chance. Just in case.'
'Jan.'
'Yes.'
'Spit it out.'
'Right. Would you be willing to talk to the Pol. Sci. Soc.'
'What's a Pol. Sci. Soc.'
'It's the university Political Science Society. Mainly Pol. Sci. students, some from Sociology and some staff. I promised I'd get a speaker for the end of the month and I thought it would be fab if you came along and gave a spiel on workers' control. But I realise it's not your bag. Is it. Nowadays. Public speaking, I mean.'
'OK.'
'OK what.'
'OK.'
'You mean you'll do it.'
'Yes.'
'You'll talk to the Pol. Sci. Soc.'
'That's right.'
She hiccuped and said 'That's great.'
'You send me gen on time and place.'
'Sure. Is a Thursday at four OK.'
'That's fine.'
'Hey. What will you call your talk. Your title.'
Joe sucked his teeth.
'We'll pinch it from that old pamphlet I told you about. *Jack's As Good As His Master.*'
'You bet. I'll advertise it. Give it a big build-up. Get the masses for you to come and harangue. And I'll be in touch about details.'
'Good.'
'Yes.'
'That's settled then.'

40

'Joe.'

'What.'

'I never thought you would.'

'You never can tell.'

'She said 'I suppose not' and was silent for a while.

'Joe.'

'Yes.'

'Afterwards, there's a sherry do in the staff room.'

'Mmm.'

'Can I take you to dinner after that.'

'Gettin' to be a habit.'

'Yeah, well, I get expenses to feed you, as well as a bit of a fee for you.'

'Right.'

'That's yes.'

'That's yes.'

'Bye, Joe.'

'Bye.'

Jan put the phone down, gave a long low whistle and said 'Lordy Lordy me.'

The university loomed up as a squat assembly of cubes. Strolling through the maze of slab-paved pathways that led to it, Joe saw it as a collection of children's building blocks but strangely without colour, all grey, the flat grey of weathered concrete, the pitted grey of stucco, the mottled grey of pre-fabricated cladding. Like a factory, Joe thought. He started to play with the idea of what kind of a factory a university might be, trying to make something out of the words fact-ory and in-dust-story before he gave up.

He could see nothing that looked like a main entrance so he started to ascend a zig-zag catwalk, lost his nerve and retreated. He halted a lanky, head-down, gum-chewing student and asked him the way to the Political Science Department. The student looked at him sadly.

'You're going to Political Science.'

'That's right.'

'Poor sod.'

He turned and pointed to a short flight of steps.

'Down there, left at the bottom, forward, till there's a big metal chimney thing blocking your way, look to your right and there it is.'

Joe asked where he studied, and the lad replied 'Fine Arts.' Joe said 'Lucky bugger' and walked down the steps. The lad shouted after him 'You look a bit old for Political Science' and Joe shouted back 'I'm a slow learner.'

He found a four-storey, stilted structure, in black glazed tile and glass, with the words Political Science sunk into one corner, in silver letters. Inside he wandered along indistinguishable corridors till he found room 109 with the name Janis Bragg lettered onto a wooden IN-OUT slide, set to IN. Above the name was a fuzzy, highly coloured, Polaroid snapshot of Jan, to the left a typed quotation from Plato which read 'Socrates is guilty of corrupting the minds of the young and believing in deities of his own invention instead of the Gods recognized by the State'. Above that was a picture of gophers standing by holes in the desert, looking up at the sky, and to the right was a strip of cartridge paper bearing, in manuscript, the words 'Abandon Talcott Parsons all ye who enter here'. Someone had crossed out Talcott Parsons and written in Karl Marx and someone else had crossed out Karl Marx and written in Pareto. Joe studied it closely, shrugged and knocked on the door.

Jan shouted 'Come in' very loudly. As he entered she scrambled from behind her desk and shook his hand vigorously, saying 'Hello' several times. They agreed that it was good to see each other, settled that Joe did not want tea, coffee or a pre-meeting sherry and removed a stack of books from an upholstered chair so that he could sit down. Jan fussed about the office being cramped, the chair not being comfortable and insisted that she could have picked Joe up in her car and brought him to the university and would have been very happy to have done so. Joe said it was no matter and Jan stressed her point again.

'It wouldn't have taken long. By car. To run out and fetch you. Save you the journey.'

'No. It's like Marlowe says.'

'Christopher Marlowe.'

'No. In Chandler. To Moose Malloy. He says I'm all grown up. I go to the bathroom alone and everything.'

Jan flushed and said 'Suit yourself.'
'I thought you might know it. Being American.'
Jan shuffled books around her desk.
'You look very smart.'
Joe patted his jacket.
'It's my Sunday best suit. In honour of the occasion.'
'Classy.'
'Thanks.'
Jan flicked at the pile of papers in front of her and pushed them away. Joe pointed to a keyboard and printer, topped by a visual display unit, to the left of the desk and said 'Impressive.'
'It's a word processor.'
'It must be grand to have your words processed.'
She patted her hair and said 'It really is good to see you, Joe.' He smiled and said 'You too.' She relaxed and sat floppily in her chair, waving an arm as she spoke.
'It looks as if there'll be quite a few staff members at the meeting. Hope you don't mind. My guess is they'll try to put the academic boot in.'
'Why.'
'Because you're an outsider. Not on the team. Bit of intellectual snobbery. That sort of thing. Are you bothered.'
Joe admired the polished toecaps of his shoes.
'Not so's you'd notice. I began my illustrious career in public speaking just after the war, doin' factory gate meetings in the rougher parts of Manchester. So I might just manage not to tremble. In front of your mob.'
'You're boasting, Joe Telford.'
'Blowing mi trumpet.'
'Sure you don't want something to drink.'
'Not even English tea.'
She peered closely at the tiny face of her wristwatch and said 'We can drift down now, if you like.' She came round the desk and as Joe got to his feet, she kissed him. He furrowed his brow and said 'What was that for.'
' 'Cos I wanted to.'
He opened the door and said 'Not a bad sort of reason.'
    The lecture theatre was bowl-shaped, with the seats steeply raked. The windows were blinded and from the high-tiled ceiling

the northern light of fluorescents poured down. Jan and Joe lounged by the high lectern, fronted by a long bench littered with television screens, overhead projectors and a console for controlling the lighting and the moveable screens. They watched the room fill up. Jan nodded towards a group in the front row and said 'Them's your lecturers. The heavy mob with the fixed smiles. The sad-looking bastard at the end, him with the pot belly and the vacant stare, is the Professor.'

'You'll look well if he can lip read.'

'I'm not certain he can read at all.'

'Your students are a solemn-looking bunch. Most of 'em have got pen an' paper out.'

'Ready to take notes.'

'You're kiddin'.'

'I'm not.'

'Suppose I talk rubbish.'

'Makes no matter. They'll take it down. Every syllable.'

The secretary of the Society came over to them, shyly introduced himself and asked if he could tape-record the lecture. Joe said 'I'll be sure to speak up.'

The room filled and a few latecomers squatted on the aisle steps. Jan poked his ribs and said 'See. You've got pulling power.'

'Amazin'. Once upon a time, at Newcastle-under-Lyme Town Hall, I addressed an audience of two. An' one of them was the Chairman's mother-in-law.'

'Well you're back in the big time now. Got any notes.'

'No. You'll have to hope inspiration strikes.'

'Ready.'

'Strainin' at the leash.'

Jan introduced him briefly, stressing his practical experience in workers' co-operatives and referring to some of his writing, before moving away from the lectern and seating herself in a chair, placed apart, at the right-hand end of the front row.

Joe folded his arms and studied his audience for a while, watching them progress from absolute stillness, to shuffling movements, to loud throat clearing noises, as they waited for him to speak. He told them, in a quiet conversational voice, that they were not to fret, a thought was bound to come to him.

After a further silence, he began to talk about the contrast

44

between the continuous public praise of representative democracy in politics and the silent and total acceptance of dictatorship in industry. He debated the belief that workers cannot manage themselves and dubbed it an untested old wives' tale, used in the tradition of the mother who told her son that he was not to go near the water till he could swim. He attacked the satirical picture of decisions lost forever in the wrangling of workers' committees. Pacing slowly to and fro behind the lectern, he speculated that apart from long-term policy referenda, industrial decisions could be taken in the process of work itself, just as a football team plays through a myriad choices using a fast-flowing, mutual understanding of its task and purpose. He got laughs spinning through a series of examples of workers propping up industrial undertakings in spite of nonsensical management decrees. Coming out from behind the lectern he sat on the long bench and leaned towards his audience, telling them about his experience of working in collectives, the kinds of problems and conflicts they presented, the opportunities they offered, the way they were politically organised and the kind of personal loyalty that was needed. He wandered back to the lectern and cast about the history of workers' movements, pondering their dreams and achievements and disasters, wandering to and fro from peasant revolts to the Swedish general strike of 1909. He stopped speaking suddenly.

Jan moved from her chair to the end of the bench and called for questions and comments. An elderly lecturer combed his beard with his fingers and said, in a languid voice, that no doubt the theory was all right in its way but surely there were hardly any cases of it being put into practice.

Joe leaned on the bench and spoke in a loud, reciting voice.

'Well, if we want a few practical examples, ancient and modern, we get Owen's New Harmony, the French government print workshops, the Guild Socialist experiments, Barcelona Tramways in the Civil War period, a good many kibbutzim, CPF Boot and Shoe, Mondragon, Brora colliery, Scott Bader, Triangle Wholefoods, Wilshaw's. . . .'

The man interrupted, his voice more energetic.

'No, no. I mean on a really vast scale. Not hole in corner. On a scale that matters, that is significant. It's never happened in a really massive way.'

45

Joe scratched his head.

'That's like saying the glorious revolution never happened, which it sure as hell didn't. A really massive workers' collective would challenge the whole class system. What you're pointing out is that history's score so far is workers nil, bosses one. Still, it's only half-time.'

Another staff member took off his glasses and waggled them at Joe.

'I suppose you have heard of Georges Sorel.'

'O aye. His mother used to do our washing.'

'I beg your pardon.'

'Granted.'

The man frowned, sat silent for a moment, before saying 'The point I'm trying to make is that one of the greatest admirers of Sorel's syndicalism was Mussolini. Benito Mussolini. The founder of fascism. Now what does that tell us.'

'I have heard Judas and Jesus were great buddies at one time.'

The man put his glasses back on and peered through them.

'I don't follow your reasoning.'

Joe shrugged.

'Like they say. You ask a silly question and you get a silly answer.'

A student at the back shouted 'It's called scholarship' and there was a rumble of foot stamping. The professor rapped the bench in front of him and spoke firmly.

'Your talk is all very entertaining, in its way, Mister Telford, but surely it belongs in sociology or even, God save the mark, economics.'

Joe stared at him.

'I'm not a lot bothered about what little boxes you like to keep your ideas in, Mister.'

The students broke in on the questioning and interrogated Joe about his political affiliations, one asserting that, at heart, Joe was a Communist.

Joe grinned at him.

'In my time, sonny, I've taken quite a few teeth out of blokes who called me that. Think about it a bit. Russian industry is about as democratic as Unilever. Main difference is that in the West political and industrial managers conspire quietly together and in the East they're officially teamed up.'

A woman member of staff came back into the discussion with a rambling discourse on Joe's naive faith in workers and was asked how she came to have such a naive faith in bosses.

The questions were coming faster and the audience was beginning to argue with itself when Jan closed the meeting, formally thanking Joe to prolonged applause and foot stamping from students and polite hand clapping from the staff.

At the gathering in the Senior Common Room, Joe wedged himself into a corner, sipped sherry and nodded and muttered amiably as he was pelted with academic comments requiring him to explain the collapse of the nineteen-twenty-six general strike, the paradox of an organised anarchist movement and his failure to give literature references for all his assertions, mixed with courteous enquiries as to where he lived and where he originally studied. When Joe replied Hanwood Grammar School it was treated as a whimsical answer.

Finally, Jan guided him to the door, distributing goodbyes. As they clattered down the main stairway she said 'You ever get drunk, Joe Telford.' Joe said it had been known and Jan said 'Great.'

Jan yawned, gave up rummaging through her bag for the door key, sat down on the step and gazed at the full moon scudding across the cloud-driven night sky. Joe was standing at the far end of the path, patting a globe-shaped privet bush and singing, quietly.

> *Jesus wants me for a sunbeam,*
> *To shine for him each day,*
> *In every way try to please him,*
> *At home, at school, at play.*

Jan fumbled in her bag again and shouted. 'Didn't know you were religious.' Joe gave the privet bush a last pat and came and sat down beside her.

'Not really and truly. Not a holy Joe. Just left over from Sunday school.'

'Parents were religious.'

'Whose parents.'

'Yours.'

'Why.'

'They sent you to Sunday school.'

47

'Only so as to have some peace on a Sunday afternoon. Chance to digest the old roast and two veg. Little snooze.'

Jan handed him her bag and told him to find the key. He dumped the contents on the concrete path and studied them. She rested her head against the door.

'I can beat that anyway. Holier than thou. Listen to this.'

She hummed to herself, searching for a tune, then sang.

> *Running over, running over,*
> *My cup is full and running over,*
> *Since the Lord saved me,*
> *I'm as happy as can be,*
> *My cup is full and running over.*

While singing, she made big rolling gestures with her hands. He squeezed her arm.

'Very sad.'

'Not sad. No way. It's happy.'

'Well, yes. But beautiful and sad as well.'

'You found the key.'

'Patience. In my father's house are many mansions. If it were not so I would have soddin' well told you.'

He fingered the bag's contents on the path, lifting items to eye level and putting them down again.

'You went to Sunday school, Jan.'

'Nope. My people sent me to a summer camp. Every year. In Canada. Kinda religious. We were called pioneers. Yessireebub.'

Joe conducted himself, arms outstretched, voice forced into bass.

> *Not for delectations sweet,*
> *Not for riches safe and palling,*
> *Not for us the tame enjoyment.*

He pom-pommed vaguely before rising to a crescendo on an elongated 'Pioneeeeeeeeers O Pioneeeeeeeeeeeers.'

Jan poked his chest and said 'No, no. Not like that. Not at all. More like this.' She sang in operetta style.

> *If she's late for morning dip,*
> *She's a Pioneer girl,*
> *If she does fatigue with a zip,*
> *She's a Pioneer girl,*

48

If she moves with a neat little stroke,
As she gracefully paddles her boat,
Sweet personality, full of rascality,
She's a Pioneer girl.

'Can you really paddle a boat.'
'Betcha. A kayak. On Clearwater lake. Straight as an arrow.'
'Like Unkas.'
'Unk who.'
'Unkas. The Mohican.'
'Who's he.'
'Fenimore Cooper. Jesus, girl. You had a funny education.'
'Never you mind. Find that key.'
'Not here.'
'Got to be there.'
'No. Everything but.'
He crooned.
'Lipsticks and dipsticks. Powder and paint. Pills and potions. Unmentionables. No key.'
'Got to be.'
'Look in your pockets.'
'Never put it in my pocket. Never ever ever. Always in my purse.'
She thrust her hand into her coat pocket and produced the key. Muttering 'Strange' she hauled herself up by the doorknob and fiddled with the lock. As the door swung inwards it seemed to pull her with it. She fumbled for the light switch and said 'Figured to carry you over the threshold but reckon I'm not up to it.'
She found the entrance light.
'Come on then.'
'Minute. Picking up your bits and bobs.'

   He presented Jan with her handbag. She shut the door and pulled him a little way into the living room. Telling him to stay put, she hung her raincoat behind the door and groped round the room, switching on tiny wall lights and a cluster of bulbs at floor level, directed so as to reflect from the ceiling. Joe's head turned in a slow semi-circle. Kneeling by the sideboard, Jan asked what he would like to drink. He said he was not sure.
'Name your booze, feller.'
'Whisky.'
'Rye.'

49

'Real whisky.'

Jan said something inaudible and fumbled with bottles and glasses. Joe paced round the room, staring intently at eighteenth-century prints, lush potted plants, a board covered with a complicated array of sea shells, a daguerreotype of Nelly Melba, a rosette-shaped horse brass, a pale blue sketch map of Chesapeake Bay and a portrait photograph of Eugene V. Debs. He stopped in front of the marble shelf jutting out above the electric heater and rubbed a soapstone carving of an Eskimo. He picked up a framed photograph of a middle-aged couple, standing by a heavily chromed car, against a background of winding mountain road.

'Your Mam and Dad.'

'Yep.'

'Handsome couple.'

'They like each other too. Big advantage. If you're married.'

He toyed with the silver figurine of a mermaid, crossed to the desk and played with a glass paperweight with tiny sea horses sealed inside it.

Jan slumped down on one end of a long sofa, a glass of whisky in each hand.

'When you've finished prowling round you can have your drink.'

Joe stayed a while longer at the desk, fondling the paperweight, before sitting at the opposite end of the sofa and taking his whisky. She raised her glass to him.

'Here's to you, baby doll. What you think of the shack.'

Joe's gaze wandered round the room.

'Posh. Reight posh.'

'You're going to turn out to be a bit of an inverted snob, Joe Telford.'

Solemnly, Joe nodded his head.

They sipped their whisky in silence. Somewhere outside there was a chorus of goodnights and take cares and car doors thudding, as a party broke up.

'Great speech you made, man. Great.'

'You said that before.'

'True. An' I'll say it again. That bit about neither master nor servant. It was a great speech.'

'The world will little note nor long remember what we say here.'

'Say here what.'
'Gettysburg.'
'Gettysburg.'
'Lincoln.'
'I know about Lincoln.'
'Didn't say you didn't.'

After a further silence she pointed out that he was still wearing his jacket. He patted his lapels.
'Take it off.'
'Take it off.'
'Looks as if you're about to leave.'
He struggled out of his jacket, clumsily changing his whisky glass from hand to hand.
'Put it somewhere.'
He hung the jacket over the back of a chair and sat down again.

She dabbled her finger in whisky, sucked on it and swung her legs up onto the sofa, resting her feet in Joe's lap.
'You can take my shoes off.'
'Yes ma'am.'
He levered her shoes off and dropped them by the side of the settee.
'You any good at foot massage, Joe.'
'Never tried it. I'm pretty good at peeling oranges. Cut round twice, skin deep and it comes away in quarters. Fetches the pith off. Sounds funny that. Pith off.'
'What's that got to do with it. Peeling oranges.'
'Nothing really. It's just something I'm good at.'
Jan nestled her head against the backrest.
'Give it a try.'
'Peeling oranges.'
'Dimwit.'
Tentatively Joe massaged her feet. She waggled them.
'They're not fragile. Not porcelain feet.'
Joe squeezed them more vigorously and said 'They're little feet.'
'Thank you.'
He skidded his knuckles along the soles and she jerked her legs and told him not to tickle. He promised not to.
'You watch it.'

'I'll watch it.'

'Right then.'

'Right.'

'Are you drunk, Joe.'

'Not so as to say drunk.'

'Me neither. Kinda sorta drunk but not regular drunk.'

She rolled off the sofa, fetched the whisky bottle and refilled both their glasses. As she sat down, Joe asked if he could have her feet back and she put them on his lap. He asked if calves were allowed. She said they were and he stroked her calves.

She sipped at her whisky and complained that Joe was not drinking. He picked his glass up from the carpet, took a large swallow, replaced it and went back to stroking her calves. She bedded herself more deeply into the sofa and spoke sleepily.

'Tell me.'

'Tell you.'

'Yes. Tell me.'

Joe cleared his throat and began to sing 'Tell Me the Old Old Story of Jesus and His Love' but Jan slapped the back of the sofa and said 'No. Not that old story. Tell me about when you lost your virginity. That one.'

'That one.'

'When, where and with who.'

'Whom.'

'Whom was whom.'

'Sybil Harrison.'

'Hey. Sybil. That's pretty classy.'

'S'right. She was the headmaster's daughter. She was only a headmaster's daughter but she certainly knew her onions. No. That was the gardener's daughter. Only a headmaster's daughter but she taught me a lesson or two. Anyway, she'd been to a progressive school. You could tell she was progressive 'cos she cut her hair short.'

Jan wriggled on to her side and her voice came to him muffled by the cushions.

'How old.'

'Sixteen. Sweet sixteen. Me and Syb.'

'Where.'

Joe retrieved his whisky and propped his forearms on her shins.

'First time was in little Walter Bailey's old uncle's seaside caravan, what he had the key to.'

'What was it like.'

Joe rattled the whisky glass against his teeth.

'Let me see now. Sweaty. It was a hot day an' the caravan was like an oven. And the sex was a bit comic opera. Well all overture really. Not much opera to speak of. And embarrassing as hell. The French letter was a hell of a problem. And fascinatin'. And frustratin'. And we couldn't wait to try again. I remember how surprised I was. Surprised by how smooth Syb was and how solid she was. I suppose I'd imagined a lass's nude body so often it was a surprise to find they were real. Funny that. You have all these fantasies. Shadowy curves and dark patches. And there she was with a real cunt and bones and she was heavy. Marvellous.'

'You love her.'

'Barmy about her. Used to write her poems and give her mi clothing coupons.'

'What's a clothing coupon.'

'It was wartime. Clothing was rationed. On coupons. An' we learned juggling together and did an act in the school concert. Star turn.'

'She love you.'

'At first. I think. Yes, she did. But after we'd been knocking about together for a year or so, her Dad took a job down south. In Worthing. Few letters then end of story. I hitchhiked down to see her once but it was a flop. Fresh fellers and pastures new. All over. Just like that.'

'Sad.'

'It seemed sad to me.'

'Wonder where she is now.'

'Long lost. What about you.'

'Virginity wise.'

'Mmm.'

'Your drink's empty. Lean over.'

She wrestled round to reach the bottle and hunched awkwardly forward to fill both glasses.

'Not like yours. Well, we were both seventeen. Bit older than you and Sybil but it was more your lust. More like your lust and curiosity. Pierce Morton Gould. Beau Gould we used to call him,

53

on account of he was real pretty. An' he was A team at football, and he was all-star baseball and he used to flash his lovely body around at basketball, an' all the girls said he was hung like a Greek statue in the Templeton gallery and they said he did it like crazy. So I chose him. I decided he was the one to start the ball rolling. So to speak.'

She tittered.

'So I got him invited over to our country place for a weekend and I snook in at night and straddled him.'

'And how was it.'

'Not bad. But not good. He was scared because I was a virgin and that surprised me. And he wanted to chicken out because my parents might get to know about it. He was a bit of a mouse, really.'

He giggled and she demanded to know what the hell he was giggling at.

'You sound like you were a pretty fearsome sort of lass.'

She pondered.

'Could be. I knew what I wanted and I meant for him to deliver the goods.'

'And what became of him.'

'Hell knows. He just disappeared into the world.'

Joe balanced his whisky glass on the sofa arm and stroked her legs, listening to her breathing become slower and more even. He let his head loll backwards and looked hazily up at the ceiling with its intricate patchwork of shadows, trying to remember a song lyric about flickering shadows that softly come and go. A clock was producing a curiously sibilant tick, like the puffing of a far-off steam engine, but he failed to locate its whereabouts. A dog barked gruffly, somewhere out on the estate, and was answered by a high yapping.

Jan spoke in a near whisper from down among the cushions.

'Know what, Joe.'

'What.'

'We've got too much light and too many clothes. You agree.'

'I agree.'

She rolled slowly off the sofa and groped from one switch to another till only the single bar of the electric fire cast a glow into the room. They undressed, clumsily scattering clothes around them. Jan sat cross-legged in front of the fire and Joe sat opposite her. They gazed at each other.

Jan reached across and ran her fingers down his ribs.

'You're a lovely bony man.'

'A bony old man.'

'A bony man.'

He touched her breasts and passed the palm of his hand lightly across her belly.

'You're as beautiful as Sybil Harrison.'

'Thank you.'

She bowed forward. Shuffling closer together they kissed and stroked and patted and squeezed each other. She pulled his hand onto her cunt and he felt the hair moistening as she rocked gently, pinning his fingers beneath her. He flinched as she stroked his prick. Suddenly she grasped his shoulders and rolled him onto his back, spreading herself across him. He mumbled 'Now I know how Beau whatsisname felt like.' She muttered 'Shut up, Joe.' She wriggled herself carefully onto him and he wrestled and jerked convulsively under her for a little while, then shuddered and went still. She murmured 'O dear O dear.' Joe sighed, pulled her head against his and whispered 'See. All overture an' no opera.' She kissed him and tugged at his hair.

'Never mind. We'll practise. Lots of practice. Till we get it right.'

She lay on him for a long time, sometimes moving a little to feel his hip bones or the flatness of his belly, rubbing her breasts against his chest.

Sliding off him and on to her side, she propped her head on one hand and paddled her fingers in the sweat on his chest.

'You all right.'

'Bit better than all right.'

She put her thigh across his legs and leaned down to kiss him. For a while she prodded and poked him till, fiddling in his navel, she pulled out a piece of fluff. Joe murmured 'A message for Garcia.'

'What is.'

'What you got from mi belly button. A message for Garcia.'

Jan flicked the piece of fluff away.

'You know Joe, you're a bit of a nut.'

'No I'm not.'

'Who's Garcia.'

He crooked an arm under his head.

'When we were kids, there was this film. Called *A Message for Garcia*. South American revolution thing. Excitin' stuff. Anyroad, it got to be a sort of catchphrase. If you saw a kid running through the village and you asked him where he was goin', he'd say, I've got a message for Garcia.'

'You're still a bit of a nut.'

His body loosened and his head lolled sideways. She pushed at him.

'Joe.'

'Mmm.'

'You falling asleep.'

'Think so.'

'Tell me one thing. First.'

'Yes.'

She propped his head up on her hand and looked at him.

'After we went out that first time. When I drove you back to your house. Why did you send me away.'

He ran his forefinger down the side of her face.

'I was afraid. I was afraid you were going to disturb my peace.'

She nodded.

'I can more or less understand that. But why did you agree to do the talk. Why did you come back.'

Joe bumped his forehead gently against hers.

'Because I think you're going to disturb my peace.'

She cuddled him.

When he had relaxed into a soft whistling snore, she disentangled herself and went upstairs. Standing in the bathroom she contemplated the shower, sniffed at herself and decided she smelled fine. She collected pillows and pulled the big duvet off the bed, dragging it behind her down the stairs. Kneeling over Joe she pushed the scattered clothing away, tucked a pillow under his head and rolled him into the duvet so that it served as a mattress and cover. She wriggled down next to him and lay staring at the ceiling. Her last thought but one, before she fell asleep, was that Joe was frail and she would have to be gentle with him.

She fell into sleep at the end of a nagging speculation about what was in the message for Garcia.

Joe's voice boomed out from the bank, across the open water of the wide pound that led up to the lock.

'You great, steaming, transatlantic twit.'

Jan stood stiffly at the stern of the narrow boat, gripping the tiller and staring straight ahead. White-faced, she ignored Joe loping along the towpath, level with the boat as it ploughed forward. He howled despairingly.

'Reverse, put it in reverse, for Christ's sake, down by your left hand.'

The boat bumped heavily into the grass bank at the point where it funnelled into the lock. Jan kept her footing by clinging to the tiller as the engine cut out and her coughing, as the breeze blew diesel fumes out onto the stern platform, broke the sudden silence. The boat started to drift away from the bank. Joe snatched at the bow rope, hauled the craft round to the lock entrance and tied it to a mooring ring, anchored in concrete. Jan was sitting on the tiller stool as he thumped along the sundeck, dropped into the stern and switched off the ignition. Her head drooped and her voice trembled.

'There was no need to shout.'

He squatted on the top step of the cockpit and stared at her.

'How do you make that out.'

She let her body relax and swivelled on the stool.

'You're a bigmouth. You are. And a bully. And what is a twit anyway.'

'It's somebody who stands like a stuffed dummy, starin' pop-eyed and doing nowt, while the bloody boat runs into the bank.'

'I couldn't think what to do, was all.'

He rolled his eyes upwards.

'Gentle Jesus. The throttle goes forward for forward, straight up for neutral and backward for reverse. Now I ask you, that hardly teks a skilled engineer, does it.'

She slapped the tiller.

'It doesn't steer right.'

'Course it does. I've told you. With a tiller, a boat's slow to

57

answer, so you make your move a bit ahead of time and compensate straight away because it'll need time to take effect.'

'You shouldn't have left me in the boat by myself. It's not fair.'

'I was goin' ahead to open the lock.'

'I'm not used to it yet.'

'Hells bells. You drive a car. If you can drive a car, in traffic, with gears and clutches, at high speed, you can surely to God tootle a boat along a canal at four miles an hour.'

'That's got nothing to do with it.'

Joe scrambled to his feet, stood over her, squeezed her throat then kissed her.

She pouted and said 'What's that for.'

'You make me feel like Buster Keaton.'

'Why Buster Keaton.'

'In *The General*. With his sweetheart. They're rushing along in this locomotive, escaping the Northerners who're shooting at 'em, and she's supposed to be piling wood into the firebox. And when he looks at her, she's throwing bits of wood away 'cos they've got knots in 'em and playing house, sweeping out the cab an' such. So he starts to strangle her then changes his mind and kisses her.'

'You mean I'm a twit.'

'Only sometimes.'

'Well there's no point in standing around. Let's get through this lock.'

'Aye, aye, helmsperson.'

He picked up a lock key and scrambled onto the towpath. Propping his back against the gate beam, he pushed open one gate, pulled the boat through into the basin and closed it. He unwound the paddles and gate blades at the far end and the boat sank down as the lock started to lose water. He sat, legs dangling into the lock, letting the bow rope slide over his knees, watching Jan pottering about in the cockpit. She tilted her head back and he waved at her as she shouted.

'Hold the rope and keep the boat in the middle. So we don't get hung up on the sill.'

Joe tugged at the rope.

'I told you that.'

'Never you mind. Just hold onto the rope.'

When the water had settled to its lowest level, Joe pushed open the gate on the low side and hauled the boat out, holding it against the bank till a motor cruiser coming up the canal had sidled past them, into the lock.

For the next mile Jan steered the boat in long snaking curves while Joe clucked at her side. Finally, she steadied it into a straight run, slightly over to the right bank, and felt enough at ease to loll against the stern rail, holding the tiller casually, with one hand. She dawdled the boat comfortably when Joe leaped ashore and heaved open a swing bridge and readily agreed that he could stay at the front, sitting on the prow. When he came back he said 'You try it. It's just like flying.'

'What do I do.'

'Sit as far forward as you can and look straight down at the water.' She crept along the outside ledge of the boat and sat on the prow for a long time. When she came back to take the tiller again, for another lock, she said 'It's just like flying.'

Through the lock, they saw a heron, standing stiffly, at the top of a small tree on the left bank. Disturbed by the approaching boat noise, it lifted clumsily into the air, retracted its legs and flapped slowly along the canal, to settle again in a sentinel stance. A second and third time it moved off, ahead of the boat, but its fourth flight brought it to the boundary of its hunting ground and it flew left in a huge semi-circle to settle back on the edge of the canal, behind the boat.

She watched Joe as he sat on the stern rail, studying the banks, intently.

'You really relate to canals, don't you, Joe.'

He furrowed his brow.

'You mean I like 'em.'

'Yes.'

He hesitated.

'I suppose I do. Nobody can find you on a canal. You've gone secret. Spying out the land in a way.'

Jan burst out laughing and pointed to the bank where the bow wave of the boat had dragged a clutch of moorhen chicks from their nest and left them bedraggled and astonished, bouncing madly up and down on the turbulent water. She leaned across the tiller and put an arm around his waist.

'We've seen a lot of those. What are they.'

59

'Moorhens.'
'Moorhens.'
'That's right.'
'Why aren't they up on the moors then.'
'They started out being called mere hens because they are a water bird but it got mispronounced into moorhens, till that's what they got called.'
She nibbled his ear.
'You're full of bits of edification, Joe.'
'Well known irrelevant gen merchant.'

They travelled on through a small town, the ruined backsides of old factories looming over them, and out into flat fields, with a sluggish river meandering alongside, till it looped away to the west. The canal entered a deep, shadowed cutting with trees springing almost horizontally from its sides and creepers trailing down into a mass of struggling rhododendron bushes. Out of the cutting they moved through the glazed green light of overhanging willows, past the white boil of a feeder stream, round a bend and into a long straight run of glass-clear water with a flight of three locks, just visible in the distance. They haggled about whether it was time to eat and agreed that he would take the boat through the locks while she got the meal ready. At the locks, two young lads gave Joe a little help and a lot of shouted suggestions, warnings and self-congratulation as they leaped from deck to lock side and hauled the narrow boat in a bumpy zig-zag through the three sets of gates. Joe paid them excessively and steered the boat half a mile on from the locks, before mooring.

Down in the galley, he watched Jan shuttling a frying pan, piled high with sliced vegetables and tinned tomatoes, over a calor gas flame.
She grumbled about the jolting of the boat coming through the locks as she ladled the mix into the bowls he was holding. Cramped on narrow seats, against the cabin table, they ate hungrily and drank their way through a bottle of cheap burgundy.
He muttered approval and asked what the meat was.
'It isn't.'
'Isn't what.'
'Meat. It's Granos. Sort of soya bean magicked into meat. Mollylecularised.'

60

'Tastes all right.'

'And it's in a stir fry. Lots of fibre and near as dammit no cooking oil gookum.'

'Is that good.'

'Course it's good. You eat too much fat, Joe Telford. And too much sugar and not enough fibre and not enough vitamins.'

'Bad as that.'

'Yup. Goin' to reorganise your diet, man. Tend to your health. For dessert you get yoghurt.'

He leaned back from his empty plate.

'Don't like yoghurt.'

'When did you eat it.'

'Didn't. I don't like it.'

'You're like a child. Not eating things you haven't tried. Well this is fruit yoghurt, so you'll like it. After a while, we'll move you on to natural yoghurt.'

'Lucky me.'

'You disputing my nutritional advice.'

'Wouldn't dare.'

They wrangled about food till the meal was finished and Jan flopped onto the double bed at the stern of the boat while Joe washed the pots. He stuffed pans into the cupboard under the sink and came and sat on the edge of the bed, unlaced and kicked off his boots and rolled alongside her. Kissing her neck, he slipped his hand under her skirt and began to stroke her thigh. She patted his face.

'What's this all about.'

'I thought we ought to have some more of that practice you're so keen on.'

'We've already had a lot of practice on this cruise, Joseph. Just a waterborne sex orgy, this canal lark.'

'Tony and Cleo, bargein' down the Nile, courtesy Inland Waterways Board.'

He slid one probing finger into her pants.

'Practice makes perfect.'

She unbuttoned his shirt and circled his chest lightly with her fingernails.

'I know what I meant to ask you about.'

He mumbled 'About two fingers being better than one' as he

61

wriggled a second finger onto her clitoris, and brushed it gently.
'No. Randy Joe. About radio. You said you'd run a pirate radio, in
politics. Giving out anarchist messages. When I said I gave a talk
once, on the radio.'
He rested his head on her chest and attended to the pulsing of his
fingers on her cunt.
'What about it.'
'Tell me about it.'
'Now.'
'Yes.'
He made a rumbling sound in his throat.
'Long, long time ago. Me and some blokes. During an election.
We ran this pirate political radio transmitter. About a thirty-mile
range. Radios. Moved it about. I had it for a while. 'Cos I had this
porter's job in a hospital and I got it set up in an old storeroom,
hidden behind some boxes, with the aerial going up by the
drainpipe to the roof.'
He sucked at the nipple of her right breast through her cotton
blouse and mumbled 'Hurrah for no bra.'
'Stop dis-gressing. How did people know how to tune in to
you.'
'We came in on the television frequency. We used to cut in four
or five times of an evening, telling people to keep their television
sets on when the programmes finished and listen to Rebel Radio
– the voice of political home truths.'
He spluttered and began to suck her nipple again.
'What are you tittering at. So to speak.'
Joe leaned his head back and grinned at her.
'I was just thinkin'. It was a comical do in its way. I'd set the thing
up in the storeroom, switch on to transmit and leave a tape
running, so the voice would start in say three minutes. Then I'd
dodge through the hospital to the nurses' lounge, where they had
the television goin'. There was only the one channel in those days.
To check if the transmitter was workin'. I'd stand at the back and
on would come my voice chantin' about Rebel Radio. Once it was
the newsreader bloke on the television an' he's looking round him
all goggle-eyed an' upset 'cos he could hear my voice on his
monitor an' he's struggling to keep goin' with the news.
Everybody in the nurses' lounge is jabbering away, wondering

62

what's happening and I'm standin' there all puffed up, on account of it was me that was happening.'

Jan undid the top button of his trousers, opened the zip a little way and walked her fingernails across his belly.

'Smug bugger.'

'It was nice bein' the only one in the know.'

He tugged at her pants and she arched her back so that he could slide them down and off.

'How come the fuzz didn't catch you with their direction-finding gizmos.'

'They tried. But they got it in their heads it was coming from the terraces behind the hospital. They did house-to-house checks on them. Anyway, it would have been a hell of a job searching a hospital.'

He pushed his hand along her thigh and hip and under her blouse to fondle her breast.

'The last night I broadcast, I came out from the hospital about midnight or so and there's detector vans and coppers and plain clothes buggers all over the place and I'm nodding an biddin' 'em goodnight as I stroll off.'

'Smartass.'

He leaned down and across her and licked gently at her cunt. She opened her legs, stretched and made a low, whistling sound.

'You are a distracting bastard. Do you think it does any good.'

He raised his head.

'Sucking your cunt.'

'The pirate radio. Broadcasting.'

He moved back to lie alongside her.

'No way of telling. Might have given somebody an idea or two. Rattled the powers that be.'

'Reason I asked.'

He flicked her nipples delicately with thumb and forefinger.

'Reason I asked.'

'Was.'

'This feller's doing an external Master's. At the university. Name's Tully. He's got a job in government computers. Home Office. An' he says he's hacked in to some sort of state secret stuff. He's a rebel type. Wants to know if it can be used at all. Politically. And if so, how.'

She jerked as he put his finger back in her cunt and rubbed it slowly up and down. She mumbled 'Wants to be a gadfly stinging the body politic sort of thing.'

'Might be.'

'If I fix up a chat will you talk to him.'

'Sure.'

'You mean that.'

'I'll talk to him.'

She rolled onto her side, trapping his finger, and pulled the zip of his trousers further down.

'What were you doing portering anyway.'

'Had all sorts of jobs. Once was a creator of non-reconditionable government jerricans. By bashing 'em.'

'What's a jerrican.'

'Petrol can.'

'Who'd have thought.'

'Like I said.'

He lifted his buttocks and she wriggled his trousers and underpants down to his knees. She cradled his prick in her hand.

'Why did you bash them.'

He shivered.

'See, this firm had a contract to recondition old jerricans. An' in the contract it said they didn't have to try to recondition them if they were damaged beyond a certain extent. Well this mob wasn't going to bother with any cans if they weren't nearly perfect to start with. They came in railway wagons on a little spur line near the factory and the bloke throws each one out at my feet.'

He wriggled hard and thrust his legs up and down till his trousers and underpants dropped onto the deck.

'Where was I.'

'You had this gasolene can at your feet.'

'Right. An' I was holding a seven-pound sledgehammer. If the can was OK I heaved it into the lorry to go off to the works. If it had a little defect I gave it a bloody big bang in the middle with mi hammer. Just where the struts cross. So it all caved in. And threw it on the reject pile. See.'

Jan said that it was a dull story and began to move the end of his prick up and down, in tiny jerks. Joe gasped and tried to steady his voice.

64

'An' every Friday a man from the Ministry came. A genuine man from the Ministry with a bowler hat and a briefcase. Honest.'

He rolled on to his side as Jan put both her arms round his neck and he fingered open the buttons on her blouse.

'And the man from the Ministry used to go through this bloody great pile of reject cans, real careful, to see if they were all proper rejects truly beyond repair.'

She rubbed the nape of his neck and he groaned and slid his thigh over her.

'I could have told him. Personal guarantee. Given him my guarantee I had personally non-reconditionablised 'em. Absolutely.'

He inched into her very slowly and lingered between each thrust and withdrawal. She gripped his buttocks and held him to the same dragging pace. Putting her mouth against his ear, she whispered 'It must be great to be a feller with a sledgehammer.' After a long time, they began to rock together more swiftly and deeply and she sobbed as she came. Gripped tightly by her thighs, he grunted and drove strongly into climax. He tried to ease himself off her but she held him and they relaxed into a sleepy embrace, listening to the slap of water against the hull of the boat and the cawing of homecoming rooks.

In the gathering dusk she whispered in a tone near to panic. 'Joe, we're being looked at. Joe.'

He mumbled 'Where.'

'Through the curtain. Somebody's head. Watching us.'

He rolled to one side. His voice copied her whisper.

'Can't see anybody. We're not on the towpath side.'

'There. There.'

He pulled the curtain open and they looked out at the huge head of a cow, its nostrils pressed against the window which was clouding in its breath. He kissed her.

'Cows are very nosy animals. They love to know what's goin' on.'

Jan fetched the second round of beer and asked Joe what he thought of her favourite pub. He sucked his bottom lip and surveyed the lounge.

'Beer's piss poor. Pork pies have got more gelatine than pork. Barman's a jokey sod. Seats are slippery. Decoration's imitation, plastic, Edwardian rubbish. Crowd is a bunch of natteracious smart alecks and the muzak's a load of 'orrible plinky plonk. Otherwise, it's a grand place.'

She kissed his cheek and murmured 'Just for a moment I thought you didn't care for it. Anyway, I thought the beer was OK.'

'This brew's never been any good since Allsop disappeared.'

'I'm sorry to hear that.'

He pulled his cuff back and looked at his watch.

'When's this Tully feller comin', anyway.'

'Give him time. He has to drive across from Manchester.'

'What's he do.'

'You know what he does. He's a computer-statistician. He works in social stats for a Home Office project.'

'He's a civil servant.'

'You make it sound like leprosy.'

'They can cure leprosy.'

Jan thickened her accent.

'Gawd, yo'all is a pree-judiced feller, Joe Telford.'

'That's true. What's he doin' a thesis on. At your university.'

'Computer models of structural social change.'

'Bai gum.'

'You're putting on your thickie act, Joe.'

'Just a bit.'

'Anyway, I've as good as promised him you'll help him blow the whistle on Her Majesty's Government, so you be nice to him.'

He swished his beer round and peered into the glass.

She started to hum to the muzak and he said 'That one translates fine.'

'What translates fine.'

'The song.'

'Don't get you.'

'Simple. All songs translate to their true meanin' if you just substitute three words.'

'How.'

'You don't know.'

'I don't know what you're talking about.'

66

He squeezed her hand and said 'You're not very cultured are you.'
'Tell me.'
'Well. For love you substitute knob. For dance you substitute wank and for heart you substitute arse. That way you get what the song is really about.'
'I don't think I like the sound of this.'
'Like you were just humming that well-known song "Knob is the Sweetest Thing, the Nice, the Neatest Thing".'
She looked at him wide-eyed.
'You can't just do that.'
'Of course, you could have sung instead that old ditty "I've Got my Knob to Keep me Warm" or "My Knob is Like a Red Red Rose" or "I Can't Give You Anything but Knob, Baby".'
Jan covered her mouth with her hand.
'What've you got.'
She shook her head.
'You've thought of one.'
'It just came into my mind. Couldn't help it.'
'Out with it.'
'There's a pop song about "Your Love is Lifting me Higher and Higher".'
'Exactly. A lady in the female superior position. Now translating dance to wank gives you such ballads as "When We're Out Together Wanking Cheek to Cheek", "I Could Have Wanked All Night" and "Wanking in the Dark".'
'That will do.'
'And arse for heart gives you that fine homosexual anthem "You are my Arse's Delight".'
'Shut up.'
'Or the gay bloke's chant of terror, "You're Breaking my Arse with Your Heaving".'
She punched his arm.
'Enough. You're going to ruin no end of songs for me, desist.'
'Not even "That's the Story, That's the Glory of".'
'Not even.'
'Refuse enlightenment you do.'

Joe was complaining of the lack of dartboard or dominoes when Jan pointed to the door where a fresh-faced young man and a dark, plump girl stood, scanning the lounge. They crossed to the table and the four stood stiffly, handshaking and nodding, while Jan introduced Chris Tully to Joe Telford and Tully introduced Evelyn Hughes to Jan and Joe. Drinks were fetched and they sat round the big iron table, making clumsy conversation. Joe said that Evelyn could be a man's name and that his Member of Parliament when he was a lad had been called Evelyn, while the girl smiled brightly and said she had never actually met a male Evelyn and Chris Tully in answer to Jan's query explained that the journey from Manchester had been easy till they left the motorway and the traffic was jammed on the narrow country roads. They all agreed that it was a fine evening and the pub was a convenient meeting point.

When the small talk dwindled into fits and starts Jan suggested that they 'get to the nitty gritty'.

Tully began with a rambling explanation of his work, its complexity, how it was administered, how all sorts of information, including committee minutes, were nowadays stored in a computer database and how he sometimes went down to London to work with a government team that was preparing new programs for analysing census statistics. Evelyn Hughes watched him admiringly as he spoke, her lips slightly parted. Joe sat slumped on the bench seat, sucking on potato crisps, and Jan finally cut in to prompt Tully to talk about the confidential material he had acquired.

Tully lit a cigar with clumsy ceremony, said 'Right, right' and puffed on it several times in quick succession. He looked round to make sure that no one was sitting near them.

'OK. So I spot early on that this London set-up must have a lot of security stuff on the mainframe. There's blokes creeping in and out of director's office for login codes, user identification codes, program file names and so on and shredding print-outs all over the place. Your briefcase and pockets are checked when you go in or out. User manuals are full of dark hints about the Official Secrets Act and stuff about levels of confidentiality and so on. If you call for listings half of 'em come up no access. The resident blokes in the know are lording it over us visiting yokels because we're not in the know. Hinting at cloak an' dagger shit. And so on. See what I mean.'

68

He drew heavily on his cigar, choked, recovered and looked intently at each of his three companions in turn.

'So I says to myself, Christopher, young feller-me-lad, let's have a peek at some of this super secret garbage. Find out what the bastards are up to. Use your craft and guile. Now, guess how I got in.'

Evelyn said excitedly ''Cos the Greeks had a word for it.'

'Exactly so, sweetheart.'

'They usually do.'

He looked at Joe.

'I've told Evelyn and Jan how I did it. Can you guess.'

'Not a clue.'

'Want to know.'

Joe tugged at his right earlobe with his thumb and forefinger.

'All ears.'

'Right. It was a bit trickier than this but I'll give you the gist. I'd noticed one time, on the director's desk, a sheet of restricted listings marked no longer in use. They'd emptied the files that these codes used to access. Right. And lo and behold every one of these codes is somebody out of Greek mythology. You know, Zeus or Jason or Mercury or whatever, followed by a two-figure number. So I set the old cortex to spike fire and given a brief brood I have the gizmo. I get a dinky little program running that contains the names of Greek gods or heroes and generates a series of all numbers 1 to 99 in a continuous loop and for each number it tries to log in to the mainframe. Took a little while but *voilà*. We get to Perseus fourteen and up it comes on the screen. There was still some diddling about before I could access the specific files but given my delicate touch up comes the deep dark secret.'

With a flourish, he took two folded sheets of computer print-out from his inside pocket. Evelyn nudged him and said 'Tell them how you got it out of the building.' Joe said 'Do tell.' Tully clamped his cigar between his teeth and grinned. 'How about that. There's the security brigade, peak caps an' all, sitting at the door, all stern and sentry-like. So what does Cock Robin do then, poor thing.'

Joe said 'Fiddle it out through the computer.'

Tully clinked his beer glass against Joe's and supped from it.

'Spot on, brother. You would not credit it. These buggers don't even know their own technology. I just switch the output over to the modem channel, dialled into my micro in Manchester and squirted the data down the line. I clear the machine at the London end, shred the print-out and when I get back to Manchester I print out there.'

Jan said 'Neat.' Tully made a bobbing bow and handed the print-out sheets to Joe who spread them on the table. Tully waved his cigar at the top sheet.

'The first part you can't make sense of. Too many coded references. And I don't know what the acronym at the top stands for. CC usually means co-ordinating committee but I don't know what LO is. But I can guess what the list is.'

Joe folded his arms and stared at the sheet.

'Phone tapping.'

'Smart feller. Go to the top of the class.'

Jan started to ask who the people on the list were when Evelyn said she would fetch another round of drinks. She took their orders, refused Joe's offer to pay and went off to the bar. Tully leaned over and jabbed his finger at the print-out, scattering cigar ash.

'Take your columns left to right. Name of person. Date of birth. That's a standard identifying datum. Phone number. Initials of requesting agency. Some I'm not sure of but obviously MOD is Ministry of Defence. HO Home Office. SB Special Branch and so on. Where it has a bracketed PO it may mean that their mail is being checked as well. The column with figures is a mystery. Might be the file numbers of the tapes. Then date surveillance begins and for a few of them, date surveillance was lifted. I don't know why some of them have asterisks. Two of them are marked actioned but God knows what action.'

He pulled the top sheet to one side.

'The sheet underneath is the one I got a month later. It's really the same with eleven names added, three dropped off and a couple more with dates for surveillance ended.'

Jan ran her finger down the list.

'But who are these people.'

Tully stubbed out his half-smoked cigar and sucked noisily at his beer.

'There's three names I can recognise. West and Valey are both

70

fairly big noises in Nuclear Disarmament and Clive Redditch I've seen on TV once. He's a political pundit of some sort.'

'You know any of them, Joe.'

'A couple, I think. There's a D.D. Crowther that's a union official, Transport I think. He's getting on in years so the date of birth is about right. Ayat Khan is from around these parts, local government, made a big fuss about immigration policy and racial discrimination.'

Tully rapped on the table and said 'Now I remember him.'

'So they're all sorts.'

'Like that list Nixon had.'

Jan repeated 'All sorts' and Joe raised his eyebrows at her. She flapped her hands.

'I mean not necessarily spies or anything like that.'

'Just troublesome citizens, sweetheart. What my old headmaster used to call agitators and troublemakers. He warned us about them. Said they were a menace to social stability.'

Evelyn came back clutching four glasses precariously to her breasts. Joe made her stand still while he took them one by one and put them on the table. As they sipped their drinks she said it was exciting, poking their noses into government secrets. Jan agreed but looked doubtfully at Tully.

'I'm not sure it'll cause all that much of a stir though, making it public. Everyone knows there's a lot of official phone tapping. They're always arguing about it in Parliament. It'll hardly come as a shock to people.'

Tully hunched forward on his stool.

'Yes but if we get the papers to publish lists of people whose phones are being tapped, your actual names, that makes it sensational. There'll be charges and counter-charges. Guessing what they're up to. Why these particular phones are being tapped. Rows galore. As you would say, Jan, hot diggedy dog.'

'I wouldn't ever say such a thing, Chris. What do you think, Joe.'

Joe chewed his thumb.

'Not that simple. Any newspaper would want proof that the list was genuine. That means you and your source would have to be revealed to some journalist. That would give the coppers a fair chance of tracing it all back, once the stuff was made public. A journalist's sources are getattable, nowadays.'

Tully looked stricken.

'Hell, that's not on. No way. Nobody's got to know this stuff came off a Home Office computer. They'd nail me for sure, once they knew that.'

Evelyn put her hand on Tully's arm comfortingly.

'You've got to understand. In my job I can't take the risk.'

Joe wagged a finger at him.

'Not to panic. Let's think a bit. Anyway, I'm not sure the papers would touch it as a straight secrets exposed deal. It's got to be made into some sort of news item for them to publish it. Do that and I think I know a journalist who'd fancy it.'

Jan said 'Sounds fine. How do you make it into a news item.'

'Without the police tracing it back to me.'

Joe sipped at his beer and grimaced. He folded his arms and the others stared at him. He stared at the ceiling.

'Suppose. Suppose I take the list. I get the address of each of these people from their local directory. The STD code tells me their locality.'

He tapped the print-out sheet.

'Let's say I write each one a letter. Standard screed, anonymous, saying did you know you have government eavesdroppers earwiggin' on your phone. Tell 'em the date it started and the agency that wanted it done.'

Jan started to interrupt and Joe flagged her to silence.

'OK. I write to my journalist mate. I do that anonymously so it doesn't put him in a spot when they get on to him. I just tell him that the following people have received detailed information about their phones being tapped. He can ask each of them to confirm this and if they do, he can publish that as a news item. That's what makes it a news item. He doesn't have to say it's true that their phones are being tapped. He just says it's true that they've been told their phone is being tapped, how they feel about it, why they think it might be being done to them and so on.'

Jan looked puzzled.

'Seems all roundabout.'

'Sort of wheels within wheels.'

'It'll do the job. There'll be questions in the House. Is it true that as reported et cetera. Government daren't issue a straight denial and their narks'll panic summat fierce 'cos it buggers up part of

72

their phone tapping system. Half the people on this list will be protesting publicly, askin' why them and so on. It'll work. We can leave out a few that are on the list so that it doesn't point to the computer record as the source.'

Tully looked at Evelyn then at Joe. He chewed his lip.

'Yes, I can see that. It makes it a scandal with names attached. You get them on your side. But we have to make sure it can't be traced back. We've got to be absolutely sure.'

'You can only ever be sure up to a certain point.'

The young man fingered the print-out sheets, scratching the surface of the paper and bending and straightening a corner.

'What I'll do. In future. I won't get a print-out at all. I won't put it up to my terminal. When I go to the London set-up, I'll put it up on the screen for just a minute or two and memorise any new names and telephone numbers.'

He paused.

'How do I get them to you.'

Joe shrugged his shoulders and said 'Write to me.'

'You must be joking. And I'm not phoning you either. There's got to be no connection between you and me from now on. Not a trace. They'd get on to it.'

'All right. How about you tell Jan and she tells me.'

Tully's voice squeaked.

'No. That won't do. They can connect me to her, through the university, and they could link her to you.'

Joe looked sideways at Jan.

'They do a grand job.'

He tapped his nose.

'How about carrier pigeon.'

Tully flushed.

'If you're not going to take it seriously.'

'No, I am serious. Honest. Just seems a bit tricky.'

Tully cupped his right elbow in his left hand and put his other hand to his forehead. After a few moments he turned to Evelyn.

'You can be the interface. Take any new names to Joe. When I pass 'em on to you. How about it.'

Evelyn looked pleased.

'I'd like that. I'd like to be part of it. The courier. I'll be the go-between.'

Tully patted her hand.

'Joe. Where do you work.'

'What's that got to do with it.'

'Where do you work.'

'Pritchard's. It's a timberyard.'

'Whereabouts.'

'In Scarby. Just by the river bridge. Where you come into town.'

'Good. Now here's the plan. When I get new info, I tell it to Evelyn. She memorises it. When do you finish work.'

'About five.'

'So, on the day she gets the new names, Evelyn waits outside your timberyard at five. When you come out she follows you until there's no one with you and tells you the names and numbers to memorise.'

He turned back to Evelyn and said 'There's to be no other link. Just repeat the list till he's got it and break contact. Is that clear.'

Evelyn's eyes widened and she nodded vigorously.

'You bet. I'll be so hush hush you'll be amazed.'

Jan whispered to Joe 'A message for Garcia' and Joe pinched his cheeks tightly between finger and thumb. Tully repeated his instructions at length and Evelyn said 'You bet' and 'Sure' and 'Right'.

When Joe had agreed to the arrangement Tully insisted on handshakes all round and repeated each part of what he called 'the master plan', seeking assurance that the journalist would be unable to guess at the original source of the information, that the anonymous letters would be posted from different parts of the country, that the print-outs he had brought would be destroyed, that Evelyn would make sure she was not identified while talking to Joe. He spoke enthusiastically of the uproar the exposures would cause and proposed a toast 'to gadflies on the body politic'. Joe added 'to flies in the ointment', Jan offered 'to crap hitting the fan' and Evelyn concluded with 'upsetting apple carts'.

Through another round of drinks the talk was jokey, full of self-congratulation and sketches of possible public outrage at phone tapping revelations. It slackened suddenly and Tully said he must take the chance, while in the district, to visit his thesis

74

supervisor. He called Joe comrade and made a short speech about not meeting again for the present but being united in the great conspiracy. Evelyn winked at Joe and said she would meet him by the third gravestone and the password was Mata Hari.

After leave taking, Joe and Jan sat in silence for a while till she said 'What do you think.' He folded the print-outs and tucked them into his inside pocket.

'He's a bit wet behind the ears.'

'But he is bright.'

'As a button.'

'What about the scheme.'

He searched in the cellophane packet for the last few slivers of potato crisp.

'Ah the scheme. Bit of a joke really. It'll not lead straight to the new Jerusalem. Still it'll squeeze the balls of the powers that be. Bring a few tears to their eyes. An' that's a jovial and righteous thing to do.'

'For a while, anyway.'

'For a while.'

She looked at the array of smeared and empty beer glasses.

'Last drink.'

'Mek it a whisky. Half water. I can't stand any more of this brew.'

She brought two whiskies and sat leaning against him, her arm tucked into his.

'What about this great book you said you'd write, Joe.'

He sipped at his whisky.

'You said I'd write it. I only said I'd think about it.'

'I can see it now. The life, times and political philosophy of Joseph Telford in two volumes, tastefully bound in hand-tooled leather with title lettered in gold leaf. No, we'll make it a paperback with a real dramatic picture of you on the cover.'

'God save us.'

'And an interview in the *Guardian* when you become one of their weekend people.'

'An' they make me Mayor of Chapel-en-le-Frith.'

'It is time you got started, though, honey lamb.'

'You know what.'

'What do I know.'

'Life's getting to be a bit hectic since you rose from the waves, young Venus.'

The small town died away in a scatter of pebble-dashed bungalows and the Oaklands nursing home came into view. From a distance it looked like a handsome Georgian mansion with a portico and lintelled front. As Jan turned the car into the drive she saw its charms diminish into peeling paintwork, shoddy columns stuck on to the doorways, badly carved transoms, ill-fitting windows of mixed sizes and a network of bodged drainpipes and gutters. She pulled onto the end of a short line of parked cars and switched off the ignition. The engine clicked and creaked as it cooled. From beyond a distant copse of trees, Sunday morning church bells were tolling, repeating four notes over and over again. Fingering the steering wheel, she stared through the windscreen at a man using a walking frame, bumping heavily across the lawn in front of the house. Joe reached out and pushed back a strand of hair that had fallen over her eye.

'You look fretted.'

'Do I.'

'You do.'

She turned towards him.

'I guess it's the idea of talking to someone who's dying. I'm afraid of upsetting him or making him angry. Being too cheerful or too solemn or too something. It's OK for you. You're his son. Well, not OK, but different. You see what I mean.'

He grinned at her and she smiled back mechanically.

'Listen. Charles Frederick's got uraemia but he's dying more or less slow and easy. He's taking his time about it and he doesn't suffer that much bar his stiffness. Dying doesn't bother him a lot, so there's no reason why it should bother you. He's content in his own way. Just say what you feel like saying, when you can get a word in edgewise. And don't mind if he drops off to sleep now and then. All right.'

'If you say so.'

'I say so.'

'What if he doesn't like me.'

'He's bound to.'

'He's not bound to at all.'

'He's bound to.'

He gave her a gentle push and she climbed out of the car and took his hand as they walked down a long, rush-matted corridor that smelled of air-freshener over carbolic and up a wide, curving staircase. From somewhere below them a radio carried the voice of a clergyman intoning the morning service.

'What sort of a joint is this.'

'It's a private nursing home. Mostly old folks. Bit shabby but comfy enough in its way. Dad was a union official for a long time, till he retired on pension. Engineering Union. When he fell ill they paid for him to come here. He nags on about it but I reckon he likes the company.'

Lift doors opened just in front of them and an elderly woman with a shock of white hair propelled her wheelchair out at a surprising speed, trundled away down the corridor, spun to her left and disappeared from view. To their right, as they moved forward, was the open door of a small lounge with half a dozen people within, some fiddling with newspapers, two with heads bowed over a board game.

Joe led the way into a four-bedded room at the end of the corridor and tiptoed past a skeleton-thin man who lay deeply asleep on one of the beds. He picked up two chairs and carried them out onto a balcony on which his father sat, in dressing gown and slippers, eyes closed, moving almost imperceptibly to and fro, in a rocking chair. Seating Jan at the far end of the balcony so that she faced his father, he placed himself half-way between them, in the window arch. When Joe said 'Morning, Dad' Jan was startled by the clear blue of the eyes that opened and looked at her from the lantern-jawed skull, with its parchment-like, jaundiced skin. His voice was throaty, but clear.

'You must be Janis.'

She blinked.

'That's right.'

'You're the scholar.'

'Sort of.'

The old man looked toward his son and said 'Mornin', Joe. You're early.'

'Came by car.'

'Things must be looking up.'

He turned his gaze back to Jan.

'He sings quite a song about you.'

She smiled, uncertainly.

'Seems smitten. An' it's a long time sin' he cared that much for a lass. One way or t'other. That right, Joe.'

'You're embarrassing her, Dad.'

'I might be. But I'll bet she's pleased, even so. It's a compliment. You are pleased, aren't you.'

Jan crossed her ankles and sat back more easily in her chair.

'Yes, I am. I'm rather partial to your son, Mister Telford.'

He regarded his son, critically.

'He's all right, I suppose. By and large. He was more likeable when he was a lad. Better looking too. But he has his points.'

He lifted his legs with his hands and propped them on the lower rail of the balcony.

'An' you call me Charles. Not Charlie. Never liked that. Sounds like an insult. Not that I'm easily insulted. Though some have tried.'

He looked out across the lawn, muttered about the church bells and said sharply 'You wrote a book about the Wobblies.'

'A thesis. Yes.'

'Good people.'

'They were.'

'Did you know they were practically the only working-class movement that really opposed the Great War. Root and branch.'

'I knew that.'

'Course you did. You were bound to. Writing a book. Still, it meant something that. All the bloody international socialists said they would stop war ever happening, refuse to fight. And come nineteen-fourteen, what happened. England, Germany, all over. The working class goes raving mad patriotic and can't wait to get theirselves killed off. Bar the old IWW.'

His vehement speech had left him out of breath and he paused.

'I was a Conchie in the Great War, you know. Went to prison. Got treated rough. Even the soddin' criminals were all patriotic King and Country buggers.'

He switched his gaze to Joe and pointed at him.

78

'He wasn't a Conchie. In the second lot. Went to be a soldier boy. Didn't you, Joe.'

Joe grimaced and looked appealingly at Jan.

'That was different, Dad. As far as wars can be justified, that one was. There was a Cause.'

The old man snorted.

'There was a Cause in nineteen-fourteen. Save poor little Belgium. Stop the Huns running over Europe. All that.'

'Not the same. Fascism had to be stopped. You've got to admit that.'

'Go on, son. Tell her how you saved the world for democracy. Tell her what a great thing it is to be a soldier.'

Jan's eyes flickered from father to son, following the argument. She leaned forward and touched Joe's knee.

'I didn't know you'd been a soldier, Joe. You never told me.'

'Go on. Tell her the tale of your heroic deeds. Put your tin hat on an' tell her a war story.'

'He only wants me to tell it becos it sounds daft.'

'It shows what it is to be a soldier. That's what it shows.'

Joe sighed, muttered 'Jesus Christ' and scowled at his father. He rested his left ankle on his right knee and fiddled with his shoelace before telling his story in a mechanical, reciting style.

'All right. How I won the war. Took my medical. Seventeen years eight months. Got called up in nineteen-forty-four. PBI.'

Jan started to ask a question and Joe said 'Poor bloody infantry.'

'Did my square bashing at Catterick and got shipped out by air with some replacements. We landed at night and got taken on in lorries and dumped in a field. Never did find out where we were. Somewhere near the Belgian border I should think. Anyway we were told to follow this officer up to the start line. So off we go, plodding along in the dark behind him, an' there's flares floating about in the sky and gun flashes way off in the distance. Some British artillery opened up behind us, with the shells going over us. Falling ahead. After a bit, some of the British shells fell short, right in the middle of us lot. We start running around in a panic, shouting an' not knowing what to do. I got a lump of shrapnel in mi back. The pain was amazing. I never knew there could be such pain. Then I got a clunk on the head and went unconscious. When I come round I'm back in an aeroplane again, going home

79

to hospital in England. And that was my war. By the time they patched me up it was all over.'

Jan took his hand.

'I think that's one of the saddest damn things I ever heard.'

Charles Frederick laughed himself into a fit of coughing and they patted his back till it died away to a wheeze and he gasped 'Bloody marvellous. Absolutely bloody marvellous. Straight off he gets clobbered by his own side. Just shows what military might can do. Joe Telford versus Hitler. Bloody marvellous.'

Joe objected mildly to his father's mockery before going off to fetch tea. Jan rebuked the old man for his lack of sympathy. He rubbed his chest and blinked at her.

'I can afford to take the mickey now. I'm glad I can. When they brought him back all smashed up I couldn't stop cryin'. I tried to but the tears just kept coming.'

The corners of Jan's mouth turned down and he held his hand out towards her and said 'No, no, you're right. I should stop goin' on at him. I'm sorry. Tell me about you.'

'What would you like to know.'

'Joe tells me your university study is on workers' control of industry.'

'That's right.'

'An' you believe in it.'

'Very much. Don't you.'

'I believe it's a grand idea but it'll never be. You listen to an old union man, lass. The best the working man can get is a near enough decent wage. An' he'll have to struggle like hell just for that. Just not to be bloody trampled on, that's your practical aim. Syndicalism'll never be more than a dream. Tek my word for it.'

Jan looked at him, quizzically.

'I'll bet when Lincoln said they should free the slaves there was a guy like you around arguing the most we could hope for was lightweight chains and no flogging on Sundays.'

The old man looked startled.

'Hey up. You're as bad as our Joe.'

'I'll take that as a compliment.'

They argued on, the old man sawing the air with his hand, slowing and deepening his voice to an oratorical style and Jan mimicking him and coining pompous slogans to match his

80

declarations. Suddenly, he dropped his voice back to a conversational tone and said 'Bugger it. I'll let you win that one.'

His head sank onto his chin and he peered at her through half-closed eyes before saying 'I gather you're attached to our Joe.'

'I'm attached.'

He raised his head.

'Ahm glad. You seem to be good for him. Put life into him. He's always been a bit inclined to draw into himself, you know. From time to time. Get broody about things. Depressed. I don't know where he gets it from. His mother was sprightly and I've always been cheerful enough. Still, since you come along, he's been a proper little bundle of joy.'

She laughed, moved over to him and put her cheek next to his. Joe came on to the balcony carrying a tea tray and said 'You manking about with my old man.'

Over tea they listened to complaints about the nursing home food, the hard beds, the cantankerous inmates, the noisy trolleys and early wakings, the bureaucratic rules. When the old man moved on to condemn the dictatorial habits of Matron, Joe protested that Matron always spoke affectionately of Charles Frederick and admired what she called his 'fine mind'. Charles paused and pondered before allowing that Matron could not help being dictatorial because it was an occupational disease of her profession and she did have her points.

Charles asked Joe how the scheme for stirring up trouble about phone tapping was coming along.

'Not bad. I've got the first few mentions in the newspapers and it seems to have started sparks flyin'.'

'You goin' on with it, then.'

'I've got plenty to come. Should blow the lid off it a bit more.'

'You want to go careful on it. Watch your step.'

Jan asked him if he disapproved of what Joe was doing.

'Not a bit of it, I'm all for it. I'm just pointing out that the powers that be are not famous for their sense of humour. They'll see nothing funny in being shown up and if they catch Joe at it they'll put the boot in, mek no mistake. That's all I'm sayin'.'

Joe promised he would be cautious.

Later he and his father went through what seemed like a well-rehearsed quarrel about whether or not to go for a walk.

81

Eventually, Charles gave in, collected his walking stick and followed them out into the grounds of the home. Jan and Joe sauntered and chatted, while the old man kept silent, his jaws clenched, leaning heavily on his stick, trying to force his stride out to keep up with them. When they reached a small pond about two hundred yards from the building, he studied a raised, bench-like part of the bank and carefully lowered himself to sit upon it. Jan sat lower down, nearer the pond, while Joe hunted about for flat stones and played skipping them on the water. They applauded when he reached eight jumps with a small piece of tile. He joined them on the grass and he and Jan talked quietly while the old man sat, hands folded on the stick, chin resting on hands, dozing in the sun.

'You don't talk a lot about your mother.'

'Our Mam.'

He held a buttercup under her chin to see if she liked butter.

'She died when I was fourteen, so I suppose she's a bit faded into the past.'

'Your Dad said she was sprightly.'

'She was that.'

'Were they a happy couple.'

He canted his head on one side and scratched his eyebrow.

'Happy as most I should think. But Mam could never stand his politics. She could never fathom why he was so bound up in it. She thought all that mattered was the people close by, what your home was like, family, that sort of thing. She used to think it was daft me doing geography at school 'cos it was about foreign places.'

He nodded towards his father.

'It was funny. If Dad went out with his mates boozing and came home merry, she'd just laugh at him. Pat him on the head and steer him off to kip. But if he stayed out late at a political do, union, anything like that, she'd bolt the doors and not let him in. He'd shout through the letter box please to let him in but she wouldn't. He'd have to go an' sleep at his mother's. My grandmother.'

She showed him a ladybird crawling over her wrist and turned her hand this way and that to keep it on her, while she tried to count the spots.

82

Their heads jerked round as he spoke.

'There's not as much in ponds as there used to be.'

'What you talking about, Dad.'

'Ponds. There's not as much in them.'

'How d'ye mean.'

The old man thought.

'When I was a lad. Before the Great War. Ponds were chock full of things. Newts, frogs and toads, tiddlers, water boatmen. All kinds of dragon flies, water spiders, sometimes a grass snake and watermoths, voles, allsorts. And they smelled more, the ponds. Wick with things. Now they seem empty. Well, not so full.'

He seemed to go back into his doze. Jan studied his face and whispered 'I'll bet he was handsome. As a young man.'

'He was. I've got some old photos. I'll show you. He used to have a tash at one time, upward curving at both ends. Reight dashing.'

Later the old man murmured, as if completing a train of thought.

'It's like they say, the working man is his own worst enemy.'

When Jan asked him what he meant, he said 'Can I have a read of the book you've written, about the Wobblies, the one Joe sets such store by.'

'It's only a thesis, just typed, but I'd be honoured if you'd read it. And tell me what you think of it.'

He pointed his stick at her.

'I'll do that all reight. I always do.'

'I'll bring it next week. When we come.'

'Course it'll take me a while to read it. I used to be a big reader but I can't concentrate for long now. I have to read a bit at a time.'

He rambled on about books he had read. How he thought Shaw was too clever clever but he admired Wells and had read everything he ever wrote. His voice died away as he said 'That last thing he wrote. *Mind at the End of its Tether*. That was a poor thing though. It was H.G. Wells's mind that was at the end of its tether. A real pity that.'

He dozed again and they woke him to watch a pair of squirrels that had come down from a tree on the far side of the pond and moved across to play within a few yards of them. One of the squirrels became angry at the other and dashed back to the tree, chattering with rage.

The dinner gong struck three times, sounding clearly from the house. Charles Frederick complained.

'You'd think we were bloody Indian colonels. Bashin' that soddin' thing. Goes through your head.'

He refused help to rise and took the time needed. At the door of the house he gripped Joe's hand. Jan kissed him. He grinned and said 'God knows you're pretty enough.' As he disappeared inside he shouted back 'Take good care of her.'

Joe lolled on the window seat, looking out at the elaborate rose gardens, patchworked into the lawns in front of the house. Jan was perched on a soliloquy chair, peering into an ornate dressing table mirror, delicately applying mascara. She spat daintily into the tiny black box in her left hand and squinted her eyes. He tapped his shoe toe-caps together and spoke to the ceiling.

'Funny the way women put make-up on with spit.'

She murmured something he failed to hear.

'Anyway, you don't usually wear war paint.'

'No.'

'So.'

'So this is a blue plate special.'

'Dinner at the family mansion.'

'Mmm.'

He rolled off the window seat and crossed to examine the big four-poster bed, rubbing the carved wooden pillars and running his fingernail noisily along the silk coverlet. Jan winced.

'Sorry. Never slept in a four-poster.'

She fluttered her eyelids at her reflection and simpered.

'Get your chance tonight, lover boy. We can play Henry the Eighth and Anne Boleyn.'

He examined the adze marks on the ceiling beams.

'Not Tudor. Jacobean. To start with. Bits put on later. What's it cost your Dad to rent this noble pile.'

She picked at the outer corner of her eye with a little finger.

'It's like the man said. If you have to ask, you can't afford it.'

He paced moodily round the room, sniffed at the lace runner on the dressing table, stared at an age-stained picture of a shepherd

84

tending his flock and kissed Jan on the neck. She pulled his hand round her, turned it over and pressed the palm to her lips. Seeing his scowl in the mirror she raised her eyebrows.

'It's your folks. Your Mam just about managed a bit of a chat but your Dad looked at me like I was rubbish.'

'Worse that that, friend. You're unclassifiable rubbish.'

She leaned back against his chest.

'And he hates to think about what we get up to in bed. More so, on account of you're the same age as he is. No way is he going to forgive you that. He's a jealous old sweetheart.'

Joe rested his chin on the top of her head.

'I'm amazed they have me here at all. All things considered and by and large.'

'They know damn well if they don't have you they won't have me.'

He stepped back and studied her face in the mirror.

'Is that a fact.'

'That's a true fact.'

She slid out of her chair, turned to him and patted his cheeks.

'Mister Telford. It's getting time you realised how important you are.'

'Me.'

'You.'

He stared at her, silently, till she said 'I kid you not' and he murmured 'I'll bear that in mind.'

She flounced the long skirt of her dress.

'How do I look.'

'Smashin'.'

'You look pretty distinguished yourself.'

She brushed his temple lightly.

'Some time, I'll dye your hair grey. Make you look even more distinguished.'

He looked at her wide-eyed.

'You can't dye somebody grey.'

'You can so.'

As they walked along the oak-panelled corridor he whispered 'What do we natter about at dinner. Is it like the officers' mess. No religion, sex or politics. Nothin' interestin'.' She took his arm, halted him for a moment at the top of the wide staircase and said 'We have to sweep down this, all dignity and grandeur. Got it.'

'Right.'

Heads up, nodding to right and left, they marched in step, very slowly, raising their knees high, down the staircase.

'You talk about what you like. They mostly talk about money and holidays.'

'Magic.'

'And whatever you say they have to pretend to like you. It's a rule.'

As they entered the dining room a tiny waitress, in a black dress and a white headband, bobbed forward with a tray and offered them a choice of dry or sweet sherry or martini and Jan's mother came across and revolved them through the guests who were standing in a large alcove, introducing them to the other five couples. She stumbled at first, blocking after presenting them as 'My daughter Janis and her. . .' but recovered and reversed it to 'Mister Joseph Telford and my daughter Janis.'

Jan whispered 'circulate' and they separated for a while, Joe nodding and smiling and giving vague answers to queries about his view of the weather, the house and the gardens, to a succession of guests. Eventually he worked his way back to Jan and when she turned to him he wobbled his head from side to side and muttered 'Can't figure out who's who, ma'am.'

Jan swopped their empty glasses for full ones from the passing tray and peered over his shoulder, keeping her voice low.

'Right buddy boy. The grey man and woman you were just talking to I know. They're the Humes. He's Sir Geoffrey, a moneybags and a merchant banker and he and Pop get together on quite a few deals when Pop's over here. They're into a conglomerate.'

'My granny used to make them but they were so sticky you could hardly get 'em down.'

'The guy in the check jacket and his wife I know from back home. Friends of the family, Art and Josie Kramer. He's a good ol' boy.'

'Sir merchant banker and a good ol' boy. Got it.'

'Don't know Mister and Missis Glover, just behind me. He's some sort of senior civil servant. And the young feller Tynan is new to me. He's in advertising and PR and he's already got a trench between his eyebrows. Miss French, with the pain in the ass smile, is his Miss French. I didn't get the names of the fussy pair with the cleavage and the dicky bow tie but he's Brussels and the Common Market.'

'This the lot.'

'For dinner. There'll be some more coming in tomorrow. For the weekend.'

'Coach parties.'

Chatter grew louder as a middle-aged manservant in a black suit lit the large candelabrum that stood in the centre of the antique plank table and Jan's father came in and circulated round the group patting backs, shaking hands and kissing cheeks before shepherding them all to their chairs. Joe found himself sitting between Lady Hume and Miss French. Jan's parents took the end of the table seats and Jan sat next to her father, diagonally opposite Joe. Soup was served by the little waitress with the headband to a firm announcement from their host that it was Stilton and broccoli and worth a round of applause, which it got. The man in black served the first wine, holding the bottle with the label carefully turned so that guests could read it. The women admired the carved ivory napkin rings and the small Grafton vases of wild flowers that were spaced down the centre of the table. Soup spoons clinked pleasantly through the babble of conversation, and the array of wine glasses and silver on highly polished wood scattered the candlelight over the table.

Joe made sympathetic noises to Miss French as she complained about having to cut her holiday short because her mother had contracted an illness with many and dramatic symptoms which was still proving a diagnostic mystery, while half-listening to Lady Hume on his left who was describing a production of *The Importance of Being Earnest* which she had long ago attended and illustrating it with a passable imitation of Edith Evans as Lady Bracknell. Miss French worked backwards to reflect that actually having cut her holiday short was not a great grief, since Venice was becoming so crowded and slummy that one would not visit it at all, were it not that friends who lived there felt so exiled and isolated. Lady Hume had worked forward to a recent production of an Albee play which was colourful, in its way, but not so witty as Wilde. The civil servant across and left of Joe leaned forward to say he was recruiting a foursome for golf on the morrow but when Joe said he did not play, he shook his head and went back to talking to the woman on his right about the tax benefit of a covenant on one's children's school fees.

Joe found he needed to offer little beyond expected affirmations till well into the sole bonne femme when Lady Hume, having introduced herself as Elsa, asked him what he did. Joe considered.

'During the week or on Saturdays.'

'Well, both.'

'In the week I'm office dogsbody for a timber merchant and on Saturdays I help out at a bookies.'

Elsa Hume blinked and said that it must be very interesting.

'No. It's not interesting.'

'Not interesting.'

'No.'

'Isn't it interesting at all.'

'There's nothing in it to be interesting.'

She looked mildly distressed.

'I'm sorry to hear that.'

Joe patted her hand.

'Don't be. It doesn't bother me. They're just jobs.'

She enquired if the work could not be made something of or alternatively if Joe could not take up something more rewarding, vocationally, so to speak. The conversation died away when Joe said no to both suggestions. She turned her attention back to him at the beginning of the entrée and urged him to visit the new Van Gogh gallery in Amsterdam. She described it in great detail, stressing that it was like the Guggenheim in New York but more human. Joe said he would certainly consider this.

Miss French asked him if he was going riding the next day. When Joe said he had never ridden she seemed shocked and said surely he had. He sucked the lip of his wine glass then smiled and said 'You're right. Well, in a way. When I was a lad I used to work on a farm sometimes and at the end of the day, they'd let us ride the farm horses back. You know, the big Shires they used to have for pulling carts. They had these great big broad backs and you'd sit up there with your legs straight out in front of you 'cos they were too wide for them to hang down. And if the field was bumpy you'd slide about on its back. It was like being on a billiard table at sea.' Miss French said it sounded great fun and he really must come riding as the Braggs' neighbours had a marvellous stable and were only too happy if you used it and he could certainly

88

borrow some gear and she could teach him. Joe called across to Jan that Miss French was going to teach him to ride. Jan choked on her quail, recovered and grinned at him.

Glowing and relaxed with one more refill of wine, Joe was listening for a while to the civil servant who had moved on to the relative tax benefits of separation and divorce, when he caught the word enterprise repeated several times by Hume, who was sitting to his right, on the opposite side of the table. He leaned forward and listened to Hume explain that, unlike his host and Americans generally and the Japanese, English businessmen lacked enterprise.

'You mean they're not greedy enough.'

Hume turned his head and fixed his eyes on Joe.

'I beg your pardon.'

'Granted.'

'I was talking about enterprise.'

'That's right. Greed.'

Hume re-arranged the cutlery on his empty plate.

'Hardly. You can't simply equate enterprise with greed.'

'Same thing.'

'Surely not.'

'Near enough.'

Hume pushed his spectacles further back on to his nose.

'Enterprise is boldness. It's being really forward-looking. It's a willingness to think in a novel way and to try and act upon one's thinking.'

'So as to get some goodies. Money and power.'

'Not necessarily.'

Joe wagged his forefinger at Hume.

'So why. Why is it when you say he's enterprising it's always talking about some bugger who's got his fist in the jam jar. You don't say Einstein's enterprising for relativity or old Ben Tillett was enterprising in his union work or enterprising Melly 'cos he's a good jazz singer. You mean free enterprise. Free to rob poor bastards blind.'

Hume looked round at the rest of the party, who had stopped talking to listen to the exchange, took off his glasses and cleaned them.

'I think that is taking a very narrow point of view. Enterprise

benefits society as a whole, rich and poor alike. It creates wealth.
If economics teaches us anything it teaches us that.'
He put his glasses back on and looked intently at Joe.
'In effect, enterprise distributes wealth.'
Joe responded with a hooray and held out his glass to the servant
who was making the rounds with the wine.
'What about you doin' an enterprising distribution an' givin' your
money to the poor an' needy. How about that.'
Hume cleared his throat.
'I don't think we should make a personal issue out of economics.'
Joe drank deeply from his refilled glass.
'Now you're wrong there. Economics is a very personal issue.
Personal as all hell. Particularly if you're poor.'
The young man, Tynan, from Joe's side of the table, spoke
sharply.
'I suppose you, of course, come from a poor family, Mister
Telford.'
Joe waved his hands expansively.
'Poor you say. By heck, lad, the only jewellery my mother ever had
was beads of sweat.'
Elsa Hume started to say she was sorry to hear that and stopped
suddenly. Missis Glover murmured 'And pearls of wisdom.' Joe
beamed at her then gazed again at Tynan.
'Poor. You talk about poor. Even the cockroaches in our house
were pitiful. Pitiful. They used to stagger about, falling down
every few steps. Half-starved they were.'
The young man whitened and said heavily 'How very distressing.'
Joe leaned to his right and patted his hand.
'You've no idea, son. Leaves its mark on you, you know. Like
indelible pencil. There's the rickets for a start.'
Jan's voice came cheerfully from the end of the table.
'And the funny habits, Joe. The way you still collect old crusts of
bread to carry about in your pockets, for fear you'll fall on hard
times again.'
He smiled fondly at her.
'Can't help myself.'
'And always checking your hair for nits, even though they're long
gone.'
'True. And mi nose still out of shape from all the times I used to

90

flatten it against the baker's shop glass, lookin' in at his cakes.'
Two of the women began to giggle and Jan's father cut in loudly.
'When you've done putting my guests on, Joe, we'll finish up and
go through for coffee.'

In the lounge, cuddling his coffee and brandy, Joe found
himself flanked by Hume and Tynan as they talked again about
the economics of enterprise. They tapped his chest and seemed
eager to be understood. Hume kept beginning his sentences with
the word 'seriously' and argued at length that a modicum of
poverty, which was only poverty relative to generally high
standards, was simply the inevitable delay that even the best
economic system experienced in taking up its own slack. The
tendency for a certain amount of wealth to crystallise, as it were,
on a central group simply reflected the fact that the group was the
absolutely necessary cutting edge of developments in the economy
as a whole. The young man from advertising and public relations
threaded in remarks about creativity being necessarily a char-
acteristic of a minority and their authority being an articulation of
the natural order. Hume granted that compassion was morally
desirable but stressed that only an effective system could make
compassion function, otherwise back to the jungle. Both accepted
the need for ultimate constraints on enterprise, Hume favouring
some limits on currency speculation and the young man coming
down heavily in favour of the advertisers' code of practice. Joe was
looking round helplessly for a refill for his brandy glass when
Hume asked if he would accept that given inevitable problema-
tics, the economic system was essentially valid. Joe sighed,
handed his empty glass to the young man and stuffed his hands in
his trouser pockets. His eyes shifted their gaze slowly from Hume
to Tynan then back again to Hume.
'All right. Let us see if we can get to the nub. You're a chap that
has got his hands on a bit of the power and the glory. So you have
to believe it's a good system because it's let you scramble to the
top. It'd tear your mind in half if you realised that a system you've
built your life on is really dead lousy.'
Hume started to speak and Joe raised his arm and said 'Hoddon.
It's my turn.' He nodded towards Tynan.
'It's like him. When he's making up adverts. It takes all of us no
end of effort to say something half-way worthwhile or true or

sensible. Even when we're trying our damndest to do just that. So what chance has he of saying owt worthwhile when he's not even trying, he's just out to sell something. Mostly rubbish at that.'

The young man pouted.

'So what am I saying. I'm saying it isn't your fault that you talk shit and I'm not blaming you for talking shit. I'm only saying that you do talk shit. Inevitable shit.'

After a short silence Hume said 'I think we'll leave it at that' and led the younger man away. Joe stared after them gloomily, hands still stuffed in pockets, swaying gently to and fro.

Elsa Hume joined him and asked him why he looked so sad. Joe blinked at her.

'I've run out of brandy and I've upset your husband.'

Elsa fetched him a glass of brandy and said that upsetting her husband was not the greatest crime in the calendar. She had done it often. Joe cheered up and Elsa pointed out to him that all of Ayckbourn's plays were about upsetting people and, truth to say, they showed that people were bound to be upset. Joe said that that must surely be so.

Side by side, on a monk's bench, Jan and Ruth Glover surveyed the gathering and talked casually about its members. Ruth Glover ruled that Miss French must have been head prefect of her school and had to explain that a head prefect was nothing like a cheer leader. They speculated about her relationship with the young man from advertising whom they saw as embittered because he never made head prefect. Elsa Hume was judged a sweetie and her husband a man practising for the next honours list. Jan explained that Josie Kramer's worried look was born of doubts about British sanitation and hygiene standards. The man from the Common Market was deemed deadly dull but his fond way of stroking his wife's behind when he thought no one was looking was approved.

Ruth Glover looked across the room towards Joe.

'Your Joe's an interesting man.'

'Only interesting.'

She eyed Jan quizzically.

'There's no "only" about being interesting, young lady. After over twenty years of a bland marriage and a few boring casual affairs I've come to the conclusion that being interesting is the best thing a man can be. Don't, as you Americans say, knock it.'

'I'm sorry. I thought you were putting him down.'

'Never. How did you find him.'

Jan put her nose inside her brandy glass and sniffed dreamily. 'I found him in books first. Bits of him. There was something about the way he wrote that had a kind of fire in it. Like you were being spoken to directly. It stirred me up. So I went hunting for him and I found him in a scutty little house on top of a muddy hill in a rainstorm.'

'Sounds romantic.'

'It is. In a way.'

'And now you're hopelessly in love with him.'

'Does it show that much.'

'It shows on both of you. You seem proud of each other.'

Jan nodded fiercely. Ruth Glover's husband approached hesitantly and asked if they wanted any more coffee.

Ruth said 'No, dear' and he drifted away again to a group gathered round Jan's father who were loudly condemning high interest rates.

'Forgive me for being nosey but do you see a future for you and Joe.'

Jan said 'Why not,' halted and began again. 'I suppose there are a few why nots. I dunno. When I found Joe he'd resigned a bit from the human race and I'm only just getting him to think about rejoining. A lot will depend on that. I suppose you're going to tell me about the age difference and the difference in background and all such hoopdidoo.'

'No. No such hoopiwhatever. I think you're a fine couple but I wouldn't push him too much if I were you. He doesn't seem like a man who'd relish being pushed.'

'You reckon.'

'I reckon.'

'Sometimes you have to push somebody for their own good.'

Jan's mother descended on them with a long explanation of how the dinner menu had been worked out and Jan excused herself and moved across to Joe who was sidling away from a conversation about perfume-free deodorants between Elsa Hume and Josie Kramer. She took his arm, pulled him down into a deep, heavily overstuffed sofa and kissed him. He held out his empty brandy glass and she poured a tot from hers into it.

'How you makin' out, Oliver Twist.'

'Not sure I want any more of the party. I want just the two of us.'

'No way we're going to get you to be upwardly socially mobile, is there, Joe.'

'Not likely.'

'We'll hang on for a bit, so as to please Mom and Pop. Then we'll sneak off to the four-poster.'

'We goin' to draw the curtains round the bed.'

'Surely are. Be all snug and uninhibited.'

'I'll show you mine, if you'll show me yours.'

'Right on.'

She hooked her shoes off with her toes and tucked her legs under her bottom.

'Not happy.'

'It's all right. Good nosh.'

He slid down and rested his head on her shoulder.

'They're a funny lot of buggers.'

'How so.'

'Not sure. I don't quite see what they're drivin' at. Not just their talking, the sort of life they lead. I mean they seem to be saying that they've chosen it, every bit of it and it's the best possible life but they're not very convincin'.'

'At least they're harmless.'

Joe shifted his head to stare up at her.

'You're not generally that daft, Jan. Cosy fuckin' chat apart, there's a lot of power assembled here. More decision making in a month than thee and me ever get around to in a lifetime. And never mind they all seem bloody genteel. If you ever threaten to take their power away, they'll rip your balls off. It's only 'cos they're sittin' comfy and safe at the top of the heap that they're so nice about it.'

Jan patted his head.

'S'pose you're right. I still tend to think of them as pussy cats.'

'Pussy cats be buggered.'

'Well, it's hard to think of your parents as the class enemy.'

He sipped the last of his brandy.

'How much longer to four-poster time.'

94

'Soon. Do you like railways.'

'I like travellin' by train. Why.'

'No, I mean do you like the history of railways. Steam, end of track and all that.'

'Fairly.'

'Well go an' talk to Art Kramer. He's a railway buff. Just say locomotives and he'll tell all. He's not bad when he talks about it. Honest.'

Awkwardly, Joe heaved himself out of the deep sofa, kissed the top of Jan's head, advanced on Art Kramer and said 'Loco-motives.'

As he reached the top of Jan's staircase, she commanded him to stop and he stood, stiffly, one leg forward, arms outstretched, blinking in the flash of the camera. The photograph slid out and she studied it as he moved to the side of the bed and peered over her shoulder. Slowly the picture resolved itself and Jan looked up at him.

'There you go. Portrait of naked man with two cups of cocoa. What do you think.'

Joe lowered the cocoa cups onto the side table.

'Not bad if you like that sort of thing.'

'What sort of thing.'

He held his arms akimbo, puffed his chest out and flexed his muscles.

'The torso terrific.'

She applauded. He thrust his hips forward, hands clasped behind his head.

'The body bestial.'

'More, more.'

He bent forward from the waist, arms extended, one leg raised in a clumsy arabesque.

'The physique phenomenal.'

'Yeah, man.'

He flopped into a knock-kneed, caved-in-chest position.

'The form frightful.'

'Wow.'

Joe lay down beside her on top of the bed, shoulders propped against the velvet headboard and passed her a cup of cocoa. She sipped it and made approving sounds.

'Good stuff.'

'You know the secret of making good cocoa.'

'I've got a feeling I'm going to learn.'

'It's all in mixing the cocoa into a real smooth paste to start with, then you pour the hot milk in, a tiny bit at a time and stir like mad.'

'Told you.'

'Did you know cocoa was supposed to be an aphrodisiac.'

'You're putting me on.'

'Accordin' to this bloke who wrote a poem about it. All about cocoa coursin' through the veins.'

'We'll check it out.'

They lay listening to 'Sunny Side of the Street' from Jan's stereo. Joe hummed along with the tune.

'Old recordin' that.'

'Dorsey and the Sentimentalists.'

'When I was a lad we used to listen to them on our six valve radio. We had a six valve radio.'

She put her thigh over his and they half-dozed through the muted, lazy surge of big band swing.

When the cocoa was finished she reversed herself on the bed, tugged him lower down and began to squeeze and prod his legs.

'What you up to.'

'Just inspectin' the physique whatever it was.'

'Phenomenal.'

'Right.'

She pillowed her head on his feet, walked her fingers over his knee and thigh and played with his prick.

'Did you know you've got some grey pubic hairs.'

Joe stroked her feet.

'Not surprising. It's satisfying the insatiable lust of a lecherous woman half my age.'

'Oh. Oh. And who said I'm satisfied.'

'There you are. Just like I said.'

She canted her head sideways, pushed between his ankles and took a line of sight on his scrotum.

'Isn't it clever the way balls have a real neat seam between them.'

'Magic.'

She poked her finger in his navel.

'You got a mention in a seminar the other day.'

'Fame at last.'

'Not by name. One of the graduate students picked on a news item about the phone tapping and said whoever was blowing the gaff on it was trivialising revolutionary endeavour.'

'That so.'

'And he said you're guilty of liberal adventurism.'

'Please, your honour, it wasn't my fault. She egged me on.'

'Did you know you've got a cute little ass.'

'Noted for it.'

Jan scratched her fingernails lightly down his groin and he shivered. He separated her toes and studied them one by one.

'Your left big toe's got a funny nail on it. Shiny and crinkled at the same time. Little ridges in it.'

'Not a nail. It's a carapace. It's what grows when the nail's gone.' Joe kissed it.

'Poor old thing. How'd you get it.'

'When I was eight I got a real bad infection under the nail. The doc promised he wouldn't hurt me but he'd palmed a little pair of pliers and when I let him hold my foot he tore the nail straight out.'

'The rotten bugger.'

'That's when I lost faith in medics. If he'd been honest with me I'd have forgiven the pain but he said he was just going to look at it. He promised faithfully he wasn't going to do anything.'

'Poor pet.'

He bent round and down and licked her belly till they were curled awkwardly inward, head to head, whispering. Clumsily she turned onto bent knees and lay head down, thighs spread and arse upwards. Joe scrambled onto his knees and entered her gently from behind.

Jan made gargled swearing sounds round the pen that was jammed crossways in her mouth, as she flipped through the wallet files and bundles of notes scattered over the table. She rooted about in the briefcase that was propped against her chair, flicked through a set of index cards, shook her head, took the pencil out of her mouth, wiped the spit from it onto her jeans and called for Joe. There was a muffled clumping of footsteps above her as he came to the head of the stairs and shouted 'Yo.'

'What d'ye mean, Yo.'

'I dunno what it means. I've heard it in US cavalry pictures with John Wayne. They all shout Yo.'

'Well come down here. I want you.'

He appeared a minute later steering an armful of bed linen round the bottom of the stairs.

'Question. Who was Exchequer in Attlee's first post-war government. Called in to pinch-hit after a year or two.'

He began stuffing the linen into a big blue plastic bag.

'Sir Stafford Cripps. Known to the masses as Sir Stifford Crapps. Why.'

'Doing the appendix bits to the post-war political context section. Question. Nationalisation of the mines. Exact date and what was that notice they put up that you told me about. Saying who runs the mines.'

He pulled a succession of crumpled shirts, singlets, underpants, socks and handkerchiefs from the rammelled bottom drawer of the dresser and thrust them into a plastic bag.

'First of January forty-seven. And the notices said "This colliery is managed by the National Coal Board on behalf of the people".'

She muttered 'Not of or by but on behalf of,' scribbled rapidly and stuck the pen back in her mouth, re-sorting the papers she had tossed around in her search. Joe hunted out an old coffee jar, filled with soap powder, from the kitchen cupboard, gathered up tea towels and a tattered tablecloth and put them into the bag. He looked round the room, checking that everything had been collected.

'Will you tek us into Scarby for the washeteria this aft, sweetheart.'

'Sure. Why don't you buy a washing machine. Get some capital equipment.'

'Nay. Scarby washeteria's my one bit of community life. I'll not give that up.'

'Big deal.'

'Did you know that you get a better wash from medium than you do from hot.'

'You don't say.'

'Took me a while to learn that.'

He leaned against the windowframe, playing with the anglepoise lamp on the table, bending the centre joint, swivelling it on its base and turning the shade up and down.

'Would you like me to switch it on for you.'

'There's plenty of light.'

'I can if you want.'

He straightened the lamp so that it stood stiffly upright, outstretched, like a searchlight perched on a narrow scaffold.

'It's a grand present this. I move it over to the sofa at night, to read by.'

'I bought it so it would light the way for you to write your book, feller.'

'Did you know you can turn this knob and have different amounts of light.'

'Yes. Now shut up while I finish this section.'

Rubbing his elbows, he mumbled that it was getting cool and knelt down to put a match to the fire. The lighters burned quickly but the coal was slow to catch and he held a sheet of newspaper across the grate to draw the fire. Watching Jan, her head bowed over a large pad of yellow lined paper, he failed to notice the newspaper turning brown from the heat of the leaping flames and when it caught fire, he hastily crumpled it and threw it into the grate. He stayed crouched by the fire rubbing his hands, then pointed to a pile of handwritten manuscript sheets on the edge of the table.

'That the political context chapter.'

'That's it.'

'Can I read it.'

'Thought you'd never ask. All yours.'

He picked up the chapter and lay down on the sofa with it, legs draped over the back, reading slowly, often stopping to gaze at the ceiling, sometimes going back to check something in the pages that he had read and dropped onto the carpet. Halfway through he went into the kitchen and made tea for the two of them. Jan refused a scone and Joe returned to his sofa, juggling with tea, scone and papers, occasionally shifting his position to squint more closely at her handwriting.

Reading finished, he lay slackly, hands clasped across his chest, seeming to stare at a calendar with a photograph of Durham Cathedral on it, that was nailed to the wall facing the sofa. Jan tapped her pen on the pad in front of her and watched him out of the corner of her eye.

'Well.'

He pretended to be startled.

'Oh. Fine. Really fine.'

'What's wrong with it.'

'Nothing's wrong with it. I said it was fine.'

'But.'

He swung his legs round, lifted himself out of the sofa and knelt by the fire to put a few lumps of coal on it, from the bucket that stood in the hearth. Wiping his hands on his trouser knees he stood up.

'Within its limits, it's a very well written survey.'

'Within its limits.'

'That's right.'

She flipped her pen onto the table, propped her chin on her fist and looked hard at him.

'Its limits being what.'

He walked the few paces to the door and returned to stand with his back to the fireplace.

'The limits you've set. Fair enough. You're entitled to set limits. You've looked at the political context for workers' control of industry. Right. What immediately surrounds it. Some of the gen on local government attitudes is new to me. Good stuff.'

'So what are you complaining about.'

'Not complainin'. It's just that you've chosen not to paint a bigger picture.'

'You mean history-wise and worldwide-wise and political theory-wise and so on.'

'Yes. If you want to put it that way.'

'So what should I have said.'

Sawing the air with his hands, he raised his voice.

'For Christ's sake, Jan. You know as well as I do.'

'Know what.'

100

'What the whole bloody political point of workers' control is. You only need to say that the whole soddin' socialist-communist movement from Marx on got it hopelessly fuckin' wrong. They thought if they got rid of capitalist private ownership they'd get rid of class society. They forgot that it's control that matters, not bloody ownership. So what we've got all over the place is a new syphilitic class system starting up. With power based on political and economic organisation instead of ownership. And Soviet soddin' Russia is a prime example. Old bloody Burnham's managerial revolution. And it's just as much a top dog-underdog bloody set up as capitalism ever was. An' the significance of a real industrial democracy is that it's the only way to get a real political democracy. Syndicalism's not just a pretty idea about a few co-operative factories, liberal crap about co-ownership, it's the only answer to class rule. And that makes it the most politically significant bloody. . . .' He stopped speaking abruptly as he noticed Jan twisting her head to and fro, looking over her shoulders.

'What's up with you.'

Jan shrugged.

'I'm just lookin' round to see if I can spot this goddamned great mass audience you're obviously addressing.'

Joe flushed.

'All right. All right. I didn't mean to shout. I'm just pointing out what's not in the chapter.'

'What you mean is I should have written a chapter nine-tenths based on Joe Telford's famous old pamphlet *Workers' Control versus Totalitarianism*.'

'You could do worse. It's not a bad pamphlet. And it was translated into French. The French went a bundle on it.'

'It's a brilliant pamphlet. But it's not what this thesis is about.'

She stood up, moved across to him, brushed some crumbs off his jersey and spoke more softly.

'Look, Joe. This is an academic thesis. Not a clarion call to the barricades. That means there are limits to what I can get away with. Everything has to be put in moderate terms, backed up with refs and evidence, balanced statements at all times. You know what I mean.'

'You mean harmless.'

She punched his chest.

101

'I don't mean harmless. An' you know I don't mean that. Look I'll go over it again and see if I can work the anti-managerial class stuff in under a survey of views that have been taken. Quote Telford J. in all his glory. How about that.'

'Only if you want to.'

'I do want to. I hadn't realised how narrow I'd made that section. Honestly.'

'You'll not quote it like an old museum piece.'

'I'll quote it with fire in it. OK.'

He put his arms round her.

'Sorry, pet. I do rant on a bit, sometimes. It's me soap box days comin' back to me.'

'I like a bit of a rant.'

For a long time they kissed till Joe said 'We can't go on kissin' like this.'

'Why not.'

'Mi bum's burning.'

Back at her note making, Jan rubbed her eyes and let her head sink till her forehead came to rest on her arms, on the table. She could hear Joe's voice outside the window, shouting something to his neighbour, and the high piping tones of Nelly Hurst shouting back. He barged through the door and scuttled over to the fireplace, putting the thermos flask he was holding on the mantelpiece. He said it was 'reight chill' outside. Seeing Jan's head resting on the table he went across and stroked her hair. 'Poor old thing. It's weary stuff this thesis writing, love. Would you like a break. Come for a walk. Blow some university cobwebs away.'

She turned her head sideways.

'Where to.'

'Up to the reservoir to see Albert Hurst at work, guardin' us water for us.'

'Why there.'

'Nelly told me he'd broken his tea flask so she's filled up mine and I've promised to take it up to him to have with his snap.'

'OK.'

She lifted her head with exaggerated slowness and began to tidy up the papers on the table while Joe fetched raincoats and scarves from the hall and held them to the fire to warm.

She kicked off her slippers and laced herself into walking shoes.

'I never know how to be with Albert Hurst anyway. I try to get on his right side but he always seems to look down his nose at us, disapproving, sort of.'

'That's 'cos he is disapproving. He thinks poorly of me on account of he reckons I'm a dirty old man practising lusts of the flesh on a girl young enough to be mi daughter. An' he disapproves of you because you're a sexy, promiscuous young woman making decent elderly citizens slaver with desire and tempting 'em into carnal sin. Especially him.'

He helped her on with her coat.

'I never try to tempt him.'

'You don't have to try. You only have to be around and his imagination does the rest.'

'You'd never know. He hardly ever talks.'

Joe pocketed the thermos flask.

'That's because Nelly has drowned him in talk all their married life. He's given up trying to have his share of chat.'

They worked their way round the end of the abandoned street and held hands as they struggled up the top slope of the hillside and onto the moor. A keen wind blew against them, causing them to talk in short jerky sentences.

'How long does it take you Joe. To get to Scarby. To work.'

'Getting on for an hour. If I go round to the main road. For the bus. A bit more if I walk. Why.'

She ducked her head against the wind.

'Just thinking.'

'What about.'

'That's only about the same time. From my house. Any time you were at my house. I could drive you to Scarby in that time.'

'It'd take you nearly an hour back. To the university. At best.'

'Yes but I'd be in the car. Not walking or waiting for a bus. Easy drive.'

'Then what. At home time.'

'I could come and fetch you.'

He slowed down, glanced at her and strode forward again.

'That's daft. It'd be getting on for four hours driving. In a day.'

103

'Well, perhaps, some days you could take the bus. It's only one change. From my home.'

'I don't follow you.'

'I'm saying if you stayed at my place. In the week. Not just weekends.'

'How often.'

'As often as you wanted to.'

He stopped and faced her.

'Just what are you suggestin'.'

'What I said. As often as you want to.'

'What if I wanted to all the time.'

'That'd be fine.'

'Are you sayin' I should come and live with you.'

'More or less. Yes. No. More. Actually.'

'Bloody hell.'

'I love you too.'

'No. I mean steady on a minute. I do love you but I shall have to think about it.'

She poked her finger at his chest.

'You really love me.'

''Course I do.'

'True fact.'

'Honest.'

'How much do you love me.'

He grinned.

'We used to have this saying. When we were keen on a lass. I'd walk barefoot, half a mile, over broken glass, just to throw stones at your shit.'

'Christ.'

'Only it's a bit sudden. About living together.'

'I've hinted before. More than once.'

'I never knew that.'

'You're no good at hints, Joe. It's a waste of time with you.'

He tucked her scarf, which was flapping about, into her collar.

'I'll think about it. It'll tek me a while but I will think about it.'

'You do that.'

'I'm much complimented.'

'So you should be.'

'Well, I am. But you must let me think about it.'
She hugged him and they both grinned at a sudden burst of cackling gossip from grouse hidden in the bracken.

Jammed at an awkward angle between sprawling stacks of timber, Joe finished counting lengths of two by four. He wriggled out backwards, looked at his notebook and muttered 'Nothing fucking like.' Back in the office he found that everyone bar Eric Pritchard, who was fiddling with a hand calculator, had gone home. He entered the figures from his notebook onto stock sheets, tidied his desk, wrestled through the torn lining into his raincoat and said goodnight to Pritchard who grunted, still crouched over the calculator, jabbing at it with a stubby forefinger.

Outside the yard gate Joe stood for a moment, gazing skywards, trying to decide whether to stroll up to the pub or go straight home. Choosing the pub he set off toward it, whistling a flat version of 'There's a Tavern in the Town'. He had walked about a hundred yards when a large car drew into the kerb alongside him, the rear door opened and a voice from within said 'Excuse me.' Assuming it was someone about to ask for directions, Joe leaned into the car and peered at the man sitting on the far side of the back seat. The man held up a small card and said pleasantly 'Mister Telford.'

Surprised to hear his name, Joe leaned further forward to look at the card. As the man in the car said 'I wonder if I could have a word with you,' Joe became aware of another man moving up behind him, taking his elbow and pushing him lightly, while half-turning him, so that he was forced to step into the car and slide onto the seat. The man from behind followed him in, sat to his right and slammed the door. As the car pulled smoothly away, Joe said 'This is bloody ridiculous' and tried to struggle to his feet but was firmly held by the elbows of the two men which were tucked neatly over his forearms. He kicked viciously at the seat in front of him and shouted 'Stop this soddin' car.' The man on his left made clucking noises and said 'Really, Mister Telford, all this fuss and you haven't even asked what we want to talk to you about.' Joe realised that his breathing had become heavy and fast. He tried to slow it down.

'All right then. What's it all about.'

'You saw my warrant card, Mister Telford.'

'I didn't see it. I was trying to look at it when this bugger started heaving me into the car.'

'Special Branch. We want you to help us with our enquiries.'

'What about.'

'Come, come, Mister Telford. You know what about. Don't you now.'

Joe felt suddenly cold.

It had to be about exposing the phone tapping. But how could they have got on to that. Questions jumbled in his head. Was anybody else being taken in. Tully. Evelyn. Jan. Did they know what was happening to him. Had the journalist guessed who was writing to him and said something. Had they got the right to take him away in a car. How much did they know. Should he ask for a lawyer or was that like a confession. If it was Special Branch and not just ordinary police did that mean it was regarded as a major offence. What was the punishment.

His thoughts skittered back over the months, little snapshots parading before his mind's eye, pictures of himself, checking the phone books in the library for addresses, posting the envelopes in boxes all over the county, sending summary sheets to the journalist, burning bits of paper that he had made notes on, collecting newspaper cuttings that reported the phone tap revelations, meeting Evelyn outside the gates of the timberyard, selecting which names to make public so that they would not tally exactly with the lists he was given, talking to Jan and his father about how the scheme was progressing, watching the image of a politician saying on the television that it was all malicious mischief making. Each segment of the work seemed to be represented by a mental picture and each picture raised the same question. Was this what they had somehow seen, somehow detected.

He became aware that the car had accelerated and looked up to see that it had turned onto the motorway and was travelling west in the fast lane. Realising that the men had asked him nothing in the time that confused ideas had been rattling through his mind, he debated whether to invite questions, so that from them he could find out something of what they knew, or to remain silent. Give himself time to work out what stand he would take. He decided to risk a question.

'What is it you want to know.'

'All in good time. We'll soon be where they do the questioning.'

'Where's that.'

'Not far.'

'Whereabouts.'

'Soon.'

Twice more Joe asked where they were going and was ignored.

Letting his hands flow delicately over the controls and flashing his headlamps through the dusk at anyone who delayed him, the driver kept the needle in the orange glow of the dashboard, wavering in the eighties, seeming to enjoy the speed, humming snatches of song to himself, drumming little tattoos on the steering wheel. Lulled by the low monotone of the motor and the hiss of the tyres, Joe watched the turn-off signs loom up and flash by, vaguely noting that the car was heading towards Manchester. Spots of rain began to splash onto the windscreen and the driver switched the wipers onto a slow intermittent sweep that fragmented the beams of light moving towards them in the other carriageway. In the gathering darkness, cat's eyes unreeled endlessly in front of them. The men on either side of Joe sat motionless, staring out of their respective windows. It passed through his mind that they were 'like a pair of fuckin' bookends'. His chin had sunk onto his chest and he was half-dozing when the driver, finding his path blocked by two huge TIR lorries, jockeyed for the lead, hooting viciously.

Joe lifted his head and looked around the gloomy interior of the car. It came to him that there was a kind of madness in the situation. He had got out of bed, cooked the same old egg breakfast, walked to work on a still autumn day, spent the morning totting invoices, his lunchtime sitting by the river, watching ducks bobbing for the bits of bread he threw to them, the afternoon stocktaking loads of untidily stacked timber, grumbling about lost delivery note copies, enjoying a fig biscuit with his mug of tea, trying to remember if there was anything good on television for the evening, deciding to have a pint of beer and a cheese and onion roll and maybe a game of darts at the pub and now here he was, sitting mute, like a dummy, locked up in a tin box, rushing through the night at eighty miles an hour, with three men he didn't know, going Christ knew where, to face Christ knew what.

His voice exploded the stillness inside the car.

'All right. You can stop this fuckin' thing right now. I'll make me own way back and you can write me a letter about it.'

The man on his right wriggled his back against the seat but no one replied.

'Come on.'

Joe waited a full minute before he spoke again.

'Right, brothers. If you don't pull up then I'm going to start lashing out. And the first thing I'm going to do is to thump that smug bastard in the driving seat in the back of the neck. And at this speed that should make it reight interesting.'

The men on either side of Joe nestled into him more closely. The one on his left yawned and spoke in an affectedly weary tone.

'Mister Telford. Before you go into your "with one bound he was free" effort, may I offer you a small piece of advice. Just one.'

He patted Joe's forearm and left his hand resting on it.

'Never force the law to commit itself. Never ever.'

'What's that supposed to mean.'

The man on Joe's right had turned in towards him, so that his knee dug hard into Joe's thigh.

'It means, old son, that you are now entangled with the law, in all its awesome majesty. That is for sure and cannot be undone. You are entangled. But what this entanglement with the law will result in, now that is an open issue. Who knows. It may be just a matter of asking you a few questions, you give the right answers and straight back home you go. All tickety-boo as they say. On the other hand, if you get stroppy and start making life hard for us, you may force us to commit ourselves. Obstructing officers in the execution of. Arrest, charges laid, prosecutions put in train, all that sort of thing. Forced into it. So that we can keep a grip on the situation, so to speak. Then there's no turning back. So my advice to you is to play it cool, co-operate, be a good boy and all may yet be well.'

He yawned again.

Staring vacantly out of the window, Joe saw that they were

108

coming off the motorway, down a steep slip road, into a dark suburban sprawl.

It seemed to Joe the meanest room he had ever been in. It was about twelve foot by fourteen, without furniture, except for the hard metal chair he was sitting on and three stacking chairs in a corner. Lit by a dim, fluorescent overhead fitting, the only window was a dirty, speckled, metal framed, narrow strip that ran along the top of the rear wall. The paintwork was a uniform matt grey-green, except for a yellow, tinny-looking radiator clipped to the right of the flush door and the black box and bell of a fire alarm unit up near the ceiling. The grey composition floor was badly pitted and tended to curl away from the base of the walls. When they had first brought him into the room, the chair had been placed dead centre, but after a period of sitting, feeling ridiculous, surrounded by empty space, he had moved it to the rear wall. Once, the door had opened and someone had stared in at him for a moment but nothing was said, the man closed the door and left. Noises were muffled, hard to identify, as if the people who made them were some distance away.

He wriggled his toes and flipped the heels of his shoes off and on. His raincoat had been hung up in the front office and his shoelaces had been taken away from him, along with his tie, penknife and watch, almost as soon as they had entered the barrack-like building. They were put in a large, stiff envelope and the contents listed on the front, for him to sign. He had been left standing, just inside the large office, while the two men from the car held a low-voiced conversation with the man at the desk. Some kind of form had been produced and they had filled it in, glancing over at him from time to time but asking him nothing. It seemed that they already had whatever information was required for the form. Then came exile to the bare room.

He looked down at his wrist and felt annoyed at forgetting, yet again, that they had taken his watch away. That must be to try and disorientate him about time. Taking shoelaces and penknife must be to stop him committing suicide but you could hardly hang yourself with a watch strap. He guessed he had been sitting in the room for about two hours, so it must be around ten o'clock at night.

Staring round the room again, he concluded there was absolutely nothing of interest in it. Perhaps that was the idea, torture by boredom, the terrors of the vacant mind, let you stew in your own juice till you were rendered down to a mental mush. He contemplated leaving the room, finding somebody and asking for a paper or a magazine to read but reflected that they would only look blankly at him, put him back in here and make him feel stupid for asking in the first place. Pondering that, by tradition, people who were taken away and kept in bare rooms tried to escape, he decided that it might not be too difficult. The door was not locked. Just sneak down the corridors till he found a way out and off into the night. Having no shoelaces would be awkward though. Escape where to. Where could he hide. And what would he be hiding from. He was not, as far as he could gather, under arrest, so what would he be escaping from and if he did sneak out would that be resisting arrest and could they arrest you for that. And could you resist arrest if you had not yet been arrested.

He went over to the door, gently pulled it ajar and peered round the jamb. To the left was a dead end, a brick wall. To the right the corridor extended in shadow for twenty feet, with one more door on his side before it turned the corner from which light was spilling. Distantly he could hear the tapping of typewriter keys. He shuffled through the door, stood for a moment looking towards the bend in the corridor then shuffled back again, closed the door and returned to his chair. If no one came soon he would simply go to the big office near the entrance and demand to see someone. Tell them in no uncertain terms that he would be kept waiting no longer. Was it possible he had been forgotten. Overlooked in some way. Perhaps the man he was supposed to see had not been told that he was here and had gone home. He wondered repeatedly what their rights were. What were his rights. Had they a right to take his watch away. Could he leave here whenever he wanted. Just walk out.

He had stopped thinking about his part in revealing official phone tapping, and how and what Special Branch knew of it, the moment he had decided to say nothing to them. Refuse to talk. That should stop them in their tracks. There could hardly be much in the way of evidence, only suspicion. Anyway, however long the interrogation and whatever they asked him, the answer was simple. He knew nothing about it. No. Never. Nothing. He felt comforted, once he had resolved that denial, simple and total denial, was to be his stance. It felt as if that would bring the whole matter to an end.

He took out his wallet and read slowly through the contents. A copy of Henley's 'Invictus' that he had put there long ago to try and memorise the third verse. He knew the rest but the third verse always slipped away from him. Not a bad poem, he thought, melodramatic but not bad. From the dates given at the top, he worked out that Henley had died at the age of fifty-four, fairly young. He read his Donor Card and admired the main wording. 'I would like to help someone to live after my death', followed by the niggling but practical instruction to 'Keep the card with you at all times in a place where it will be found quickly'. The list of organs on the reverse side intrigued him because he had known they could use kidneys, eyes, heart and liver but had not realised they could transplant his pancreas. He wondered what his pancreas was like and what it did and resolved to look it up in a reference book when he next got the chance. He studied a smiling picture of his mother standing against a washing line post. He must have taken it with the family Box Brownie because the print had a yellowing border with deckled edges. He studied the picture of Wellington on the back of a five-pound note, reflecting that Wellington was quite a good-looking chap who had lived to be eighty-three years old, much longer than Henley. The little battle scene seemed unconvincing but the chariot-driving lady on the front was quite dashing. He wondered if it was Boadicea and concluded it more or less had to be. She seemed to be the only chariot-driving lady in history. Bored by the bus timetable, he deciphered the scribble on the bottom as a recipe for ginger wine given to him by Milly at the bookmaker's but never tried. The print on the back of the old receipt for a registered letter was too small to read in the poor light.

He put the wallet away, folded his arms and stared at the door. He concluded again that they were almost certainly overstepping their powers and had nearly made up his mind to find someone and tell them he would wait no longer when the door opened. A big man in a check jacket crooked a finger at him and said 'Come on.' Joe followed him through a maze of corridors, feeling like an absurd old man as he shambled along, scuffing his shoes on the floor, to keep them from slipping off. The man in the check jacket opened a door and motioned him inside. He pointed to a chair in front of a desk and as Joe sat down, he closed the door and came and stood behind him and to his right. The man behind the desk rotated slowly in a big swivel chair, examining papers in a large, red folder. In what seemed like a long period of silence, broken only by the creaking of the swivel chair, Joe studied the man, noting his thin face, eyes set deep behind steel-rimmed spectacles, long spatulate fingers, white shirt, black tie, jacket on the back of the chair, relaxed manner. Framing his head were tiers of shelves carrying regimented rows of box files. The desk was bare save for the file, one empty set of wire trays and a neat assembly of pens, bowl of paper clips, stapler, hand dictaphone and ruler.

The man scratched his forehead, pushed the file of papers away from him, closed its cover and tapped it.

'Telford J.'

He swivelled his chair back to a central position.

'Sorry to keep you waiting. Took time to verify all the facts of your case. My name is Sanson, by the way.'

His voice was a pleasant baritone and he paused between each sentence.

'So as not to prolong this and in fairness to you, I think we should come straight to the key question. The only question really.'

He tapped the file again.

'The names of the people whose phones were being tapped. Where did you get them from.'

Joe licked his lips and tried to sit more at ease on his chair.

'I don't know what you're talking about.'

Sanson looked surprised, shook his head slowly and swivelled his chair again, to and fro.

'It really is a bit late in the day for that sort of nonsense, Telford. Now, how did you learn which people were under surveillance.'

'I don't know what you're talking about.'

Sanson rubbed his temples and stared first at his desk then at Joe.

'Ah, me. I really had hoped for a brief and sensible interview. Still, let's try again. Joseph Telford, I put it to you that for the past several months you have been revealing to various individuals that their phones were being tapped by government agencies. At the same time you have been sending details of the surveillance to a national newspaper. This is true.'

He paused. Joe folded his arms and spoke loudly.

'No. I deny it.'

Sanson opened the cover of the file in front of him.

'You are a bare-faced liar, Telford. And what is more you are a foolish liar. Only· foolish liars deny what can easily be proved.'

He picked up the top sheet of paper from the file and studied it.

'Item. Tests show conclusively that all three of the form letters warning the recipients of telephonic surveillance which are held in evidence, were typed on the L.C. Smith typewriter, serial number 40787, the property of Joseph Telford, found at his address at 1, Hannover Street, Moorhill. Matching characteristics of type face and alignment are listed below and et cetera and et cetera. Proof fairly positive, wouldn't you say.'

Joe's face darkened.

'You've been in my house, you bastard.'

Sanson turned the paper face down on the right-hand cover of the file and took up a second sheet.

'Item. The right-hand end of the silk ribbon of the L.C. Smith typewriter et cetera was typed on only once, owing to premature reversal of spool direction and the two words visible on this section of ribbon, namely 'since they', occur in the form letter warning recipients et cetera held in evidence. Highly significant, yes.'

He took a third sheet from the file.

'Item. One twenty-seven by twenty-seven envelope found in the top left dresser drawer in the living room of 1, Hannover Street, Moorhill and so on, contained cuttings from national newspapers all directly reporting or commenting on the warning letters being sent to individuals, alleged to be subject to telephonic surveillance by government agencies et cetera. Fairly indicative, is it not.'

'Anybody can collect press clippings, if they want to.'

Sanson took off his spectacles and pinched the bridge of his nose.

'Now that really is pathetic, Telford. All this is cumulative and well you know it. You're an intelligent man, so do me the courtesy of not talking like an idiot. Shall I go on.'

He waited a few moments before fingering another sheet of paper out of the file, replacing his spectacles and peering at it.

'Item. Found at the address et cetera, forty-four sheets of white weave, A4, seventy-grammage, ship-watermarked paper, in packaging designed for one hundred sheets, of the exact kind on which were typed the three letters held in evidence, warning et cetera, et cetera. Would you like more.'

Joe tightened his folded arms and stared at the floor. Sanson slapped the file sharply.

'Look, Telford. I have enough evidence here to convict you under the Official Secrets Act half a dozen times over. So don't piss me around. Tell me where you got your information and we may be able to let the whole matter rest there. If we can put a stop to the leak, that's the main thing. That's what we have to know. So show some sense. Where did you get the information.'

'You had no right to go into my house.'

'Rubbish. We were justified by what we found there.'

Joe flapped his arms and started to shout, spit coming out with his words.

'You're a fuckin' thief. You can just keep out of my house. Keep right out. You an' all your fuckin' friends, you half-baked prick.'

Sanson smiled pleasantly at him and nodded. The fist caught Joe high on the cheek and slammed him out of the chair. He cannoned into the wall, slumped onto the floor in a sprawling heap. At first he was shocked and numb, then aware of sharpening pain, the side of his head seeming to be swelling out. He lifted himself on his left elbow and groaned with the effort of turning his head to look upwards. The man in the check jacket was sucking the knuckles of his right hand, while Sanson leaned back in his chair, swivelling it slowly from side to side. One of Joe's shoes had fallen off and he twisted his body, groping across the floor to get hold of it, and put it back on. He shuffled back to the wall and propped himself against it, in a sitting position, gasping for breath. Sanson put his fingers on his desk, like a man about to play the piano, and stared at them.

'Pick him up.'

He was lifted, dragged back to the chair and dropped on to it. For a while the man kept his hands on Joe's shoulders to stop him toppling to the floor. Sanson contemplated him for a while and leaned forward.

'It has been a long and tiring day, Mister Telford, and I will tolerate no vulgar abuse from you. You are in grave danger of suffering from the old falling down the station steps syndrome. So let us show some respect and have no more savage attacks on the sergeant's fist with your head. Understand.'

Joe grunted.

'Now, back to the beginning. Same question. Where did you get the names from.'

He shuffled the papers back into the file and squared them off.

'Who gave them to you.'

Joe touched the side of his head gently, with the palm of his hand.

'How did you find out who was having their phone tapped.'

Joe opened his mouth and breathed deeply.

'If I may stress the obvious, Telford. You are in deep trouble and getting in deeper by the minute. Your whistle-blowing antics are over and if you don't want to pay a very heavy price for them you had best co-operate. So stop messing about and answer the question. What was the source of your information.'

'You can go fuck yourself, spiral-wise.'

Joe hunched his right shoulder as he spoke, turned his head away from the sergeant and flinched as Sanson pointed a finger at him.

'You really are a very stupid man, Telford.'

He paused.

'One last time. Who told you about the phone tapping.'

Joe probed his cheekbone with his forefinger and winced.

'You've fuckin' had it. If it's down to thumpin' you can get stuffed. I'm saying no more to you.'

Sanson sighed.

'You haven't exactly said a great deal so far.'

For a minute he looked at the papers in the file before flipping the cover shut.

'All right. We'll give you time to ponder. Come to your senses. Then we'll start again. Take him away.'

The sergeant pulled Joe to his feet, hustled him along the corridors and pushed him through a heavy door into a room with a ceiling bulb behind a wire mesh, a narrow bed on the right, a chemical closet against the rear wall and a sink with one tap on the left. As the door thumped and locked behind him the word cell came into his head.

He looked at the bed and the sink and stood wobbling indecisively for a moment before going over to the sink, turning on the tap and splashing cold water, carefully, onto the side of his head. Patting his cheek with the rough towel that hung by the sink he shuffled to the bed, slipped his shoes off and slumped onto it. Lying back, his hand resting on his chest, he closed his eyes. After a while he opened them and looked around for a light switch but failed to find one. He rolled sideways onto the bed, closed his eyes and muttered 'Don't listen to the fuckers.'

When the man patted his shoulder, Joe tucked his knees up into his stomach and curled his head into his chest, trying to stay asleep. The man shook him and told him to wake up. Joe covered his eyes with his hand.

'What time is it.'

'Time to answer some questions. Get up.'

'I've hardly slept.'

'Get up.'

'I'm tired.'

'Come on.'

Struggling upright he pushed his feet into his shoes and sat on the edge of the bed, lolling forward. When the man took his arm he pulled free and scuffed across to the sink. He splashed water onto his face and swore as he touched the bruised cheekbone. After dabbing himself with the towel, he slopped obediently behind the man, along the dimly lit corridors, till he was thrust into an office. His guide left immediately, closing the door behind him.

Joe stared at a plump little man with a shiny bald head, who was standing by a bench which ran down one side of the office, his hands clasped tightly round an electric kettle. Noticing that Joe was staring at him he said 'It seems to be heating all right. Sometimes it doesn't. A loose connection, most likely.' After a pause Joe said 'Most likely.' The man took his hands off the kettle and assembled mugs, spoons, milk bottle, sugar bowl and coffee jar next to it.

116

'Please. Have a seat. Rest your weary bones. Expect they're weary bones.'

Joe lowered himself into the comfortable, rounded, leather-upholstered chair that faced the desk.

'I'm Welbeck. You're Telford, I gather.'

'Yes.'

'Would you like some instant coffee. Not decaff, I'm afraid.'

'Don't mind.'

'Milk and sugar.'

'One sugar.'

As he made the coffee, Welbeck chattered, cheerfully.

'Have got some Polish stuff. A kind of brown powder. Called Barley Cup. Hardly ever offer it, though. Sort of stuff only a Pole could drink. Mark you, in certain moods, I have been known. For that matter I had a herbal tea period once. Jasmine, camomile, mint, that sort of thing. But it didn't last. Came back to the old instant. Funny thing, making a drink on the night turn like this. Always seems specially enjoyable. Reminds me of when I was a boy at school. Being up late in the dormitory, having something to eat or drink, always seemed like the very devil of a thing. Sort of adventure. Know what I mean.'

'O aye.'

'Fresh out of biscuits, I'm afraid. Damn poor commissariat. Sorry about that.'

'I don't mind.'

'Keen on the old instant, myself. People make a lot of fuss about coffee. Blue Mountain, Mocha, Jamaica, that sort of stuff. Nothing against it but it's finicky to prepare and I'm just as happy with the old instant. Personally.'

Joe blinked, lifted his head and said 'Me too.'

Welbeck added milk and sugar, stirred the two mugs vigorously, handed one to Joe and took the other to the chair behind the desk. He drank noisily.

'There. How's that.'

Joe sipped his coffee.

'Fine.'

'Good. Revive the old flagging spirits. Expect your spirits have begun to flag a bit.'

'Not so's you'd notice.'

'Good for you.'

He pulled open the centre drawer of his desk, took out what looked to Joe like the same red file he had seen earlier and fiddled with the papers in it. He seemed to be talking half to himself. 'It's being political, y'see. Makes it tricky. Now criminal is straightforward enough. Chap commits a crime. Deserves to be punished. All there is to it. But political. Horse of a different colour. Always two sides to the question. Have to appreciate the other chap's point of view.'

Joe felt his head nodding forward onto his chest again but straightened up when Welbeck said 'Had a look at Sanson's notes about you' and waved two A4 sheets, covered with small, crabbed handwriting. He ran his finger along the lines, sucking his teeth. 'Gather he made pretty heavy weather of it.'

'You could say that.'

'Could be you made pretty heavy weather of it, yourself.'

'No.'

'Well the two of you didn't exactly get along. Rather got at loggerheads. Shall we say that. And, by the way, you can certainly believe me when I say that I in no way approve of the sergeant using his fists. Quite out of order. Quite.'

Joe shrugged his shoulders. Welbeck opened the centre drawer of his desk again and fumbled about with a pipe, tobacco pouch, packet of cigarettes, small tin of cigars and a lighter.

'Do you smoke. Got 'em all here.'

'No.'

'Sensible chap. Don't mind if I do. Never could break myself. 'Course they say a pipe's not half as dangeous as cigarettes. Come to that.'

'That's all right.'

Welbeck packed his pipe, slowly and carefully, tamping each layer of tobacco, waving the flame of the lighter delicately across the bowl, talking all the time.

'Joe, I may call you Joe. I'm Harold. Parents called me Harold. Never understand why I couldn't be a Harry. Rather fancied Harry. Less formal. Always seemed doomed to be a Harold.'

'What's Sanson.'

Welbeck raised his eyebrows.

'Roger, as it happens.'

118

'Roger, the lodger, the sod.'

He pointed his pipe at Joe.

'Certainly understand how you feel. He's a good man, mark you. Make no mistake about that. But perhaps a bit over-zealous. Doesn't really appreciate your point of view, Joe.'

'And you do.'

'I'm trying to. I really am. Key thing. Understand the other chap's point of view. Suppose I tell you how I think you see things and you correct me if I'm wrong. How about that.'

He paused and when Joe said nothing, he began again.

'To start with, you obviously feel it was the right thing to do, exposing the phone taps. You didn't do it for profit. Not out of malice. You did it because you thought it socially useful, isn't that so.'

'I never said I exposed any phone taps.'

Welbeck blew a series of grey puffs of smoke down at his desk.

'I'm not asking you to sign any statement, Joe. Nothing's being taken down as evidence. Just coming to terms. All above board. This chat is purely between us.'

'Tape recorder.'

Welbeck said 'Ah' and rattled the stem of his pipe between his teeth.

'As a matter of fact there isn't a tape recorder but I can see why you'd be suspicious. Natural in the circumstances. Quite understand. Tell you what. No need to commit yourself. You don't admit anything for the moment but hear me out. Right.'

'What time is it.'

Welbeck looked surprised. Joe held his wrist up.

'They took my watch away.'

'Silly that. Do apologise. It's just after three.'

'Thanks.'

'Not at all. Now, we were talking about your point of view, were we not. First there's your conviction that you were doing what was right by your standards. Political principles and all that. Fair enough.' He paused.

'Second. In addition to your political beliefs you have your personal loyalties. Naturally, you don't want to land anyone, friends perhaps, in the soup. Only right and proper. Don't want to feel you betrayed anybody. Do I read you right.'

'That'd be true of anybody.'

'Not invariably. I do assure you. Still, we'll leave that aside. Now, other side of the coin. Let's turn to the official point of view. I'll try and interpret it for you.'

He seemed to ponder awhile, wagging his head slowly from side to side.

'Part of it is hurt official dignity. Punctured pride. That sort of thing. They might not admit to it but it's bound to be so. You've made them look like fools. One man, boldly and ingeniously, upsets large official apple cart and they are understandably angry. But that's not their major concern. What's at the heart of their view of the matter, the nub, is the practical issue. How can they restore an effective system of telephone surveillance when they haven't located the ultimate source of the leak. The mole as it is popularly put. Targets could still be warned, even if it weren't made public in the press.'

'And so.'

Welbeck looked at him sadly.

'Joe, Joe. You still aren't trying to see their point of view. They don't tap phones for fun or out of spite. They are trying to find a way into a spider's web of things that threaten all of us. Terrorism, espionage, subversion, criminal conspiracy, all on a scale that grows day by day. Phone tapping, along with other types of surveillance, is absolutely essential, believe me.'

'Are you telling me that all the people they earwig on are spies and so on.'

'Not at all. Wouldn't claim any such thing. Quite often the people whose phones are being tapped are as innocent as the day is long. They're an unknowing part of a chain. They don't realise they have suspect contacts who have to be tracked down. You're a mature, experienced chap, think about it.'

'And what price freedom.'

Welbeck jabbed the air with the stem of his pipe.

'The price of liberty, Joe, is eternal vigilance.'

'By Christ you've got it turned round, flower.'

'What do you mean, Joe.'

'That bit about the price of liberty. That was Curran trying to remind poor buggers to keep an eye on the government, 'cos they're liable to get you by the short and curlies. It's not about government narks needing to spy on people.'

120

'It's on behalf of the people, Joe.'

Joe slammed his coffee mug down on the desk.

'Be buggered. You twist things, you do. It's like the bloody Russians with the old socialist slogan. The bit that used to say from each according to his ability, to each according to his need. Did you know what the Russians say now. They say from each according to his ability, to each according to his worth. They distort it like that. And most of 'em don't even know it's been changed.'

Welbeck tapped his pipe on an ashtray and sucked on it so that it made bubbling noises.

'We are wandering a bit from the point, Joe. Though I will take on board your argument. The key thing is for us to negotiate an agreement.'

'What agreement.'

'Let me put it in a nutshell. Nobody necessarily wants to punish you, Joe. Nor do they necessarily want to punish whoever gave you your information. If we can make sure that the leak is stopped and it doesn't happen again, that is of the essence. Just let us get an important part of the security services' investigative system working again. We'll settle for that believe me.'

'It'd be a right mug that believed you.'

Welbeck put his pipe back into the drawer and clasped his hands together.

'I don't think I deserve that from you, Joe. I'm trying to be reasonable. I'm trying to understand your point of view and get you to understand mine.'

Joe yawned.

'You haven't got a point of view. You're just a fuckin' cog in the machine. If they told you to drown me in shit, you'd drop your trousers and strain.'

Welbeck unclasped his hands, studied his fingernails for a while then pressed the buzzer on the inside ledge of his desk.

'I'm sorry you take that attitude, Joe. I really am. Your position is not an enviable one and you could do with an ally.'

He pulled the file towards him and took a gold pen out of his inside jacket pocket.

'I'll try and keep some sort of reasonable offer open and trust that when we meet again you'll have understood that I am sincerely trying to help you to make the best of a very bad job.'

121

A few seconds later, the man who had woken Joe came in and led him back to his cell. Alone, he paced around it then sat on the bed, staring at the sink. He muttered 'Silly bastards'd do better if they tried the cosy fuckin' chat bit first not after they've bashed you.' Later, in a mimic posh voice, he said 'And goodnight to you, Harold dear.'

Joe slept fitfully and woke early. He tried to remember what he had been dreaming but could only recall that he had been the train announcer at a large railway station but they had not given him a timetable from which to make his announcements. He had kept saying vaguely that trains would be arriving shortly.

When the man appeared at the door, Joe was sitting hunched sideways on the bed, back propped against the wall, his ankles crossed, massaging his toes.

'On your feet.'

'Where's mi breakfast.'

'Later.'

'When.'

'After you've talked some more. Come on.'

'I'll have a cup of tea, first.'

'Ask 'em in the interview room.'

'No. I want my tea here, in my room. Alone.'

The man moved into the cell and stood over him.

'Not till you've finished singin' your song. Now move.'

Joe flattened his back to the wall and braced his heels against the iron frame of the bed.

'I want a cup of tea.'

'Stop playing silly buggers and get off the bed.'

'I want a cup of tea.'

The man leaned over and gripped Joe's arms, tightly.

'Listen to me, friend. If I have to bounce you out of here, I can and I will. You hear me. Now which is it to be, walk on your own feet or get dragged there.'

Joe brought his head forward so that their faces touched and the man pulled back a little.

'If you get me a cup of tea, I'll trot along wherever you want. Like

122

a good little dog. If I don't get a cup of tea, you're going to have to drag me around and I'll say bugger all to anybody when you get me there. So you can please yourself.'

The man shook Joe so that he flopped back and forth like a rag doll. He lifted him half off the bed, let him fall back in a heap and shouted 'For fuck's sake.' Joe mumbled 'Milk and one sugar.' The man stamped out of the cell, slamming the door after him. Joe scrambled back into a cross-legged position and sat rubbing his arms, quietly singing snatches of 'Christians Awake, Salute the Happy Morn'.

In fifteen minutes the man came back with a mug of tea. Joe said 'Thank you very much' and stretched out on the bed, sipping it slowly. The man leaned against the door, arms folded, shuffling his feet. When Joe said 'By, but it's good,' he gave a snort of disgust. The tea finished, Joe slipped into his shoes and followed the man along the corridors to a seat in the office where he had first been questioned. Sanson sat behind the desk but there was no sign of the sergeant, and the man who had conducted him there left immediately.

'Had any second thoughts, Telford.'

He spoke without looking up from the red file in which he was scribbling. Joe waited till he had stopped writing and lifted his head.

'Thoughts on what.'

Sanson put his pen down and tilted his chair back.

'The question doesn't go away just because you refuse to answer it, you know. It stays with us till it gets settled. So once more from the top. Where did you get your information from, about the phone tapping.'

'What information.'

'OK. Let's go back one stage. In your home we found indisputable evidence that you are the person who has been warning people about their phones being tapped. What do you say to that.'

'I dispute it.'

'Don't talk rubbish. How can you dispute it. The evidence was there. Typewriter, paper, overtyped ribbon, the lot. What more do you want. It was in your house. It proves you're our man. Beyond all reasonable doubt. You have to admit that.'

'Don't see why I should.'

'The tools that did the job were found in your house.'

'So.'

'So how did they get there.'

'Maybe you put 'em there.'

Sanson dry washed his face.

'You're acting the idiot again, Telford. Evidence is evidence. It won't go away. You've been nicked. A proper collar. No two ways about it. And you have only one choice to make. The choice between staying stumm and carrying the can or co-operating with us and we'll work out a deal.'

'Isn't it time I got to see a solicitor.'

'Stop daydreaming and face facts. You had a good run for your money but it's all over. Finished. Get that into your head and tell us what we want to know. Then we'll see what can be done for you.'

'I'm entitled to a solicitor. Isn't that so.'

Sanson pulled himself out of his chair and went over to stare out of the shoulder height window. Joe's eyes followed him. As far as he could see the window looked onto the side of another building, a few feet away. From somewhere nearby came the harsh, scissor grinding sound of a car starter motor, revving over and over again but failing to fire the engine. Sanson turned and faced him.

'Let's be clear, Telford. We are talking about prison. Years of rotting in some lousy stinking prison. We are not talking about fines or probation or a telling off by the magistrate or any such damn sort of thing. We are talking about a nasty stretch inside. Think on that and think about your only chance of avoiding it. Now who gave you the names.'

'Am I entitled to a solicitor.'

'Damn it. You haven't been charged yet. The whole idea is that we might not have to charge you. If you co-operate.'

'What would you charge me with.'

'What the hell does it matter. There's plenty of charges. The whole idea is to get this settled quietly. There's been enough publicity as it is. Tell us where you get your names from and there doesn't have to be a charge.'

Joe pulled at his earlobe and gazed down at his feet which were resting on top of his shoes. He scratched his chin and said 'There's nothin' to shave with in that cell.'

'I'll see you get something to shave with.'
'There's not even any soap.'
'There'll be soap. Now what about it.'
'What charge would it be. If there were one.'
'Sod it. Official Secrets Act. One seven eight. One seven nine. Anything you like. What's it matter.'
'I'd have to ask a solicitor about that. I mean what am I supposed to have done. What sort of harm I mean.'
Sanson went back to his chair and swung in it, hands clasped behind his head. When he spoke, his voice was quieter.
'Telford. You must have given it some thought. Made the odd guess. Maybe even come to a conclusion.'
Joe wriggled his feet.
'What about.'
'The sixty-four dollar question. The big mystery. The thing you can't be sure about and then again perhaps you are sure. Absolutely sure.'
'What the hell are you talkin' about.'
'Come on, Telford. Don't try and tell me it hasn't been going round and round in your head ever since you got here. Round and round. One question. Like a crazy white mouse on a wheel.'
Joe folded his arms and rested his chin on his chest. Sanson spoke slowly.
'The key question. How did we get onto you. How did we sniff you out. What led us to your house and all the incriminating goodies, eh, Mister Telford. Is not that a fascinating question.'
He waited, then carrried on, smiling as he spoke.
'Like me to tell you. Give you a hint as to how come we tracked you down. Or can you guess. Bet you can guess. 'Course you can. A pinch that neat. Had to be the one thing, didn't it, feller. Just the one thing. Plain as plain can be. Stares you in the face.'
He paused, flipping the folder cover open and shut with his pen.
'Our old friend. Acting on information received. The anonymous phone call. The tip. The snitch. The grass. Had to be, comrade, didn't it.'
The swivel chair creaked merrily in the silence.
'But when you think about it, and I'm sure you're thinking about it, the answer to that question sort of raises another question, does it not. Like the old Chinese boxes. Inside the box there is

another box. So. If we nabbed you because a little birdie whispered in our ear, you may well ask yourself, who is that little birdie. A significant question for you to ponder on, Mister Telford. Who blew the whistle on the whistle blower. Who is Mister X. Judas.'

Joe swallowed and said 'I haven't admitted anything.'

Sanson licked his middle finger and leafed slowly through the papers in the red file. He separated one sheet, read it through slowly and looked at Joe, his head canted to one side.

'The record of the fatal phone call. Interested.'

'No.'

'What a poor liar you are, Telford. Let's see now.'

He moved his forefinger slowly down the page.

'Logged at nineteen forty-three. Coin operated call box. Male voice. Subject sounded angry and excited. Why angry I wonder. Mild northern accent. Rang off abruptly. Could be afraid of a trace. Maybe rang on impulse and started to change his mind. Fascinatin' to speculate on, don't you think.'

'Please yourself.'

'You know what I think.'

'I'm not bothered about what you think.'

'Lying again, Telford. You really won't go to heaven. I think you know who it was.'

'It's nothing to do with me.'

'I think you know who it was.'

'Get stuffed.'

'I'll go further than that. Make a little guess. Try an inspired thought. I think it was maybe the very chap we keep asking about. Your source of information. The man with the phone tap names. How about that.'

'When you've finished, I'd like some breakfast.'

'Well, well. Irony of fate, old son, irony of fate. Here you sit, ready to go into the slammer to protect the man who shopped you. Just how unbelievably stupid can you get.'

'Sausages would be all right.'

'Not only get the dirty end of the stick but suck on it.'

'And fried bread.'

'You really are a puzzle, Joseph Telford. But I'm a patient man. I believe the light will dawn, even on you. So we'll put you back and

126

let you think about it for a while. Give you some meditation time. Just ask yourself the question. Why should you go to the wall for the bloke who put the boot in.'

Back in his cell, Joe loudly demanded his breakfast. When it came he nibbled at it and pushed it around the plate, finding he had no appetite.

Jan leaned across the counter top and gently tapped the sergeant's chest.

'And the longer we talk, the more I figure there's something you can tell me.'

He combed his moustache with the knuckle of his forefinger.

'What makes you think that.'

'Because you're being cagey. Nice to me and sympathetic but cagey. And because I suspect there's not much goes on in this locality that you don't know something about.'

He straightened himself and fingered the flap buttons on his breast pockets.

'It's true, I do keep tabs on things. Keep an eye out. Draw my own conclusions. Still, I can honestly say I don't know where your Mister Telford is.'

'Maybe so, sergeant, but that doesn't mean you know nothing at all. Surely you can give me a clue, a lead or whatever it is you call it. Just a hint. Please. I appeal to you.'

'You're American aren't you.'

'That's right.'

'Tell by your accent.'

A young constable came out of the office with a long-spouted, green plastic watering can and advanced on the potted plants that were ranged along the wide window shelf. The sergeant said 'Later' and the constable went back into the office.

'You can't be sure he hasn't just gallivanted off somewhere and not let you know.'

'I can.'

'It happens.'

'Not with Joe.'

'You're a bit partial to him.'

'Very partial to him.'

'He's a lucky lad.'

'Thank you for saying so. I appreciate the compliment.'

He squared the big desk book with the edge of the counter.

'I'm not sure there's anything we can really do for you, lass. There's nothing in our books, I can promise you that.'

'Sergeant. Will you tell me something. Honestly. One thing.'

'Do mi best.'

'Why are you so disinclined to enter him as a missing person. Get the wheels rolling. Start an official search.'

'He's barely been gone twenty-four hours. It's early days yet.'

'Is that the only reason.'

The sergeant studied the telephone on the far end of the counter.

'What other reason could there be.'

'Because you suspect he's not just privately gone astray. You think the police are involved.'

'He's not been through our hands. That's for sure.'

'OK. I believe you. So whose hands has he been through.'

'Ah.'

Jan smiled and gazed straight at the sergeant who looked down at the counter top, patting it softly, as if he were drumming to a tricky rhythm.

'Just hang on a bit an' I'll see what I can do. I'll go an' have a quiet word with the gaffer. See what he says. Mark you, if he says we know nothing, we know nothing. That'll have to be it. Personal sympathy notwithstanding.'

'Fair enough.'

'You'll accept his decision.'

'Of course.'

The sergeant disappeared into the office.

Jan murmured 'Like hell I will' and turned the desk book round to check the entries for the previous days. She scanned quickly through reports of lost property, a stolen car listing, time of a prisoner on remand leaving the station, details of statements taken, constables logging on and off duty, magistrates court attendances and driving licence and insurance documents verified. She was puzzling out an entry to do with transfer of evidence dockets to county when she heard footsteps and hastily shut and turned the book as the constable with the watering can

128

came through the door into the reception area. He said 'Evening' and Jan nodded in reply to his greeting. His watering was painstaking. He prodded the soil of each pot, moving the thin spout carefully round the edges. He broke off dead bits of leaf, checked the training of a variegated ivy round its wire triangle and turned each pot so that the foliage previously away from the window came fully into the light.

He had just finished and was going back into the office when the sergeant returned.

'Now then, Miss Bragg. I've had a quiet word with the Inspector. You do understand that I'm speaking more or less unofficially.'

'Of course.'

'Off the record, so to speak. Merely by way of general conversation.'

'Sure.'

'Dealing informally with public requests for information.'

'You bet.'

'You might, for instance, casually ask me if there had been any enquiries to us, concerning Mister Joseph Telford, of late.'

'Have there been any enquiries to you, concerning Joseph Telford, of late.'

'Funny you should ask that. Day before yesterday we did have an enquiry, as it happens. From Special Branch. Matter of routine, we were given to understand. Just, did we know of Mister Telford's home address, place of work, any other facts about him that might have come to our notice.'

'What did you say.'

'Just gave the addresses, home and work. Nothing much else we know for that matter. We said we've nothing against Mister Telford.'

'Why did they want the information.'

'No idea, miss.'

'Do you think they've arrested him.'

'Haven't a clue. Outside our province.'

'Would you care to make a guess.'

'Sorry, miss. Can't do that.'

'And how do I get hold of Special Branch.'

'That's not easy. Bit of a hole in a corner sort of mob. Best I can do is give you a phone number.'

He consulted a thin, grey directory, tore a strip from a memo pad, scribbled on it and passed it to her.

'You can try that but they're not very forthcoming. You're not bound to learn much. Keep themselves to themselves.'

'They can't just take people away and hold on to them.'

'I'm afraid I'm not at liberty to comment on that, miss.'

'Yes but there must be laws.'

'True. But you'd be better off checking that with a good solicitor.'

'Anyone you'd recommend.'

The sergeant glanced over his shoulder at the office.

'You might try Desmond Unwin, King Street. He's not what you'd call popular in this building but he's a right terrier.'

Jan leaned across and kissed the sergeant on the cheek.

'I am grateful.' He grinned and said 'All part of public relations.' As Jan reached the door he said 'Love' and when she turned, he said 'I hope you find your feller all right.'

A new man shook him awake, with a command that he only half-caught, something about wake up Cinderella, time for the ball. Joe turned onto his side and pulled the coarse grey blanket over his head, the man tugged it down and they sawed it back and forth till Joe's effort dwindled and the blanket was shaken free and thrown onto the floor.

'Sod it.'

'Wakey, wakey.'

'Bugger off.'

'Rise and shine, sunny boy.'

Joe rolled onto his back and looked up at the grinning face.

'You let me sit on my arse all day. All on my own. Nobody comes near or by. Then as soon as I get my head down at night, some fucker wants to talk to me. Where's the sense in that.'

The man chattered as he swung Joe's legs round and heaved him into a sitting position.

'All part of the round-the-clock service. The show must go on. We never close. Now shoes and socks and let's go see the man.'

Joe looked blearily around him and patted the bed.

'Lost mi socks.'

The man tut-tutted and searched the bed before finding the socks under it. He held them aloft and dropped them onto Joe's lap.

'Come on, my little chickadee. Look lively.'

'I'm tired, honest to God. I'm worn out.'

'All in the mind. Think positive and pull your socks up.'

'Do I have to come.'

'Absolutely. So stop messin' about.'

Joe put on his socks and shoes and shuffled after the man, head down, hands stuffed into trouser pockets, muttering to himself about the daftness of doing everything in the middle of the night. He was led into Sanson's office, dumped on the hard chair and left. Sanson opened the red file in front of him and began to speak in a slow, even tone.

'Mister Telford, you've had a full day to think about your situation and decide what you want to do. Before you make your choice let me formally put the alternatives to you. They are simple and obvious. You can choose to co-operate and tell us the source of your information about phone tapping. In which case we shall settle the matter out of court, non-punitively. Our interest lies solely in plugging the leak. Or you can choose to go on shielding the man who has betrayed you. In which case you will go to jail, probably for a very long time. He will be left scot-free, rejoicing in the fact that he threw you to the wolves and you were too gutless even to protest. It's a straightforward choice between looking after your own reasonable interests or sacrificing yourself for someone who clearly has nothing but contempt for you. Bearing that in mind, what do you choose to do.'

Joe hitched further back to ease his position on the uncomfortable chair.

'What happened to Harold. I thought Harold the coffee man did the night shift chats.'

'Are you going to co-operate.'

'It must make a hell of a long day for you.'

'Where did you get your information from.'

'Of course, if you get double time for night work. I mean, if you did, it'd be worthwhile. Up to a point, anyway.'

After a long silence, Sanson began again. Somewhat mechanically, he recited the evidence that pointed to Joe as the man who

131

warned people that their phones were being tapped, stressing that preventing further interference with legal investigative routines was the main concern of the authorities, repeating that Joe owed nothing to a man who had not hesitated to betray him and that a prison sentence was inevitable if co-operation was not forthcoming. He asked, several times, for the name of the person who was the source of the information about phone taps. Joe ignored what was said or claimed that he did not know what Sanson was talking about or asked when he was going to be allowed a solicitor or complained that he was tired and protested that the chemical closet in his cell was smelly and needed emptying. When Sanson once more threatened him with prison he leaned forward and wagged a finger at him.

'And you listen to me, flower. I've thought quite a bit about all these serious charges you keep on about and how I'm bound to go to prison and I'm not sure but what you might be just bullshitting. Even if I had written to people about their phones being tapped, which I don't admit to, even so I'm not at all convinced it's against the law. It's got up your nose for sure but that doesn't necessarily make it a crime. So we'll wait to hear what the lawyers say about that.'

Sanson took off his glasses and gently stroked his eyes with the thumb and middle finger of his left hand. Replacing the spectacles he flicked idly through the papers in the file, closed it, left his chair and walked round the office, disappearing for a while behind Joe, who could hear him whistling tunelessly between his teeth. Finally, he came back to his chair and considered Joe carefully, before speaking in a louder, more authoritative tone. 'Think about this before you get too chirpy, Mister Telford. If we can clear up the one offence concerning the phone tap names, we are prepared to leave other matters out of account. However, if you persist in being unco-operative in the one area, we shall have to pay attention to other issues and add further charges to the indictment. Perhaps more serious charges.'

Joe rubbed his head with the heel of his hand.

'What's that mean. Further charges.'

Sanson picked up a pen and tapped the file with it. 'Charges arising out of your possession of highly secret Ministry of Defence documents, including confidential military reports.'

132

'What bloody documents.'

'Documents found in your house along with the evidence that you have been involved in exposing phone surveillance details.'

Joe took a deep breath.

'You are fuckin' crazy. There was never any defence documents in my house. You know damn well there wasn't.'

Sanson tapped the file again.

'I have formal depositions from my officers specifying that a number of Ministry of Defence documents were found during the search of your premises.'

Joe shouted 'The lying bastards, it's not true' and stood up to lean towards Sanson. Tripping over his loose shoes, he put the palms of his hands on the desk to steady himself.

'Look, what would I want with secret documents. Military documents. Why would I have such things.'

'For legal purposes we don't need to know that. But we could point out that it is in keeping with your subversive past.'

Joe waved his hands, gagging on his words.

'Subversive past. What the hell does that mean. Subversive past.'

Sanson opened the file and thumbed through it, looking up for a moment to say 'Sit down, please.' Joe sat down and wriggled his feet back into his shoes.

'Let's see now. Here we are. Interesting bit of history. The first entry we have for Joseph Telford is at the tender age of twenty-two. An MI6 file lists you as one of those who held dockside meetings at Hull in nineteen-forty-eight, in contravention of the Emergency Powers Act then in force.'

'For Christ's sake. Why dig that up. They were just ordinary political meetings with the dockers.'

'They were not ordinary political meetings. They were illegal and subversive.'

'Look, just because some crazy buggers in the government panicked at the dock strike and brought in Emergency Powers, it doesn't make a political meeting subversive.'

Sanson shook his head.

'You really are a very naive man, Mister Telford. It does exactly that.'

'Well it's got nothing to do with you planting bloody documents on me. You know I didn't take 'em.'

133

'I don't know anything of the sort. What I do know is that we have irrefutable evidence that you were in possession of documents marked secret, and which shall, in the words of the Act, "be deemed to have been collected by you for a purpose prejudicial to the safety and interests of the state unless the contrary is proved".'

He intoned the latter part of his speech in a mock legal manner. Joe slapped the desk.

'It's a complete fuckin' lie from start to finish.'

'Interesting that "unless the contrary is proved" bit. Sort of reverses innocent until proved guilty. You have to convince the court you weren't going to do anything wicked with the stuff.'

'Where did I get them from then, these documents. Just how am I supposed to have got hold of 'em. Tell me that.'

'Perhaps from the man who gave you the names of the people listed for phone tapping.'

Joe sat back in his chair, his arms hanging slackly at his side.

'You twisted bastard.'

Sanson pursed his lips.

'You're much too inclined to profanity, Telford. It does you no good. Actually, we have two possible routes by which the documents might have come to you. Speculatively, there is a second possibility.'

Joe spoke dully.

'What's that.'

'The CND demonstration at Weyford. Two months ago. In all the pushing and shoving some of the demonstrators got over the wire and into the compound. The documents could have been taken then. When we check we may find that their copies are missing.'

'I wasn't anywhere near the compound. I was at the other side of the perimeter fence thing.'

'Now isn't that odd. I just happen to have an officer on the staff who was there and claims he spotted you climbing the fence. Of course, he didn't know who you were at the time but he recognised you when we nabbed you. So it could all add up. Motive, means and the very documents in question, tucked away in your dresser drawer. How about that for a tidy case.'

'It's fuckin' rubbish.'

'No, Telford. It is not, as you put it, fuckin' rubbish. It's the skids down which you could slide to an even longer stretch in clink.

Could be quite a blight on your autumnal years, could it not.'
Joe folded his arms and slouched on his chair. Sanson waited a while before he spoke.

'Think about the bargain you're being offered. It's a sizeable bargain. For our part, we drop the Ministry of Defence papers indictment and any charges arising out of your unlawful interference with phone tapping. All in all, we let you off a certain long jail sentence. In return you give us the name of the character who landed you in this mess in the first place.'

He waited again.

'Believe you me, you are lucky, Telford. You may not think it but you have dropped lucky. Normally, we would propel you into the slammer fast and think it a good job well done. None of this friendly persuasion. As it happens, we are under very heavy pressure to find out how the tap names were leaked and put a stop to it. I make no bones about it. We are under pressure from on high. So we have to offer you a more than generous deal and forgive and forget once you tell us your source. Now if we can be that reasonable, surely you can reciprocate. How about it.'

Joe straightened up.

'If I don't play ball are you really prepared to book me for stealing documents you know soddin' well I had nothing to do with.'

'We are prepared to charge you with the unlawful possession of Ministry of Defence documents found in your house. Yes. If you refuse to tell us what we need to know.'

'So you'd send me down on false evidence.'

'We will make the charges I have specified, if you do not co-operate.'

Joe got to his feet and stood stiffly by the chair. He spoke quietly.

'You miserable bastard. You have fuckin' had it as far as I'm concerned. You have totally fuckin' had it. Chat time is all over. So you might as well send me back to bed.'

Sanson stared at Joe for a long time, then said 'Think about it' as he pressed the buzzer on the inside edge of his desk.

Joe was deeply tired. His bones ached and even the low light in the office ceiling hurt his eyes. It seemed to him that Welbeck's voice was coming from a long way off. A bit, he thought, like the shushing sound you get when you hold a seashell to your ear or the humming noise you can hear inside a telegraph pole. He felt a great surge of gratitude for the comfort of the chair in which he was sprawled and he interrupted a speech about the need for a negotiated settlement.

'I'm grateful for the chair. Being so comfortable. Very grateful.' Welbeck smiled vaguely.

'Yes. Quite. Glad you appreciate it. Well. As I was saying. Upshot of all this is that you've a bit driven Sanson into a corner. Not left him much in the way of options. None, really. So he's liable to come down very hard on you. You having left him no room to manoeuvre, as it were. You appreciate that.'

Joe rested his elbow on the chair arm and carefully propped his forehead on his hand.

'Yes. Understand that. It happens. Had a teacher once, just the same. Name of Good. Gummi Good, we used to call him. 'Cos *Gummi* is German for rubber. He'd say you leave me no options boy. Leave me no options. And bang with the cane. Big man with a Hitler moustache. Like a toothbrush. Came from the south of England. Hampshire or Hertfordshire. One of those places, like that. Might have been Gloucestershire. That's more west, though.' Welbeck twitched at his tie and pointed his pipe stem at Joe.

'You all right.'

'Fine.'

'Get you some coffee. If you like. Pick up.'

'No thanks. Nice of you to offer me some, though. Thank you. Nothing against coffee.'

Heavy footsteps sounded in the corridor outside, getting louder as they approached, before dying away. Joe giggled as they brought to mind a myriad of footsteps in old radio comedy programmes. Like *The Goon Show*. Whole concerts of footsteps, marching, plodding, running, echoing, melodramas of clattering boots. Often ending in a splash or the long fading scream of someone falling to a great depth.

'Sure you're all right.'

'Fine.'

Welbeck made gurgling noises as he sucked on his empty pipe.

'Fact of the matter is that Sanson's about at the end of his tether.

136

Tried every angle. No stone unturned. Can't think of any other way to make things clear to you. Question is, can you.'
'What.'
'Put it another way. What do you want. From your point of view.'
Joe changed the position of his hand so that it propped his chin instead of his forehead. He felt that he should make a big effort to be thoughtful and to the point.
'More sleep. And some books to read. And get rid of that chemical bucket and let me go to a proper bog. And give me my watch back.'
'Yes, we can do that sort of thing. More generally I mean.'
'Beer. And let me go home. And don't ever mither me again.'
'Be serious.'
'I am serious.'
Welbeck alternately clenched and relaxed his teeth so that his pipe bobbed up and down.
'Do make an effort to understand our position, Joe. We're trying to do the decent thing by you. Now you tell us. What sort of bargain are you willing to make.'
Joe yawned, rubbed his eyes and recited.

> *I'll tell you what I'll do*
> *I'll let you play with*
> *My four by two.*

Welbeck made clucking sounds of disapproval.
'There's simply no point in rudeness.'
'Not rude. Bet you don't even know what a four by two is.'
'It's hardly relevant.'
'It's a pull through. To clean a rifle barrel. Piece of cloth, four inches by two. Old army saying.'
'Good God, man. Are you never prepared to listen to reason.'
Joe used both arms to prop his head up.
'Reason away.'
'Can you not see that it is in your best interest to co-operate with us.'
'My best interest.'
'Your best interest.'
'Ten per cent.'
'What does that mean.'

'Not a lot.'

Welbeck fumbled a tobacco pouch out of the desk drawer and began to fill his pipe.

'I really can't believe that an intelligent man like you is going to throw his future away. Just throw it away. Makes no sense. Can't accept it.'

He rammed tobacco into the pipe bowl with his thumb.

'What sort of bargain do you want, Joe. Seriously.'

'Seriously. Can't bargain with cheats.'

'That's not fair.'

' 'Tis so. You're a load of fuckin' cheats. You bugger about with evidence. Plant it on me. You talk any old crap you think will soften me up. You try to make me so dozy you can trick me. Swindlers.'

'It's not like that. Really it isn't.'

Joe let his head loll onto the chair backrest and began to croon 'I hear them gentle voices calling poor black Joe'. Welbeck lit his pipe, puffed vigorously and began to argue that it was precisely their reluctance to put Joe beyond rescue that had caused them to have recourse to additional legal possibilities.

Jan gripped the phone tightly and struggled to quieten her voice.

'Well, have you got a list of people who are coming to you. In the near future, the next few days.'

'I keep telling you. He'd only be here if he was on remand. From the magistrates' court.'

'Have you checked to see if a Joseph Telford is listed to come to you.'

'He's not on any list. We've no knowledge of him.'

'Are you sure.'

'I've told you.'

'Have you checked.'

'Madam. I'm sorry but we can't help you. You'll have to try elsewhere. I hope you get the information you want.'

Jan began to panic and shouted.

'No. Don't hang up. Please. Listen. It's been several days so he

must be due to come to a court. And you're bound to be informed.
If he's remanded.'
'Only if it's in our area.'
'But he must be brought to court by now.'
'Not necessarily. I mean if he was being questioned under the
Prevention of Terrorism Act for instance.'
'What the hell are you talking about. He's not a terrorist.'
'I didn't say he was, madam. Not exactly. I'm just trying to point
out the possibilities.'
'Can I speak to the governor.'
'There really isn't any point.'
'The deputy governor then.'
'Look, with the best will in the world, we just haven't any
information for you. I'm sorry but there it is.'
'Well, who should I try then. Who might know something.'
'You could try the Citizens' Advice Bureau.'
'That's a bloody stupid suggestion. What are they going to know
about Joe.'
'I didn't mean they'd know anything specific. They might be able
to suggest channels.'
'What channels.'
'I don't know what channels. That's why I made the sugges-
tion.'
'Look, I'm sorry I shouted. Just tell me. When do you get your
next list. Of people who are going to be sent to you. In the future.'

Sanson swivelled his chair to face the side wall and his voice
dulled to a drone as he rambled through a long question about the
background of the journalist who had first written about the
phone tapping and his possible relationship to Joe. When the
question was ignored he pondered the notes on a sheet of paper in
the red file, swung his chair so that he was looking straight at Joe
and spoke sharply.
'What about Critiewicz.'
Joe clasped his hands on the top of his head.
'What about Critiewicz.'
'Leonard Critiewicz.'

139

'I know his name. We used to call him Elsie because of his initials. He never cared a lot for that.'

'He was of Polish extraction.'

'He was an old-style Polish socialist. Real fierce buggers they were. He survived the Germans in the Warsaw uprising and got to England when the Stalinists moved in.'

'What about your association with him.'

'What about it.'

'In nineteen-fifty-four you wrote an extremist pamphlet with him. Entitled *The Doctrine of Encroaching Control in Industry*. You admit that.'

'You've got a fuckin' peculiar way of putting things. I don't admit it, I'm proud of it. It was a good pamphlet, as pamphlets go. I did your actual writing. Leonard's English was always a bit wild and woolly. Anyway it was a good pamphlet. Not that all that many bothered to read it.'

'You continued to associate with Critiewicz.'

'Did you ever read it.'

'No.'

'Pity. Improve your mind a bit.'

'Did you continue to associate with Critiewicz.'

'There you go again. Associate with. What does it mean. You'd think we were bot buddies.'

'Did you stay in contact.'

'For a while.'

'Three years later he was arrested during a sit-in, at a works in Birmingham. As a ringleader.'

'That's another of them words. Ringleader.'

'Never mind about that. He was arrested. When he was released he left the country. Went to Paris.'

'So what.'

'So are you still in touch with him.'

'Be tricky.'

'Why so.'

'Been dead ten years. At least.'

He looked sharply at Joe.

'We've no record of that.'

'He must have forgotten to tell you.'

Sanson scribbled on his sheet of paper.

140

'What about Foster. The man who published the pamphlet.'

'Did you know old Elsie was a hell of a pianist. Has it got that down there. Played like an angel. Funny thing was he had short stubby fingers. Not a bit like you think of a pianist's fingers.'

'What about Foster.'

Joe stood up, rubbed his back, turned his chair round and sat on it as if it were a saddle, chest pressed against the backrest, stockinged feet resting on the stretchers. Sanson seemed surprised.

'I never said you could sit like that.'

'Do you like your job.'

'I was asking about Foster.'

'No. I'm serious. Do you like your job.'

'It's a necessary job.'

'So's cleaning out shithouses. Question is do you like it.'

'It has to be done.'

'You said that. Do you like it.'

Sanson plucked at his lower lip.

'It's fair enough. When I was a child I always wanted to be a policeman when I grew up.'

'Why so.'

He yawned and said 'Not sure. Think I wanted to be certain I was on the right side.'

'Did it work out like that.'

'We're getting off the point. I asked you about Foster.'

Joe rested his chin on his forearms and closed his eyes.

The clock on the squat tower of the town hall boomed eleven times and Jan automatically glanced at her watch. The three men sitting on the bench beside her stirred at the reminder of time and began a muttered conversation. She stood up, stretched and looked out of the tall window to the left of the bench. Rain, swept by a driving wind, lashed at huddled figures scurrying across the town square, viciously flapped shop awnings and the sodden blue flag that hung above a hotel facade. It ruffled the miniature lake that had formed around a blocked drain in front of the war memorial. She rested her forehead on the cold glass for a while,

141

turned and glanced at the brass knobbed double door of the office opposite and scowled. At the far end of the corridor, a woman in a green nylon apron appeared, pushing a tea trolley. She knocked at each door in turn, bringing two or three people out for a fussy interchange about tea and biscuits before they vanished back into their offices and she moved on. At the other end of the corridor a porter appeared in a heavy blue serge uniform and marched its full length in a guardsman's stride, before disappearing round a corner. From somewhere behind the building came the strident warbling of an ambulance, travelling along the ring road. Jan looked at her watch again and sat down.

One of the double doors opened. A young man stepped out, coughed and said 'Miss Bragg. Mister Oldfield will see you now.' The three men stood up and moved with Jan, towards the door. The young man seemed startled and skipped back as if to block their way.

'Excuse me, Miss Bragg, your appointment with Mister Oldfield.' He gestured at the three men.

'We understood, it was for you. With Mister Oldfield.'

'I'd like to have these gentlemen present when I talk to him.'

The young man muttered 'I'm not sure, perhaps, if you could wait a moment' and slipped back into the office. The woman with the tea trolley was now close enough for them to hear a hushed conversation favouring rich tea rather than ginger biscuits and complaints about failures to offer exact change for items purchased. A tall man with a mane of white hair appeared in the doorway and regarded them.

'Miss Bragg. I'm John Oldfield. I understand you have a delegation of some sort with you.'

Jan stepped a little to one side so that he could see the three men.

'This is Alan Bateman, my lawyer. Chris King from a civil liberties group that's interested and a newspaperman, Den Fletcher.'

Oldfield repeated their names, shook hands with each in turn and stood for a moment, smiling and shaking his head at the same time.

'Gentlemen, I appreciate your interest but I really don't think a committee session is called for at this point. It might well confuse matters. If it's all the same to you, I would prefer to speak to Miss Bragg on her own.'

'It concerns them.'

'I rather hope it doesn't. In any case, I think we would do better to discuss the matter informally. The two of us.'

'I want them to hear what you have to say.'

'I really cannot accept that I am under public examination, Miss Bragg.'

Jan started to speak again and Bateman took her by the elbow, muttered 'Give me a minute' to the others and guided her a little way down the corridor.

'Listen. These regional Home Office types are a bit taken up with their own dignity. Just for a start you might do better on your own. One to one. He might go entirely on the defensive in a group. He probably sees us as the heavy mob come to lean on him.'

'That's what you are. I want the bastard pressured.'

He squeezed her arm.

'Fine. But see how he responds to sweet reason first. He knows we're in the picture so we'll be inside his noodle, whether we're in the room or not.'

'What if he clams up and I can't get anything out of him.'

'Then we'll all go into action. But use us as a last resort.'

'If you're sure it's best.'

Bateman reassured her and led her back to the group. After courtesies the three men sat down again on the corridor bench. Jan followed Oldfield into the outer office, where the young man had buried himself in papers at a desk and a thin woman stood sentry by a filing cabinet. Oldfield led the way into his room. He held the back of a reproduction Chippendale while she sat down and moved to the far side of an ornate walnut desk. Sitting and steepling his hands, he rested his chin on the points of his fingers.

'That is quite a little army you've brought, Miss Bragg. The law, the press and the civil rights person. All in their serried ranks. Don't you think perhaps you're over-reacting, as they say. A shade.'

'No. I'm just tired of being given the runaround.'

'I can hardly believe you've been given the runaround, as you put it.'

Jan grimaced.

'Hardly believe be buggered. Before I got to you I tried contacting Special Branch, MI5, MI6, the Director of Public Prosecutions and every cop shop, magistrates clerk and local jail around. All I get is fobbed off with crap about it must be somebody else's pigeon or they'll make enquiries in due course or it'll all work out if I just sit on my arse and wait. Mostly they talk as if I made Joe Telford up or he's off sowing wild oats and he'll be back in a while.'

'I gather you don't believe the latter.'

'You gather right.'

Oldfield ran a thumb round his shirt cuffs, aligning them with the ends of his jacket sleeves.

'Actually, if you'll forgive my saying so, a lot of the approaches you made were wildly inappropriate, in a case of this sort.'

'What would have been appropriate.'

'Hard to say. Locating the whereabouts of one person in the complexities of a nationwide judicial process is difficult and it takes time.'

Jan tugged at her hair with both hands.

'Jesus. You see what I mean. That is exactly the kind of bullshit I've been getting in bucketloads for the last five days.'

Oldfield flushed.

'Really, Miss Bragg.'

'Really, Mister Oldfield, sir. For a start you don't need to check through any nationwide process. I told you when I phoned you. Joe was snatched in Scarby by your Special Branch people. You start from there.'

'We do not snatch people. Anyway you can't be sure of that.'

'Tell me, did you start from there and what information did you get. Or do they feed you the kind of crap they feed me.'

He picked up a pen and doodled on the memo pad in front of him. Without looking up he said 'I'm not sure that, strictly speaking, you're entitled to information since you're not related to Joseph Telford.' Jan leaned forward, bringing her head close to his.

'OK. So you want to play official games. I'm enquiring on behalf of his father, Charles Frederick Telford. And I can give you a telephone number so you can check that out. Next point.'

He sighed and leaned back in his chair.

'You really are misconstruing the situation.'

'And what is this situation that I am misconstruing.'

'It is within the usual parameters for this type of investigation.'

'What investigation.'

He sighed and flapped his hands.

144

'I will go so far as to say that it does appear that Joseph Telford is helping the authorities with some enquiries.'

'Where is he.'

'I'm not at liberty to divulge that.'

'What are the enquiries about.'

'That too is a security matter.'

'Who's got him.'

'I can't be specific on that point.'

'Proper little mine of information, aren't you.'

She chewed at her lip, seeming to look through him.

'You say enquiries. That means he hasn't been charged yet.'

'Not to my knowledge.'

'Right. I want my lawyer in here.'

He held out his hands, palms upward.

'Surely that isn't necessary. I've told you what you need to know.'

'Listen, friend. Let's see if I've got this straight. As my lawyer gave it to me, you're allowed to hold Joe twenty-four hours for questioning, then you have to let him go or charge him. If he's charged he comes up at a magistrates' court and after that he's out on bail or if not he can have visits from me and his lawyer. That's something called Judges rules. Am I right.'

'Not necessarily. Judges rules are not that specific. They allow for weekend periods. They refer to being held for questioning for a reasonable time.'

Ian raised her voice.

'Reasonable goddamn time. You've had him five days. What kind of reasonable time is that.'

'He has not objected. Apparently. He has been voluntarily co-operating. With ongoing enquiries.'

Ian's voice went harsh and flat and her accent became more marked.

'Right, buster. This is the end of the line. I have now had it up to here and here is where we light the blue touch paper. A big fat newspaper story playing up the British Gestapo angle, civil rights lobbying everybody in sight and writs of all shapes and sizes coming in like confetti. I've got the money to scream good and loud with, so you can fasten your seat belt, Mister, on account of, like the lady said, you're in for a bumpy ride.'

'Miss Bragg, I will not be threatened.'

145

'You, bub, are being threatened.'

She started to get up and he said sharply 'Sit down,' then more mildly, 'Please.' Jan sat down and glared at him. He cleared his throat.

'Will you let me persuade you to wait just two days. Let matters resolve themselves.'

'No way.'

For a while he twisted a signet ring round and round on his finger, looking away from Jan towards a set of hunting prints on the wall to his right. He said 'If only you would try and appreciate the complexity of the situation' and fell silent before abruptly muttering 'Let me make a call.' He left the room. Through the partly open door Jan could hear the dialling of the phone and the mumble of a prolonged conversation. When Oldfield came back he stood behind his desk and spoke in a self-consciously official tone.

'It seems that Joseph Telford will appear at Scarby magistrates' court tomorrow morning and will be formally charged. I trust that is satisfactory.'

Jan grinned as she stood up.

'I wouldn't call it satisfactory but at least it gets Joe out into the daylight.'

She did not reply to Oldfield's 'Good day' as she left.

Joe had finished his breakfast and was bending over, stiff-legged, feet wide apart, pressing the floor with his fingertips and giving long mock groans, when the cell door opened and a man came in and offered him a pair of shoelaces. He took them and looked questioningly at the man.

'How come I get these. Queen's birthday or what.'

'You're being shifted. Get your shoes on.'

Joe sat on the bed and began to lace up his shoes.

'These are not my laces, you know. Mine were flat laces, these are round.'

'Get your shoes on.'

'Round laces are a bugger. They slip. Can't think why they make 'em. You have to tie a double bow or they come loose.'

146

'Speed it up.'

'Flat laces are better every time.'

The man jerked his head towards the cell door.

'I notice you've got flat laces.'

'Stop jabberin'.'

Joe put his shoes on, tied them tightly and marched round the cell, stamping his feet.

'By but it makes you feel a new man. Havin' your shoes laced up. I would never have thought.'

'Get your jacket on.'

'Feels grand.'

He put on his jacket, tugged it straight and buttoned it.

'Where am I goin' then.'

The man went out into the corridor and Joe followed him.

In the office he remembered from the first evening, he was given his watch and penknife. He made a ceremony out of checking that the watch was showing the right time before he strapped it on. Left sitting by the window, his raincoat in his lap, he admired the blue morning sky, with huge banks of grey cloud promenading across it. He asked the man at the desk if he might open the window and was told to please himself. He unlatched it, pushed it wide open and sniffed at the cold moist air. He tap danced his feet on the board floor and asked the clerk if there was anywhere he could get a bar of chocolate but the clerk ignored him. A white Transit van was driven into the yard and a uniformed policeman got out of the cab, lit a cigarette, stretched himself and strolled to and fro. Joe watched him for a while before leaning his head out of the window and shouting 'Heyup.' The policeman walked across, cupping the cigarette behind his back, and looked down at him. 'I thought you might like to know. I've come to prefer mi coppers in uniform. Better than the types in civvy suits.'

The policeman shrugged his shoulders and said 'Right.'

'I'm not that keen on coppers in uniform, mark you, but if it comes to a choice.'

The policeman said 'Right' once more and when Joe said that this preference had come as a surprise, he nodded and went back to stand by the van. Joe put his feet up on a radiator, whistled 'We are les beaux gendarmes' and played at checking his watch, minute by minute, against the big electric clock on the opposite wall.

147

About a quarter of an hour later, the man who had fetched him from his cell came back and took him into the next door office, where an elderly official whom Joe had not seen before was glancing at a familiar red file and filling out a form. Joe was not asked to sit down and stood slackly in front of the desk. When he had completed the form the older man signed it with a flourish and looked up.

'You'll be taken to a police station where you'll be formally charged and brought before the magistrates.'

'Charged with what.'

'Under the Official Secrets Act.'

'Does that include that shit about me pinchin' Ministry of Defence papers.'

The man behind the desk folded the form, tucked it into an envelope and handed it to Joe's escort.

'Van's in the side yard.'

As Joe was led out through the front entrance, Sanson appeared at the door to the main office. For a moment he seemed about to come over to him but when Joe thrust two fingers into the air he went back into the office.

Standing in the queue that straggled along a railing inside the courtyard, Jan looked up at the sheer, thick walls and the huge, iron-studded gate and realised that though, all her life, this had been her mental picture of a prison, she was still shocked by the massive reality. It seemed strange that there was traffic and people and shops and houses, just on the other side of the wall, yet she felt entirely cut off from the town.

She shivered in the chill December wind and regretted being too lightly dressed. Half-smiling, she remembered how long she had pondered what to wear. Maybe she should have written to one of the women's magazines, posing it as a serious feminine problem for their advice. What should one wear when visiting one's lover in prison. Surely, to dress in a stylish and flamboyant way might seem a mockery of the poor man's condition, while to dress sexily would only arouse a desire that could not, under the circumstances, be satisfied. Yet to be deliberately dowdy could be

148

depressing for all concerned. Perhaps a sensible, well-tailored suit in an autumnal shade, not too bright, not too sombre, would be ideal.

She looked along the line of visitors and noticed that it was composed almost entirely of women. She wondered if the situation would be reversed at a women's prison or whether visiting prison was essentially a female activity. The line surged as the door at its head was half-opened and settled again as it was closed, with no one let through.

Jan asked the woman in front of her how long they would have to wait.

'They please theirselves, dear. It shouldn't be long now.'

She touched Jan's arm and said 'Your first time. Visitin'.'

'Yes. Does it show.'

'You looked a bit lost when they let us through the gate. You'll soon get used to it.'

'Do you come often. I mean have you come for a long time.'

The woman tittered.

'With our Arthur I spend half mi life visitin'. He's a right silly bugger.'

'I'm sorry. It must be hard for you.'

'You get used to it. Not exactly a bed of roses for him, I don't suppose.'

'What do you say to him. Talk about.'

'Depends. Mostly it's best to give 'em news. Any little thing that's happened. They like to be kept in touch. They get suspicious if they feel left out.'

Jan started to ask another question when the door opened wide and the queue concertina-ed and pushed into a large stone-floored room, in which prison officers checked everyone off, before letting them through into the visiting area.

Clutching her blue visiting form, she gave her name and address and Joe's name to the warder, who entered the details on his clip board. She hesitated when he asked her relationship to the prisoner before saying 'Friend', and blinked when he followed Joe's name with a recital of his prison number. She was directed to a place on a bench facing a long table with a raised board down the centre. She watched a line of prisoners in military-style tunics and trousers come through the far door. Joe

had almost reached his place opposite her before she recognised
him. He sat down and they stared at each other and smiled. They
sat mute, till Jan said 'I didn't spot you at first.' Joe fingered the
lapel of his tunic.

'It's this effort. Makes you look like an old Raf erk.'

'What's a Raf erk.'

'Doesn't matter. It's good to see you.'

'You too.'

'It's very good to see you.'

She put a hand on the raised board but the prison officer,
standing behind and to the left of Joe, wagged his finger so she put
her hand back in her lap.

'How are you keeping.'

'Fair to middlin'.'

'What's it like. In here.'

Joe pondered.

'It's a poor sort of place.'

'Yes.'

'I didn't like the bit when I first came in. You get stripped and
shouted at and left standing about.'

Jan heard a woman on her left say sharply 'It's no good you goin'
on about it's up to me to keep him in order and control him more.
I can't control him an' that's that. He's just runnin' wild.'

She tried to say 'I'm sorry we couldn't get you allowed bail' and
choked on the words. Joe shushed her fiercely.

'None o' that. It's not your fault. The lawyer you got me did his
best an' he's a good bloke. He warned me they'd be a bit
vindictive.'

'I'm still sorry.'

'And he told me how you played merry hell with 'em to get me out
of that interrogation place.'

He shook his head.

'When I was in there it was like nobody would ever think about
me. I should have known.'

Jan wiped her nose.

'It all seems a bit crazy. He says they're not bringing the phone
tapping into the case at all. The sods are just going to try and stick
you with this rubbish about stolen Ministry papers.'

Joe nodded.

150

'I suppose it's all square from their point of view. I was naughty and I have to be clobbered, even if they have to fit me up. Tit for tat. Anyway, the phone tap effort is a hard one to make a charge out of. I gather.'

They were silent for a while. Joe fingering at his poorly fitting tunic, Jan fiddling with her handkerchief. The silence grew painful and Jan said, suddenly and loudly, 'It was Tully, wasn't it. Who told them. And that was about you and his girlfriend. Wasn't it.' She flushed, looked around and saw that nobody was taking any notice of her.

'I tried to get in touch with him as soon as I knew they'd taken you. They said he'd gone on leave, unexpectedly. He'd moved digs and when I rang his works yesterday they said he's resigned his post. And when I tried to get hold of her, her friend said they'd broken up. So it has to be him and I'll bet it's because you've been screwin' whatshername.'

'Evelyn.'

'Dear Evelyn.'

She waited a moment before saying, sharply, 'Well.'

Joe stared around the crowded room.

'I suppose that was it.'

'What was it.'

'I suppose it happened like you said.'

Jan muttered 'O Christ,' groped for her handkerchief and snivelled into it. When she spoke again her voice was low and steady.

'I want to know exactly what happened.'

'I can't see the details matter a lot.'

'They do to me. How did it start.'

Joe flapped his hands and looked down at the table.

She hissed at him.

'What happened.'

'What does it matter.'

'What happened.'

'It turned out she'd never seen the Blackpool illuminations.'

'Ah, the poor dear. And you just had to show them to her. How kind.'

He hunched his shoulders and folded his arms. She glared at him and said 'All right. I won't interrupt. Get on with it.'

'We went for a drink. The last time she came with names. And it turned out she's a lapsed Catholic and we got to talkin' about heaven and hell. I told her that when I was a lad I knew what they both looked like. Heaven looked like the Blackpool illuminations and hell was like looking down into the Rother valley at night, when we used to come back on the bus from Sheffield. They had these open furnaces you could see, in the steel mills, like the fires of hell they talked about at Sunday school. Anyway, she said she'd never seen the Blackpool illuminations so we took a train there and stayed the night.'

'What a sweet story. And I suppose she just loved the illuminations.'

'She thought they were pretty good.'

'And she was randy as hell and it was just ecstatic in bed.'

Joe whistled softly between his teeth.

'Don't tell me it was a disappointment and it wasn't ecstatic in bed.'

He grinned at her sadly.

'Look, sweetheart. I'm on a hidin' to nothin' here. Whatever I say it's not going to suit. So you must just take up whatever attitude you think best.'

'And just what do you think my attitude ought to be.'

'That's up to you. Yon trip to Blackpool was nice enough but it wasn't a matter of any great importance. Either to Evelyn or to me.'

'So why did you go.'

He shrugged his shoulders.

'She just had to simper at you and you got randy.'

'You could say that.'

'It makes it seem as if I'm not enough.'

'That's not the way I look at it.'

The babble of talk washed over them till Jan sighed and said 'I suppose it's all my fault, really. If it comes to guilt allocation.'

'How so.'

She scrubbed her mouth with the handkerchief.

'I introduced you to Tully. It was me that wanted you to do something about the phone tapping stuff. It was even me that badgered you into going on that demo where they made out you stole the papers. I stirred the pot and started the whole thing off, so I'm to blame.'

152

He shook his head.

'Not when you get right down to it, love. I wanted to take it on. Fancied mi old expertise at direct action politics. Thought I was a cunning feller. Basically, it was a good idea. Worth a try. Only I buggered it up.'

Jan looked venomous.

'No you didn't. It was that stupid, silly bitch telling Tully about you and her screwing and Tully being such a shitty fink. If ever I locate the son of a bitch I'll break his balls.'

Joe smiled.

'It's a nice thought, love, but not to bother. Poor bugger's probably sweatin' blood in case I shop him. Main thing is to have a good bash when the trial comes up and get me out of here.'

'Bateman's pressing for an early trial.'

He pointed a finger at her.

'An' about that. Every time I ask him about fees and legal aid an' such, he just says it's all taken care of. What gives.'

'Pa gives.'

'Your Dad.'

'You bet. The old sod is always trying to give me money so I'm letting him pay for your defence. It's a howl. You're the last thing he wants to spend money on but he can't refuse me. He's between a rock and a hard place. He's liable to blow a gasket.'

'Poor old bugger.'

'Never mind him. I phoned him last night and he said you've got to have the best defence money can buy and he hopes you get life.'

'See his point.'

Slowly, their talk dwindled till there were long gaps between each brief topic.

'What's the food like in here.'

'Not what the Ronay bloke would give a lot of stars to.'

'I suppose not.'

'Lumpy porridge.'

'English greens with the guts boiled out of 'em, I'll bet.'

'Just about keeps you alive.'

'Yes.'

Joe tugged repeatedly at the tight collar of his shirt.

'How's the mighty thesis coming along.'

'Fine. Churning out the great thoughts.'

'Where you up to.'

'I'm doing my way back in history section. Bits of primitive syndicalism. Mediaeval guilds and such.'

'Lot of romantic claptrap written on them. Dig back to old John Ball. Basic egalitarian stuff. Who was then the gentleman and all that. It starts the theme.'

'I'll do that. John Ball.'

'Like he used to say, John Ball hath rungen your bell.'

'Good slogan.'

Jan's head turned to follow the prison officer who strolled back and forth on Joe's side of the table.

'It's funny. I've been longing to come and see you and now it feels like seeing somebody off on a train. Not knowing what to say while you wait till it starts.'

'I know what you mean.'

'It's not being able to hold you.'

'Yes. It does seem odd.'

'It is great to see you.'

'You look grand.'

'D'you like the scarf.'

'It's the one I bought you.'

'That's right.'

The woman on Jan's right was complaining bitterly about being neglected by her social worker.

'I still think you're a rotten sod. Screwing whatshername.'

'Maybe.'

'Are you sorry.'

'It is turning out to be a bit costly.'

'Serves you right. No it doesn't. That was a stupid thing to say.'

'Not necessarily.'

'No. I shouldn't have said that.'

When the prison officer had moved right away Jan reached across and squeezed his hand.

'Your Dad says he's going to write to you. Give you lots of advice on how to get along in prison. Practical hints and tips. Be very helpful.'

'Not sure. Judging by his old stories the place seems a lot more crowded and more time banged up in your cell than it was in his day.'

154

'You can compare notes next time you get together.'
'Sure.'
'I'm going to see him again on Sunday.'
'Bless you. Tell him I'm fine. Tell him I'm really sorry I can't come to see him.'
'I'll see he doesn't want for visits.'
'Bless you.'

They talked on till the end of visiting time was called and visitors and prisoners began disentangling themselves from the benches and shuffling towards the doors. Jan sat, shoulders slumped.

'I miss you, Joe.'
'Miss you.'
'Love you.'
'Me too.'
'I'll come again as soon as they let me. And I'll write to you.'
'Fine.'

She turned at the door, to wave, but the prisoners had already been herded out of the hall.

Joe shuffled along the prison landing in the slow-moving line of men returning to their cells, after slopping out. He sniffed the smell of shit which still hung about them and swung his plastic chamber pot to and fro, singing softly to himself. 'Sweet violets, sweeter than all the roses.' The young prison officer tapped his shoulder and pointed to the wall. Obediently, Joe stepped out of line and stood to attention. When the column had moved off, the officer turned and studied him, swinging his keys in a circle, on the end of the chain that hooked them to his belt.

'Telford.'
'Yes.'
'Yes what.'
'Yes, Mister Fisher.'
'We are new, aren't we.'
'I am, Mister Fisher. I don't know about you.'
Fisher stopped swinging his keys and tucked them into his trouser pocket.

'And we are cheeky with it, aren't we. Stop fiddling with your pot.'

Joe held the pot stiffly at his side.

'Now, Telford. You being new and cheeky you are in need of instruction. So let us see if you can grasp the simple basics of marching back from slopping out. Basic number one is marching back, not skipping, not mincing, not tripping the light fantastic, just marching. Clear. Is that clear, Telford.'

'Yes, Mister Fisher.'

Fisher leaned against the rails which bordered the second floor landing.

'Basic number two is that we carry our pot. Just carry it. We do not juggle with it or hold it on high or swing it as if we were the leader of the band. Clear.'

'Yes, Mister Fisher.'

'Basic number three, we march in silence. We do not talk, hum or whistle and above all we do not sing. We are not a nightingale, Telford, we are a scruffy prisoner carrying our smelly pot back from slopping out. Clear.'

'Yes, Mister Fisher.'

'Good. Now let us see if this has sunk in. Go to the end of the landing and march back to me in the proper manner, remembering your basics. Off you go, Telford.'

Joe walked to the end of the landing, turned, gripped his pot in the crook of his forearm and marched back with military precision, stamping to a halt as he reached Fisher. The officer pursed his lips and shook his head.

'Well, well, we are a cheeky old man, aren't we. Have you read prison rules, Telford.'

'Yes, Mister Fisher.'

'What about Rule Thirteen.'

'I can't remember them by number.'

'Mister Fisher.'

'Mister Fisher.'

'Then let me refresh your memory. Rule Thirteen forbids you to treat an officer with disrespect, Telford. And in my opinion, the comical little performance you just put on, was a clear case of disrespect.'

'Yes, Mister Fisher.'

156

'And we will have no more of it, will we.'

'No, Mister Fisher.'

'You are also on the verge of violating Rule Twenty, Telford. What is Rule Twenty.'

'Don't know the rules by number, Mister Fisher.'

'Then learn them. Rule Twenty forbids you, in any way, to offend against good order or discipline.'

'Yes, Mister Fisher.'

'But seeing as you are new and slow on the uptake, we will not charge you this time, we will help you to mend your ways.'

'Yes, Mister Fisher.'

'Now we'll try again, Telford.'

Joe walked to the end of the landing, turned and walked back. Fisher tapped his chest.

'Do we know the old army term dumb insolence, Telford.'

'Yes, Mister Fisher.'

'What does it mean, Telford.'

'Silent contempt, Mister Fisher.'

'Correct. And if you know what is good for you, you will desist forthwith. Understood.'

'Yes, Mister Fisher.'

'Right. Back you go and walk to me in the correct manner.'

Joe walked to the end of the landing, turned and walked back.

'A slight improvement, Telford, but practice makes perfect. Back you go. Head up, eyes looking straight ahead, face blank.'

He ordered him back and forth, four more times, before sending him back to his cell.

Joe stretched out on the top bunk and the man on the lower bunk leaned his head out and said 'Where you bin, Joe.'

Joe tucked his hands under his neck.

'Nowhere particular, Mickey. Young Fisher had me marchin' up and down the landing, just to show who's boss.'

The man on the bed opposite the double bunk spat on the shoe he was polishing.

'Real dog, that young bugger. And doesn't he love the sound of his voice. Always tryin' to make you feel like a big Jesse. I hope he didn't get your goat.'

Joe smiled.

'Not to fret, Dave. I kept in mind which one of us was actin' like a twat.'

Puzzling about what to write to you, my love, I realised that the problem is that we have never before written letters to each other. We were able to meet so often in the flesh (I like that phrase) so we never wrote and I have no idea what kind of letters you like. Do you fancy passing news of my mundane doings or my thought for the day or a short essay on God and the Cosmos. Anyway (or anyroad as you insist on saying) most important thing of all to say is that I love you dearly and I miss you desperately and think of you most often.

I am amazed and delighted to find all kinds of mementos of you about the place to dwell on – sure signs of Joe. The neighbour's cat that you made friends with still visits me and walks about disconsolate because she can't find you. So I give her the cream off the top of the milk (never had that back home, our milk was all homogenised and the cream taken out for fear of cholesterol) and we sit together and comfort each other in our missing of Joe. The shelf you put in by the corner of the stairs still stands firm and I put my favourite bits of bric-a-brac on it. It shines brightly from your varnishing. Most of all I love to read through my thesis notes and come across the bits where you scribbled in the margin in your beautiful big scraggly handwriting. I treasure even the insulting bits. The other day I came across a passage where I said there were syndicalist themes in the 1926 General Strike and you scribbled on it that there were fairies at the bottom of your garden.

Hey, did you know that you are a verified handsome feller. I got an enlargement done of the photo I took the day we went to Fountains Abbey. The one of you standing with a sad smile, all noble and dignified amid the ruins. It hangs framed above the bureau. And my friend Nina (the one with the blonde curtain hairdo) saw it and pronounced you a splendid beast. How about that. She has gone way up in my estimation. A woman of taste.

I went up to your house last weekend. (Why the hell did they never finish that road, it's a real trudge up there.) Had a long chat with Nelly Hurst next door (my but that woman can talk) and she agreed to pop in once in a while and give it a dust over, clean the windows, check for clogged guttering, leaks and suchlike. So, your property will be kept ship shape and Bristol (why Bristol for crying out loud) fashion, not to worry.

Which brings us to the soon end of thy wicked imprisonment. You will have gathered from our shyster that they are going reasonably smartly through all the pre-trial fol de rols. All the stuff about presenting prosecution evidence and re-reviewing it and so forth. He reckons three months, thereabouts, and all will be sorted out and their knavish tricks frustrated. May they burn in hell. Seems a long time, my love. Still, when you come triumphantly forth, I will utterly smother you in fuss and loving and fine wine and loving and walks up hills and down dales and cream cakes and old Tommy Dorsey music and loving. So there. You have been warned.

History department has got a copy of a film about your old hero, Winstanley. Strange sort of film. Bit amateurish but you can smell the cold and the mud on that funny old bleak hill where he set up his commune. Should I include Master Gerald in the way back in olden times bit of my thesis? You can explain to me why Cromwell and his buddies had such a down on him. Didn't know he just sort of disappeared. Nobody seems to know what happened to him. Maybe he was so downcast by failure that he just walked off into the wide blue yonder.

Miss you most at cocoa time.

The steady hiss of the downpour was broken only by the clatter of raindrops spattered by swirls of wind against the barred windows of the cell. Dave looked up from the letter he was writing and said 'Makes it feel cosy.' Mickey's voice grumbled from behind the big cut-out book he was looking through.

'Don't be fuckin' daft. Nothin' makes a nick feel cosy.'

'Yes it does. Rain outside does. Makes it feel cosy inside.'

'Does it fuck as like.'

'Well it does for me.'

'That's 'cos you're going a bit daft.'

'I'm not. Anybody else'd say I'm right. Except you.'

'Would they fuck as like.'

'Yes they would.'

When the little spat of talk ended, Joe tried again to

concentrate on the book he had borrowed from the prison library. He found its solemn account of Livingstone's life dull but read slowly, trying to savour each sentence, so that the remaining few pages would last till they turned out the lights. He tried to feel for the old missionary making one final attempt to discover the source of the Nile and found himself trapped into speculations about how much water would be required before you could label it the source of a river. He visualised a few drops trickling between blades of grass and decided they were too uncertain and might dry up. He remembered a spring that bubbled endlessly out of a clay bank, near where he lived as a child. Something like that could be a source. He tilted the book to the light to examine the blurred woodcut of Chitambo that preceded the description of Livingstone's death but could make little of it and was left uncertain whether the huts were made of grass or mud. He chose to delay starting on the death scene and asked Mickey what he was reading.

'It's about this Chrysler building. The feller that built it kept it a secret. He was going to stick a point on top so nobody knew how high it would be.'

He held the book up showing the picture on the front.

'Why the Chrysler building.'

'Buggered if I know. The wife brought it for me. It's a cut-out. You're supposed to make a model out of it. A big 'un.'

'Are you going to make it.'

Mickey flipped the book onto the table.

'Never.'

'Why not.'

'Bloody hopeless. You ever tried 'em. You got to cut up thousands of bits and bend 'em an' glue A to B to C and half the time you can't tell which is which. Gets to be a right mess.'

'Why'd she buy it for you then.'

'She's got it fixed in her head, I'm good at it. Good with mi hands. She thinks I enjoy it.'

Dave sucked the point of his pencil and said 'He cheats.'

'No I don't.'

'You bloody do. He gives 'em to Derry Shea on Threes, he makes up the model, real smart, and buggerlugs here gives it back to his wife all done up an' takes the credit.'

160

'That's not cheatin'.'

'If that's not cheatin', I'd like to know what is. It's a bloody swindle.'

'I only do it to please the wife. She'd be upset otherwise.'

'You're pretendin' to do something you can't do.'

'Only 'cos she likes to think she's bringing me somethin' I want.'

'It's still cheatin'.'

'Not if it pleases her.'

'What you reckon, Joe. It's a bloody fiddle, in't it.'

Joe pondered while he stared at the picture of Chitambo.

'It is an' it isn't. He's not trying to deceive us and it is in aid of pleasing his wife.'

'He knows he couldn't trick us. He could no more mek one of them things than he could fly.'

Mickey flicked his thumb and forefinger at the book.

'I didn't say I could. But it'd upset Liz no end if I said they were no use to me.'

'You lie to her, an' a lie's a lie. So you cheat.'

'No I don't.'

Joe settled again to his book and wondered if the natives were really as grief-stricken by Livingstone's death as the author claimed. Perhaps they had always regarded him as a pain in the arse. Like a sort of early travelling Jehovah's Witness who knocks on your door while you are comfortably snoozing, in order to nag you endlessly about God. Maybe the drums used to beat out messages – hide in the jungle, old Livingstone's coming to carry on about Christ.

Mickey said 'What you readin' anyway.' Joe held the book so he could see the title.

'It's about Livingstone. The missionary.'

'Doctor Livingstone, I presume.'

'That's the feller.'

'I saw a film about him once. It had Spencer Tracy in it. I don't think he was Livingstone, though.'

'He was Stanley.'

'That's right, Livingstone was lost.'

Joe scratched his forehead with the book.

'Sort of. More that people had lost him.'

Mickey sorted through a tin of cigarette stubs, breaking some up to roll a new cigarette.

'See what you mean. I think.'

Reading the last few pages of his book, Joe became angry at the way the London Missionary Society was being given the credit for practically everything that Livingstone had ever done. He turned back to the title page and nodded to himself on discovering that the author was an official of the society. He was pondering whether Livingstone's significant contribution had been to religion or geography when Dave asked him if he thought Manchester City would draw with Villa.

'Not likely. City's a bit up and down this year, win or lose. You doin' the pools.'

Mickey rested his stockinged feet on the bottom of Dave's bed and interrupted.

'Not him. He's writing a letter, would you believe. An' it's really all his list of draws for his wife to put on the coupon. Bloody sheets of 'em. His letters are always like that.'

Dave scowled.

'What the bloody hell's it to do with you.'

'Some letter that. Writin' out a pools form, from the paper.'

'There's nobody at home knows anything about football.'

'I suppose you fill up the rest with horse racin' tips.'

'I'll put what I like.'

'You can tell her what greyhounds to back.'

Dave looked towards Joe.

'It's not so bloody easy. If you say owt about what goes on in stir, the screws are liable to stop your letter. So what's there to write about.'

Mickey coughed at the dryness of the cigarette he had rolled.

'Summat besides football pools. I'll bet they really look forward to your letter at home. Can't wait to find out where to put their crosses.'

Dave smacked at Mickey's ankles.

'Take your fuckin' smelly feet off my bed.'

Mickey shifted his feet and muttered 'Bloody grand letters.'

Joe turned to the map insert at the front of his book and tried to concentrate on the dotted lines marking Livingstone's journeys. He was beginning to panic because soon the lights would be switched out and it was in the darkness that he most felt the suffocation of being in prison.

Trudging along under a slate grey sky, in a four-abreast column, past the lines of cladded drainpipes, wreathed in barbed wire, that ran up the four storeys of D Wing, Joe tried to sing under his breath.

In't it a pity, she's only one titty
For me to swing upon

Finding the pace too slow for the tune he shortened and quickened his stride but the rhythms still did not match and he gave up the attempt. He looked to his right at the long narrow beds of miserable, winter-stripped rose bushes, standing black and thorny in the thin soil, and wondered how they would look when summer came. Abreast of them loomed the chapel and he turned right to march past its three perpendicular windows and the bulging cross, made of pebbles, embedded in the wall. As they turned again, by the tall spiked railings that fenced off the workshops, they passed the dog handler with his Alsatian squatting at his heels. Joe cocked his head to one side, made a low growling sound and put out his tongue but the dog sat motionless, staring unblinkingly at the men marching slowly by. The loose grit on the surface of the exercise yard crunched under the men's feet and the low mutter of talk was occasionally overlaid by a prison officer pointlessly shouting 'No talking.' They turned again, where more railings ran from the high outer wall to the back of the boiler house, on past the narrow archway that led through to the reception building, to come, once more, to D Wing.

Joe had long since worked out that the circuit was seven hundred and twenty paces, that it took nearly three minutes to go round, that they circled it ten or eleven times in one half-hour exercise period. What he could not decide was whether he liked doing it or not. True, the two exercise spells did make breaks in the long monotonous day. They were events of a sort, they marked the passing of time, so they helped to convince you that time was passing. Moreover, they let you find out what the

163

weather was like and reminded you how many different kinds of sky and wind and light and air and rain there were. Being locked away from the weather for much of the time made you take great notice of it when you came out into it. And even the cramped old yard seemed like true space compared with the cells and landings, the workrooms and the narrow hall they used for association. Still, he hated the way exercise told you how completely controlled you were, how docile and puppet-like, at their bloody beck and call. It was worse than being banged up in your cell. At least there you were just locked up, not told what to do. You could mess about more or less as you pleased. Here you were not taking exercise, you were being exercised. Just like that bloody dog handler would exercise his dog. Like the way parents put reins on little kids and hauled them up and down. And you were not going anywhere, just round and round in a circle.

He strained to catch the mumble of conversation between the two men on his left.

'An' he told the AG straight out why he wanted a transfer.'

'Straight out.'

'About the shit.'

'He says, can't stand it, sir. He shits all night and the smell is rank, sir. Can't stand it any longer.'

'An' he got a transfer just for that.'

'Well he played it up a bit. He went on about how it was driving him mad an' he was frightened he might lose his control an' kill old Sammy.'

'An' they believed him.'

'Alec says he was only half-kiddin', he was that desperate. You ever smelt old Sammy's shit.'

'Can't be worse than some I've smelt.'

'That's what you think. I used to be three cells down from him in B Wing and it used to make me gag.'

'An' they've transferred Alec.'

'Last night.'

'Where to.'

'He's three'd up now with Tim Wilkins and the big Geordie.'

'Who they put with Sammy.'

'Bert Clark. They reckon he's such a dummy, he'll not notice.'

164

'Bob Simpson got a transfer once. Said he couldn't stand the other bloke's stutter.'

'You're havin' me on.'

Joe watched his feet marching and felt a little proud of them because they pointed neatly forward. In front of him he could see two men with feet splayed out at ten to two, while one further ahead was pigeon-toed. His eyes wandered up and down the column noting styles of walking. There was a man turning by the chapel who walked in a crouch, legs half-bent at the knees, and behind him there was Squinty Evans, who walked with a swing and a hitch. Behind him was a man who flung each foot outward as it went forward. Joe reflected that if he had been a dog in a show he would have been marked down for throwing. Examining his own walk he decided it was good enough though he detected a slight forward lean of his spine. He straightened himself and drew his shoulders back.

The man on his right spoke through the side of his mouth. 'Joe. If they was to turn us left when we come round to the archway again and lead us through the front yard, out the gate and down the hill to the saloon bar of the Duke of Cumberland, what would you order.'

Joe thought for a moment.

'Drinks on you.'

'Drinks on me.'

'A malt whisky.'

The man snapped his fingers.

'No. You're wrong there, Joe. I used to think something like that. An expensive drink. Somethin' special. Then it come to me. That'd be all wrong. Pint of bitter. That's what you'd have. Just that. Not even necessary to be best bitter. Just a pint of bitter. You think about it.'

A faded image of a long-ago circle he had marched in came into Joe's mind. It took him a while to recognise it as Empire Day. He had trooped along on Empire Day when he was at junior school. He pictured the hundreds of children, shuffling in straggling columns, round and round the playing field, till whistle blowing teachers finally herded them into ranks, facing the flagpole with its huge Union Jack so high you had to crane your neck to look up at it. The headmaster, speaking slowly, so that he

165

could keep his voice to a loud boom, telling them about the glories of the Empire, how it had stood against the might of the Hun in the Great War, repeating phrases like 'red upon the map', 'the sun never sets', 'the British system of justice' and even more mysterious words like 'Durbar' and 'Spion Kop' and all the children's reedy voices singing 'Land of Hope and Glory'. He struggled to recall the headmaster's name and it came to him, Mappin, Edward Henry Mappin, the mad sod. Fine summer afternoons, when you could have been off up to the quarry or down to Tilts lake, and he would keep all the children of the top three forms in after school because it was the anniversary of 'A Famous British Battle' and he was going to give a talk on it. Agincourt, Trafalgar, the storming of Quebec, there seemed to be no end to them. And you sat on the floor in the school hall, listening to the voices of younger kids shouting in the streets outside, while old Mappin droned on and on, tapping his stick at a chart full of squares and circles and saying 'now pay attention, the black squares are English infantry, the white circles with dots are French cavalry.' Joe remembered his father telling him that Mappin had been stationmaster at Kirk Walton and was never called up in the Great War because it was a reserved occupation. And in 1916, there had been such a shortage of staff at the village school they had made him a part-time teacher and later headmaster. Perhaps that was why the old sod made such a fuss about battles. He felt guilty about never serving in the Great War and getting his job because they killed off teachers at such a rate.

As they came round past the boilerhouse wall, the man on the left of Joe's line of four looked towards the prison officer who stood to attention by the archway and said, half-aloud, 'Fancy meeting you again, Mister Rayburn.' The warder jerked his head round sharply, stepped toward the column and shouted 'What was that, Phillips.'

'Nothing, Mister Rayburn, just clearing my throat.'

The officer scowled and went back to his place by the archway.

Joe, noticing that the watchers were flexing their stiffened legs and the Alsatian was on its feet looking up at its handler, guessed that exercise time was at an end. He took a last look at the sky. The door in D Wing opened, the circle broke and the column thinned to two abreast as the men were shepherded through it.

There are a lot worse blokes I could be locked up with. Dave is a bit of a morose bugger at times and Mickey can be a noisy sod but they both have a sense of fairness about living together and Christ knows we need that in this little cubby hole. They whittle on at each other a lot but it's a funny sort of quarrelling. Like an old married couple that really need each other to nag at. From where I am on my top bunk I can see Mickey at the table setting out a jigsaw of the Hay Wain. *He's put it together more times than enough but he still takes a delight in it. Point is he'll start to spread the pieces wider and wider as he fishes about till it gets in Dave's way. Dave's sitting end on at the table, reading a paper spread out in front of him. And a row will start. Bet you.*

I am most sad to be locked away from you in this grey place, my love. Did I ever tell you I keep clear pictures of you in my head. Good visual imagery as they say in the books. One I cherish is of you lecturing, from when I used to come up early some Fridays to pick you up at your university and I would slip into the big hall to catch sight of you enlightening the masses. Did you know you're a great walker, lass, when you're lecturing, rambling up and down, waving your arms about, singing your song about the Protestant ethic or reification or some such and looking and sounding so beautiful. I just got absorbed by you and lost track of what you were saying. By God I used to envy all those young sods sitting at your feet. I wished I was one of them. It was like they owned you.

Can you get a little present, on my behalf, sweetheart, and take it to Dad from me. It's a book of old photographs of the West Riding. Gen is in the newspaper cutting with this letter. The old man is a bit soppy about photographs and judging by what the newspaper says they should remind him of when he was a lad. He was a keen cycling type and used to get all over the shop. He'll know most of the places in the photographs. He'll explain them all to you. Tell him I miss him a lot. And tell him I finally got to sew some mailbags. I'm quite nifty with a machine though we go slow to stretch the work out on account of there isn't much. Seemed strange when I was doing it. I thought to myself about being part of a bloody great tradition stretching way back. Me and all the other

167

benighted sods, sewing us mailbags to pay our debt to society. Even when I was a kid I knew convicts sewed mailbags. It was a natural state of affairs. Like negroes pick cotton.

Incidentally, a bit back the squabble started as forecast but I was wrong about the cause. Dave reminded Mickey that he owed him a fag and even when Mickey gave it to him he carried on about having to ask for it and if he didn't ask he would never have got it. Mickey claimed he always paid up and Dave was the one you had to keep a close eye on and so it goes. Nag nag.

Brooding on your thesis, sweetheart, it strikes me you ought to bring to light more failures – failures of socialist political thinkers to fathom the significance of self-government in industry. All because they couldn't grasp the totalitarian nature of undiluted state control. Even with Soviet Russia staring them in the face. Good example is Orwell. Suggest you dig out and analyse his pamphlet in 1946 or thereabouts, attacking Burnham's theory of the managerial revolution. Orwell's failure to understand Burnham seems all the more crazy when you remember that in 1984 he gives the best picture to date of a managerial society. Look at Laski from the same angle.

Worst thing here is bad dreams. Can't seem to stop the bastards. Must be something about prisons. Reminds me of the bloke in Shakespeare in a dungeon who said he wouldn't mind being confined in a nutshell if it were not for the bad dreams. Last night I dreamed about waiting to be born but I knew that my mother had been told I was dead in the womb so she wasn't going to try to give birth to me and there was no way I could tell her I was alive. Not very hard to interpret when you think about it.

Salvation here is the prison library which is a rare collection of odds and sods. I'm becoming an expert in things you never heard of. For instance, my lovely precious degree-qualified mastermind, did you know there was such a thing as the Women's Gas Federation and Young Homemakers. Bet you didn't. Originally the Women's Gas Council back in 1935. First branch founded in Harrogate, first national president the Marchioness of Londonderry. They promote scientific home management and appreciation of the services provided by gas. How about that. We live and learn. And they had a stand at the British Empire Exhibition in Glasgow which was visited by the Queen. The one before this one.

Like your feller Bateman's visits. For a lawyer he's remarkably like a human being. He's always bright and breezy but somehow I don't

resent it. He keeps my mind fixed on the trial, on how near it's getting
and reminds me I'm not lost forever. Always says what a fine character
you are so we have an agreeable time mutually singing your praises.

Now Dave has started on about the spreading of the jigsaw parts. I get
a bit fed up of it.

Trying to prolong the game, Joe moved his knight to a weak, cramped position on the edge of the board. Adams pushed his king forward onto an even more exposed square. The prison officer standing behind Adams winked at Joe and set off again on his slow patrol down the long narrow hall that was used for Association. Four moves later Joe was forced to checkmate Adams's suicidal king, which had plunged into the middle of his pieces. Adams surveyed the final position.

'You've done it again, you bugger. And it's like last time. I've still taken more of your men than you have of mine.'

Joe broke a square of chocolate from the bar which lay on his side of the chessboard and popped it into his mouth.

'That's your weakness, Benjy. You play chess like it was draughts. Just a matter of grabbin' the other bloke's pieces.'

Adams wobbled his king about with his forefinger.

'That's the bit I never seen the point of. Checkmating. I mean I know what it is but why can't you take the king. Make it the bloke that takes the king wins. Why mess about saying you win when his king's bound to be taken, whatever he does with it.'

'Got to dig back in history for that one, Benjy. Old notions about the Divine Right of Kings. You see the person of the King was sacred. You could plot against him. Even push him off his throne but you were not allowed to kill him.'

'Who says.'

'It was the theory.'

'Some fuckin' theory.'

Joe's shoulders slumped as Adams started to set out the pieces for another game.

'You'd have got on all right with Oliver Cromwell, Benjy.'

'You reckon.'

'After he'd had King Charles's head chopped off people started

to play a new kind of chess for a bit. While Cromwell was top dog
Sort of a republican chess where you could take the king just like
any other piece.'

'That right.'

'Scout's honour.'

'You've got a head full of little bits like that, 'aven't you.'

'Not a lot of use.'

The tall sallow man, sitting next to Adams, fiddling with a
crossword puzzle, looked up and said 'Heyup, men. It's mi pet
screw just come in. We'll get the news.' He swung his legs to the
outside of the bench and set off up the hall. Joe watched him go

'What news is that he's after.'

'Last day of Mitchell Binns's trial today, wasn't it. And Wilson is
by way of being a big mate of his, isn't he. So he wants to know
what Mitch drew.'

He held out his fists and Joe tapped the one with the black pawn
so the board stayed in the same position. Adams moved his
queen's court knight and said 'It's funny you like exactly the same
chocolate as I do. Fruit and nut.'

Joe broke a piece off and passed it to him.

'That's three bits you owe me.'

By the time Wilson came back, Adams had both his king and his
queen well advanced. He looked up from the board.

'What did he get.'

'Seven years.'

'Fuckin' hell. That's a bit rough.'

'It's his record. Way Mitch is set up they thump him harder each
time.'

'Has he gone.'

'They ghosted him out while we were at tea.'

'Still, seven years. It's fuckin' hard.'

For a few minutes, Wilson went back to his crossword while
Adams brought his pieces forward in great leaps, across the board
Joe tried to give the game some interest by setting, as a target
mating Adams without taking more than six of his pieces. Wilson
asked what was another word for 'dry' and Joe suggested 'arid'.

Suddenly, Wilson snapped his pencil and spoke in a strained
growling voice.

'People in this country love the nick. They fuckin' worship it

170

Nothin' gives them their jollies like sending poor fuckers to prison. They crave for it.'

Adams took a pawn and left his queen under attack.

'You've said that before.'

'It's true. Right from being kids they long to have buggers banged up. It's the national sport.'

Joe ignored the queen and checked Adams for the first time. Adams pushed his king farther forward.

'You exaggerate, you do.'

'I bloody don't.'

Wilson pointed a finger at Joe.

'Did you know that bar Turkey we've more cons per head than anywhere in Europe.'

Joe re-checked Adams's king.

'I didn't know that, Des.'

'Well it's time you bloody thought about it. When a judge sends a bloke down he's our little tin god. There's millions of people readin' their papers and slaverin' with joy when they read about blokes goin' to clink. And when there's really big bird, like thirty years for the train robbers, they come in their pants. And I can tell you why.'

Adams sucked thoughtfully on the head of his knight.

'He'll tell you all right.'

'Why is that, Des.'

'It's because it makes them feel like they're gettin' their own back. They're pure and they're getting rid of evil. Every time some little runt gets put in stir, people feel like it's a bit of evil safely locked away. They think if we lock enough up then outside it'll be perfect for them. It makes 'em feel all warm and cosy thinking of us banged up in boxes. They think we're like sewerage locked well away in the drains. They never think the shit's comin' from them. It's their shit.'

He stopped, breathless. Adams said 'Steady on, kid.'

After he had lost the game, Adams said 'Anyway, you'll be scaring young Joe half to death. His trial comes up soon.'

'I'd forgotten. When is it.'

'Next week.'

'You reckon you'll get off.'

'I've got a good brief.'

171

'That's not allus enough. You've got a handicap as well.'
'What's that.'
Wilson played with the broken pieces of his pencil.
'I heard you said you'd been fitted up.'
'That's right.'
'Makes it dicey.'
'Why.'
Adams said 'You're a great fuckin' comfort, you are' but Wilson ignored him.
'Set up like yours, the old bugger on the bench has two choices. He can tell the jury that the case the filth have rigged is watertight or he can admit they might have planted stuff on you. Now if he hints they've fiddled, he brings the whole bloody system into doubt. What price the law if coppers are liars. So odds on he'll say it's you that's telling lies.'
'I haven't been convicted of anything up to now.'
'And your brief's a bit on stony ground when it comes to the plea in mitigation as well.'
'I don't see that.'
Adams looked up at the clock and started to put the chessmen back into the box.
'You're a political. For your average con, you plead remorse. He's seen the error of his ways, wishes to turn over a new leaf, your honour, give up his life of crime. Politicals can't be sorry for their crime 'cos they didn't think it was a crime in the first place. Awkward to make a plea.'
Joe folded the chessboard and rested his chin on it.
'See your point.'
Wilson shook his head and sighed.
'No. It's like Benjy says. I'm exaggeratin'. I always do. If you've got a good brief you'll breeze through it. Take no notice of me. I'm a moody bugger.'
'Sorry about Mitch Binns.'
'Yeah. Thanks.'
   After Wilson had left to join the line shuffling up the spiral staircase at the end of the hall, Adams leaned across and patted Joe's arm.
'He said it himself, Joe. You should tek no gaum on him. He allus looks on the black side.'

172

Joe pocketed the remains of his bar of chocolate and said 'Sure.'

The steel-legged tables with green plastic tops were laid in rows of eight, parallel to the canteen counter. Jan stood on tiptoe in the doorway, peering through the crowd of people milling to and from cake stands, tea urn and cash register, to wedge themselves in groups around the tables, till she saw Joe sitting in the corner to her right, with two cups of tea, covered by their saucers, in front of him. She worked her way across and he stood up as she reached him. They hesitated before kissing. She stepped back and said 'It seems funny to be able to do that.' He put his hand out and touched her face. They kissed again.

Seated at the table, Joe uncovered the cups of tea and placed them in their saucers.

'Milk and no sugar.'

'That's right.'

They sipped tea and Jan waved her hands at the surroundings.

'All this. It's better than the other prison. I didn't expect.'

Joe looked round the crowded room.

'It was the other being a local jail. Less facilities in some ways. Visiting's more relaxed here. We're still mostly three to a cell though.'

'Sorry about that.'

'It's not too bad.'

'What are they like. The other characters.'

'Arnold. He's all right. Argumentative. Talks a lot.'

'Keeps things lively.'

'Trouble is you haven't any choice.'

'No.'

'Wiggsy's t'other way round. He's a bit dead. Been in stir too long.'

She followed Joe's gaze to the counter where the queue at the tea urn had dwindled.

'Is there anything I can get you.'

'If you want to.'

'I really do.'

173

'There's some little custards. I fancy one of them.'

'Anything else.'

'A bar of chocolate.'

'Come on Joe, think big.'

'Twenty fags.'

'You don't smoke.'

'No, but you can trade 'em.'

'That all.'

'According to the rules we have to use up anything we buy during visiting time but they're a bit slack if we don't overdo it.'

'Fine. You're sure that's everything.'

'Yes.'

She joined the line at the counter and Joe watched her point to what she wanted and smile at the old man on the cash register as she waited for her change. Back at the table she sat heavily on her chair and stared down at the things in her hands. Without looking up she muttered 'Joe, I don't know what to say. About the trial.'

He smiled.

'I thought you said it all when His Lordship sentenced me and you shouted out "you bastard". I was looking straight at his face and I thought he was going to do the heart failure bit.'

'I couldn't help myself. I was in such a rage.'

'Did you get into trouble about it.'

'No. After they'd taken you away, I was hauled in front of some official type and he gave me a lecture and said I was in danger of being charged with contempt of court. I told him there was no way I could express my contempt of his court. He said I was a hysterical female and I stalked off but they didn't do anything about it.'

He reached out and took the custard from her hands.

'Don't mind about the hysterical female crack, sweetheart. Calling the judge a bastard was the most thoughtful thing anybody said in that court.'

She pushed the bar of chocolate and the packet of cigarettes across to him then gripped her arms and shivered.

'I could still have killed the old goat when he said two years.'

He peeled the paper cup away from the custard and bit into it.

'Not to fret. I should get eight months' remission for good behaviour and I've already served four months on remand. So I'll be out about a year from now. That's not so long.'

174

'It's a bloody long time, Joe. It's not right. It's not fair.'
He took another bite of his custard.
'You sound like the mother. In the monologue.'
'What mother.'
He looked down at the table and furrowed his brows.

> *Ma said, fair's fair young feller*
> *And I think it's a shame and a sin*
> *For a lion to go and eat Albert*
> *And after we've paid to come in.*

Jan rubbed her eyes with her knuckles.
'You're a nut, Joe Telford.'
'It's something we used to recite at parties. When I was a lad.'
'Well, we're still in business. Bateman's asked for leave to appeal.'
Joe finished his custard.
'Good custard that. Plenty of nutmeg on top. You should tell him not to waste his time, love. They've done a nice neat job of sewing me up. Made a good boy of me. They'll not back down on it.'
'Don't be so bloody philosophical, Joe. I want you with me. Not shut away in this goddamn dungeon.'
'Share your feelings, love. I crave for you too. I've stared at your picture on mi wall till it's wearing through with looking.'
'I feel so damn helpless, Joe. What can I do for you.'
'Well, for a start you can get me another cup of tea.'
She grinned, said 'Sod you' and went off to the counter. When she came back with two teas, he was carefully peeling back the paper on the bar of chocolate. She accepted the square he offered. He took one for himself and refolded the covering.
'There's one thing about the trial that does get up my nose.'
'It was a fix from start to finish.'
'That it was. It's just a little dream I used to have. Seems a bit daft when I think about it.'
He paused and she said 'Go on.'
'It's from donkey's years ago. You see I got into all sorts of radical politics from early on and there always seemed to be the chance that the powers that be might crack down one day, put you on trial, send you to the Bastille. Tyrants trample on rebels, it's an ancient tradition. It happened to Dad. Happens to lots of people.'
Jan watched him open the packet of cigarettes, run his thumb

175

along the tips and close the packet again. She reached across and ruffled his hair.

'That's for sure, baby doll.'

'Aye. So, I always had this picture in my mind. When the time came for my trial I was going to deliver a hell of an harangue. Speak up for the common people. Put the whole lousy top dog and underdog system on trial. Silence 'em by my fiery eloquence. Used to work out bits of speech ready, in advance.'

'Like for instance.'

He tipped his chair back and clasped his hands on top of his head.

'Pretty pompous stuff.'

'Try me.'

He stared at the ceiling.

'Despite worlds of ceremony, vast institutions like ancient pyramids and the deadly authority of official language, the hearts of our masters are worm-eaten by the knowledge that they have no true right to their power.'

'It's good.'

'Lots like that. But. Come my trial. They tricked me out of my say. When they put reporting restrictions on because of the official secrets shit, it was for sure the world wasn't goin' to hear or stand amazed at me carrying on. Not being on trial for what I'd really done made the whole bloody thing a Comic Cuts effort. And when I tried to get going and open my mouth you heard the crafty old bugger on the Bench come in sharp, about what I was saying not being to the issue before the court. It made me feel like a little kid talking out of turn and being told by the grown-ups I should be seen and not heard. It was a shambles.'

Jan knuckled her eyes again.

'I know, love. I hated the way they kept everything going clickety-click. Spending hours on bits of law that had nothing to do with anything then moving on slick as grease. I wanted to shout at them to stop, so we could just think for a minute, about what was happening.'

'Hell of a do.'

Jan hitched her chair forward and they held hands.

Joe nodded towards a tall, hook-nosed man who was sitting two tables beyond them, talking to an elderly woman.

'You know what he's in for.'

176

'What.'

'Usually you don't know a lot about what fellers are in for but he's famous.'

'Million pound bank robbery.'

'Not exactly. He hires a car and drives off to where this bloke lives. Turns out the bloke only has four pounds in cash or so he says. So Hooky does his demanding money with menaces bit, takes the four quid and drives off. Bloke notes the number of the car, rings the filth, they check it out and find it's a hire job. When Hooky gets back to the agency, they're waitin' for him and before they arrest him they make him pay twelve quid car hire to the firm.'

'That's rotten.'

'Hooky thought it was a bit much.'

'Way back when, there used to be a film series in the States called *Crime Does Not Pay*. Your Hooky would have been fine for that.'

After a silence Joe slumped in his chair. He rubbed his mouth harshly with the back of his hand and spoke in a thick voice.

'How did Dad take it. The sentence.'

'He was angry. Like you'd expect. He says you're not to let the bastards grind you down. Says it shows you really got to the sods. We talk a lot about you. You're our favourite subject.'

'How is he.'

She hesitated, fingering her cup and saucer.

'Not very well, Joe. I checked with the doctor who visits the place. He said he's weaker.'

Joe pushed his cup away from him, mumbled 'Sod it' and slapped at the table.

'I shall not see him again.'

'Don't say that, Joe. He's a tough old bird. You've said so yourself.'

'He's on his way out, Jan. What I say won't alter it.' After a pause, he said 'You will go to see him, now and then.'

'You bet. Wouldn't miss my get-togethers with Charles Frederick for worlds.'

'I wouldn't like him to be alone.'

'He won't be.'

'I feel a bit guilty.'

'As your Dad would say, don't be daft.'

'Right.'

He pulled her hand to him and kissed it.

'How's the magnum opus coming along.'

'In the home straight now. Doing the reflections on the future bit.'

'Wholemeal bread communes.'

'Don't knock 'em, Joe. Just because you're an old industrial workers' agitprop man.'

Joe tapped the table top.

'Listen. There's some business and government outfits that are managerial as hell overall, big hierarchies. But they've got subversive bits in 'em. Contract gangs, small departments and so on, organised as democratic collectives. They're a bit obscured from view but try and get on to one or two to use as examples. Check with the Industrial Democracy mob.'

'Right.'

'You can do a bit about their significance for the future.'

'Yes, O great wise chief.'

'Bugger off and get us some more tea, while I sort out some great thoughts for you.'

'Yassa.'

She collected the empty cups and balanced them back to the counter while Joe considered his bar of chocolate and decided to allow himself another piece.

The bed frame around Joe juddered and creaked as Arnold masturbated in the top bunk. It seemed to Joe an endless, joyless effort. He lay eyes open in the darkness of the cell, visualising the man above him gripping his cock, fist fashion, holding it upright, jerking it in a slow, violent, unvarying rhythm. He listened to the counterpoint between Arnold's grunting and the soft plopping on the outbreath coming from Wiggsy in the bed across from him. Turning clumsily, pushing the pillow against the top wall, he settled himself face down, hands clasped on the back of his head, feet sticking out over the end of the bunk. He willed himself to feel weary, ready for sleep, yet knew that since there was so little to do in prison he was only bored, not tired. He reflected that maybe hard labour, all that breaking of rocks, had not been such a bad thing. At least you would sleep at night, maybe even a dreamless sleeping.

Above him Arnold gasped, shuddered and was suddenly still. The smell of spunk drifted down. Wiggsy seemed disturbed by the stillness and rolled over muttering to himself. Arnold sighed, shuffled onto his side, pulled his knees into his stomach and lapsed into a soft growling snore.

Joe felt the darkness of the cell begin to smother him and drive him through the steps of his nightly logic. *If I cannot stand being locked up, if I really cannot stand it any more, what will I do. I will scream and pound on the door and smash things and howl and scream. They will have to come and take me out of the cell. They will try and calm me down but if I shriek at them and throw myself about they will take me to the prison hospital. They will drug me and when I come round and howl to be let out they will drug me again. But in the end they will put me back in a cell. There is nothing else they can do. They will not let me out. However much I beg and plead and bang my head against the wall they will not let me out. I am sentenced to be here. So it makes no sense to say what if I cannot stand being locked up. It does not matter whether I can stand it or not. I stay locked up. It's like if they take you to be executed. What is the point of saying to the hangman I cannot bear the thought of being hanged.*

Somewhere in the distance someone banged shut a heavy door and the sound echoed like an earth tremor along the landings. Wiggsy snorted as if his nose was blocked and flung out his arm so that his knuckles rapped against the wall. A while later Joe heard the ring of a prison officer's studded shoes as he crossed a metal grill on his night patrol. The heating pipes gurgled and clicked. He reflected that they were all inside sounds. No sound from outside the prison ever seemed to penetrate.

Turning onto his back, he looked down his body, trying to see his feet. He wiggled them but they were invisible in the pit-like darkness. He moved his hand towards his face till, close up, he could sense the blur of its shape. As the beginnings of panic came, he told himself that his fears were ridiculous. True, this was a bad place to be but nothing hurtful was going to happen. You could say that he was safely locked up, really secure. What could get at him or threaten him. The night would wear away and dawn would find him intact, miserable maybe but unharmed and a day nearer freedom.

179

With frightening clarity he felt the slow thud of his heartbeat. Squeezing his eyes shut, seeking comfort, he set out, slowly and carefully, on his fantasy.

You slide off the bunk and begin to dress, putting your clothes on with exquisite care so as not to wake Arnold and Wiggsy. Shirt and socks from under the pillow. Lean against the wall when you pull your socks on, so as not to topple over. Trousers from under the bed, concertina them and get both feet through the legs before you pull them up. Pause to check that neither of the men is stirring before running your hand gently along the wall, till it comes to your jacket, hanging on its hook. Jacket on, beware of the swishing sound your hands make as they rub against the lining. Now, pick your shoes up from under the bed, hold them both in your left hand, taking care not to let them knock together. Slide to the door, open it just far enough to ease through while not letting the light from the landing shine onto your sleeping cellmates. Close it, barest click, peep through the judas hole to check they're still sleeping, tip-toe, in your stockinged feet, to the end of the landing and down the spiral staircase before putting your shoes on. Quietly up to the screw, sitting by the end door. He winks and you make a gesture with your hand, a pressing down movement that tells him he must not scrape his chair when he gets up or jangle his keys when he opens the door. Along to the office, peer in at the window and point towards the main gate. Screw nods, turns off the radio he was listening to and comes out. He hands you the raincoat you need to cover your prison clothes and leads the way across the yard to the little wicket door let into the main gate. As you step over the ledge he speaks in a low voice. 'Sorry, but you know we have to keep this quiet Joe, so you've got to be back well before knock up. OK.' And you say 'Understood, Boss.'

Once outside, you stand for a while, breathing deeply, very deeply. You look downhill at the streetlights of the town, little puff balls of yellow, looping and criss-crossing as if put there for decoration. You set off on your stroll. Not a lot to see of course, hardly anyone about at this hour of the morning but when you see someone you murmur a quiet 'Evening'. You stop in front of a few lighted shop windows, purse your lips at the prices, admire the gleaming cars in the big showroom, check how the building of the

180

new office block is coming along, look to see what's showing at the local cinema, glance at the posters outside the municipal buildings, strain to make out the wording on the plaques under the town square statues by the glimmer of the electric imitation torches that the surrounding stone nymphs are holding. You sniff the air and whistle quietly to yourself as your shoes tap along the pavement.

As always, you arrive at the all-night café and the door bell tinkles cheerfully as you go inside. You order your tea and while it's being brewed you saunter along the counter and select a bun and a bar of chocolate. As he gives you your change, he reaches under the counter and brings out the daily paper which he kindly lets you borrow. Sitting by the window, in the nearly empty café, you sip your tea, nibble your bun and chocolate and read the paper avidly, item by item, page by page. Occasionally you glance out of the steamed-up plate glass window at night workers in the big bus garage opposite. Half-way through the paper you fetch yourself a fresh cup of tea.

All finished, you say a friendly goodnight to the man at the counter, as you give him back his newspaper. Pausing in the doorway, you work out a route back that will take you through a different part of town. You tuck your collar up around your ears because the air has gotten a little chill and make your way, at a leisurely pace, back to the prison.

Once there, you are a bit smart and business-like, ringing the outer bell, handing back the raincoat, nodding silently to the screws and slipping quickly back along the corridors to your cell. Time is moving on. You hold your breath while you slip out of your clothes.

One look round in the glimmering dawnlight, to see that everything is in its place. You slide stealthily back into bed, turn onto your side, close your eyes, smile to yourself and fall into a deep sleep.

Cell visiting gossip was in its last phase, in the few minutes before the end of Association. Arnold squatted cross-legged on the top bunk. Tyler sprawled on Wiggsy's bed and Joe sat at the table. All three looked towards Jones, whose long body was draped like a question mark in the jamb of the open cell door. Hands thrust in pockets, he spoke softly, a tattered Welsh lilt sounding in his voice as he answered Arnold, who had just said that he had heard the tale before and it sounded like a right made-up yarn.

'Life is ridiculous enough as it is, boyo. There's no need to make up stories. And if you don't fancy it, we don't have to bother.'

Joe and Tyler protested that they wanted to hear it and Arnold admitted that it was a good story so Jones carried on.

'Point is, I wouldn't have gone to Big Jack's in the first place, if I wasn't pushed to find cheap digs. Never liked the feller, though he was by way of being an old friend of my father like. After he agrees I can stay, we end up gettin' supper from the Chinky takeaway and she appears, his daughter. I'd heard he had one but never seen her. Tess she was, seventeen, slim young thing, long black hair, nice titties, forward pointing. Well at supper she was showin' herself off to me, mischievous-like. Playin' the sweet lass, just bein' nice to the old lodger but lettin' me know she was a woman, if you see what I mean.'

Tyler drummed a little tattoo on the iron bed frame and said 'Get the picture.'

'I could see from the start that Big Jack wasn't keen on her making up to me. He kept scowling at me like it was my fault and a couple of times he talked up loud about his little girl. Little girl see.'

'Hands off like.'

'Just so, Arnold. Now point is there was no way I wanted to get the wrong side of Jack. Built like that old boxer Two-Ton Tony Galento, if you remember him. And widely known for his bad temper. Show you. One time, in this pub in Porthcawl, this bloke with a bloody great black dog disagrees with Jack about what won the Leger in nineteen-eight. Bloke got so heated he tries to set his dog on Jack and Jack picks the dog up by its collar and back leg and starts to hit him with it.'

Tyler sucked noisily on the cigarette stub he had just lit.

'He hit him with the dog.'

'True, boyo. My Dad was there an' he said the dog was yelping like mad, the bloke was crouched down on the floor beggin' for his life and there's Jack thumpin' the poor bloody animal down on top of him. Took 'em a while to talk him into stoppin' and they had to have the dog put down.'

182

'Sounds like a hard man.'

'So you can see I was in a bit of a cleft stick. All very nice havin' young Tess twinklin' away at me but I made up mi mind to be good as gold where Big Jack was concerned, so as not to upset him. Later on, when we go to bed, it turns out I've got mi own bed but in the same room as Jack. He shuffles about a bit before he settles down to snorin' and I'm beginnin' to nod off too.'

Tyler groaned.

'You old bugger. You're goin' to tell us this lass sneaked in and got into your bed.'

'That's right.'

'Never.'

'Not a word of a lie. First thing is a bit of a draught when the door comes open and closed. Not a whisper of a sound and she's in with me, arms round my neck, clinging on and not a stitch on her, nor me neither.'

Jones paused and folded his arms. Joe tilted his chair back.

'Let me guess, Gwynne. You pushed her firmly away from you and said it is not that I find you undesirable, young lady, 'tis just that I am a true gentleman and cannot bring myself to take advantage of you.'

Arnold giggled and Jones wagged his head thoughtfully.

'That's very close, Joe. On the tip of mi tongue to say that, bar by the time I'd grasped what was goin' on mi prick was as stiff as a truncheon and she's wriggled herself onto it. An' she was that wet an' easy I could tell it wasn't the first time she'd been pronged on a cock. Apart from which I'm sweatin' blood because she's makin' little chortly sounds an' I figure any time now Big Jack wakes up, finds me rammed up his little girl and hammers me into the ground like a tent peg.'

Tyler tapped out his cigarette end, broke open the paper with his thumbnail and tipped the remaining shreds of tobacco into a tin.

'That's all very well, Jonesy, but accordin' to you this lass had come into your bed, not you in hers. And she'd come with nowt on. Surely to Christ this Jack would have seen that she was makin' all the runnin' an' it wasn't your fault.'

Joe clucked his tongue.

'Not necessarily so. Most likely Jack was besotted with his little Tess. He'd reckon she'd been led astray by the villainous Jonesy

183

who'd enticed her on. No fault of hers if her innocence falls victim to the wiles of the randy Taff.'

'Very nicely put, Joe. Not that I was thinkin' so clearly at the time.'

'Tell us what you did then.'

'Bear in mind that she's got her legs wrapped right round mine, so there wasn't much chance of a quiet pulling apart, so to speak.'

'Who you kiddin', Jonesy. You didn't bloody want to do any pullin' apart.'

'Well, yes and no. That's what I keep tryin' to explain to you. It was a tricky situation. What you might call the horns of a dilemma.'

'So what did you do.'

'First I put my hand on her mouth, signin' to her for God's sake to be quiet. Then I tries a real careful pulling half-way out an' slow slide back in and bugger me if the bed don't creak, loud and clear. Paralysed I was, listening to his snoring, till I realised this time I'd got away with it. But it was clear as the nose on your face I couldn't shag her in the usual way, poppin' it in and out. However careful I done it the old bed would have creaked like mad and certain to wake Jack and start a riot.'

'Tricky.'

'So what did you do for Christ's sake.'

'You must listen careful because it's hard to tell. Was like this. I held her tight, made sure my prick was as deep as it would go and at the same time I pressed against the curve of her cunt. Like I was in as far as I could go but I pushed in and up as if I was goin' further. An' I squeezed to make my prick harder and sort of bigger inside of her. I eased off, waited a few seconds and did it again, see. After a bit she got the hang of it and pressed down and sort of clinched my prick each time. Point is we were going at it without moving. Well at least, not enough to twang the bedsprings. Clever, don't you reckon.'

'Did you come.'

'After a while but I could tell she hadn't. So I slipped out slowly and tossed her off with the old walking out finger. Mark you, I had to pin her down when she came or she'd have made things rattle.'

'What then.'

Jones uncramped himself from the door jamb and stretched.

184

'Just a bit of kiss and cuddle and she slid off. Not a murmur from Jack.'

Tyler leaned back against the wall and whistled his breath out. 'You were on to a good thing there, lad. Cheap digs and digging in every night.'

'Don't be foolish, man. Next day I told Jack I'd changed my mind about the job and I was going back home. And back home I went.'

'You gave up a nice bit like that.'

'Think about it, Tyler. A week and I would have been a nervous bloody wreck. Cock forever as limp as a wet lettuce I wouldn't be surprised.'

They argued the point casually till the bell shrilled for the end of Association. With Jones and Tyler gone and Wiggsy back they tidied up the cell ready for the night count. Arnold stood at the door watching the prison officers work their way along the landings.

'How many times a day do these buggers count us.'

Joe mumbled from under the bunk, where he was searching for a coin that had rolled away.

'Never counted.'

'Bloody mad. Counting us all every five minutes.'

'Makes you feel important. Shows they don't want to lose you.'

Running past the end of the village – it's a two cross streets with green in the middle affair like we used to call Hicksville, Hick County back home – was a canal with a lock. The before Sunday dinner custom with the Hammonds is to walk up to the lock and watch the boat characters heaving their way through. Jesus but it brought back our time on the canal. Remember that flight of locks or steps or whichever you call it and we got it wrong and lost our water (sounds like something else that). When we looked down into it there was the crazy boat sitting on a pile of gravel at the bottom. And it was such a lazy, dawdling, loving sort of time. Having our own floating home, accountable to nobody, drifting about, making a big deal out of exploring that old abandoned factory place and you showing me how to look for birds' eggs. Guess you're right about the true speed of the human soul being four miles an hour. Wonder if those two adolescents are still earning extra bucks fishing up all those golf balls that folk sailed into the canal.

185

Jolly farce at the degree mill last week. Student Union set up to debate a Tobacco Should be Policed Like Heroin motion. They got a guy from ASH and some young buffer called Fordham from the Tobacco Council. I got the job of hosting this Fordham character around. It all got a bit steamy with students waving placards saying FORDHAM YOU ARE A WALKING DISEASE and GO HOME MASS MURDERER and a lot of jostling when I took him into the hall. When he spoke there was so much shouting you could hardly hear him garbaging on about how much the tobacco industry gave to research and the arts and sports the need for freedom of choice (but not for heroin) and we should not jump to conclusions on very complicated medical issues. Afterwards, we had to comfort — I mean comfort on account of he was really distressed — this pin-striped weirdo in the Senior Common Room. I mean, here was this elegant, courteous, absolutely decent type who makes a very fat cat living out of spreading cancer round the globe and he could not, for the life of him, comprehend. Man I mean he JUST COULD NOT UNDERSTAND why people got so upset about it all. Puzzled to the depths of his well-bred soul, he was.

Dad goes along fine, all things considered. He lets me call him Chuck (American for Charlie) and pretends to like it. Last Sunday I was complimented as all get-out because when I got there he had the family photos in a big box, to show me. Did we have a ball. Not that I got to see you naked on a bearskin rug but next best thing. Tiny Joe on beach with pot belly and sand structure. Joe on Mama's lap, velvet trousers and frilly blouse and wasn't your mother a beauty. Joe in goal keeper's jersey, Joe accepting school prize (creep), Joe at ballroom dance (didn't know about that phase of your life) with your hair all in oily little ridges. Joe addressing some sort of meeting, banner in background, looking like we were just off to the barricades. And who and what was the fast little blonde you were hugging in a group picture in front of the building with pillars. Dad says he can't remember but may just be covering up. One made me feel sad. You in army uniform with comrades, all beaming at the camera ready to go off to war. One taken in soft light of you in some sort of library with books spread out in front of you and you pointing with a pencil and laughing. So damn like you, it was a heart stopper. Not going to tell you which ones but Charles let me steal a few. Also I got him to give me one of himself as a lad with a drum in some long-lost village band that looked like real frozen history. It was a lovely visit and we both had a good cry.

Joe, I know prison can't be a very stimulating place but think about using the time there to start your book on life and great thoughts of. I spoke to your buddy Neil about it when I went to see him about progress on my IWW volume. He says he's told you several times he'll take a book by you ANYTIME. Promise you'll give it a try, sweetheart. If only jotting down some notes. And when you come out I'll fix you up with real writer's fancy dressing gown and typewriter (electronic) and desk with gilt-framed picture of Tom Paine, all to inspire you. And I'll keep rushing in with fresh cups of coffee. Promise.

Now we're moving up to the great examination orgy and students are all looking brave and sickly.

Knowing the task would not last the work time, Joe made a ceremony of laying out the parts of the electrical plugs he was going to put together. First he mimed the assembly with his hands, rehearsing the order in which he would take up the pieces. Begin with bottom plate in left hand, small leather cable holder held down by left thumb, insert two screws and drive home through holes in plate and strap, pick up and position L pin with fuse holder, clip in fuse, pick up and position N pin, pick up and position E pin, pick up top plate, place in position, pick up long screw, drive home through bottom plate to top plate. He nodded as he completed the assembly of the imagined plug and emptied his cardbord box of parts onto the table, lining them across the top in order of use, from bottom plates and cable holder straps on the far left to top plates and long screws on the far right. He counted out each component and muttered 'All present and correct, sir' when he found he had exactly enough parts for thirty complete plugs. Placing his two screwdrivers, a small one for the cable strap screws and a slightly larger one for the casing screw, to his right, he checked that his rolled-up shirt cuffs were securely tucked back and adjusted his chair to an easier working angle in relation to the table. For a few seconds he sat, left hand poised over a lower plate and right-hand thumb and forefinger just above a cable strap, staring at the wall clock, to check how much time his elaborate preparations had used up, before beginning the assembly.

When the first plug was complete, he twisted and tugged at it, finding everything firm except the earth pin which wobbled. He scowled, unscrewed the two plates and examined the seating of the loose pin. After poking it to and fro and twice screwing the plates tightly back together, he concluded that the housing of the pin had been made slightly too large, allowing play. He assembled four more plugs, checked them and found the earth pin wobbled in each one. He lined up the completed plugs in front of him and waved his arm at the prison officer who was sitting reading a newspaper, perched on a tall stool, at the front of the workshop. The officer folded his newspaper and came across to him.

'All these earth pins are loose. Too much play in the channel.' Joe wobbled each of the earth pins in turn to demonstrate his point.

'So.'

'If I could have some sort of cementing stuff. Say Polyfilla. I could pack a bit down the side of the housing and when it dried the pin'd be firm.'

The officer stared at Joe.

'Don't be so fuckin' soft. Get on with the job.'

'Anythin'. Something like wood glue, say.'

'Just put the bloody things together.'

Joe muttered 'Whatever happened to British workmanship' but the officer failed to hear him as he went back to his stool and opened out his newspaper.

Sighing, Joe picked at his nose. He unscrewed one of the plugs and poked at the loose pin, his tongue sticking out between clenched teeth. His eyes wandered over the assembled plugs, the array of components and the box perched on the corner of the table. He pulled the box to him, peered into it and tugged out one of the flat cardboard partitions. Pressing the piece of cardboard hard to the table, he cut out a tiny rectangle with the blade of the small screwdriver, packed it into the housing of the earth pin and re-assembled the plug. The pin had less play but could still be shifted a fraction, from side to side. He undid the plug, dug out the scrap of cardboard and eyed it while he cut a slightly larger piece. Packed with the larger piece of cardboard the earth pin was firm. Opening up the plug again, he dug out his piece of cardboard and, using it as a template, he painstakingly hacked out

188

twenty-nine more pieces from the partition. These he lined up between the earth pins and the top plates in his array of components, and after opening up the completed plugs he began again, adding one of his tiny strips of cardboard to each assembly.

As he worked, Joe laboriously calculated that, given his hours per week and rate of pay, he would become a millionaire in a little more than twenty-four thousand years, less if they allowed him interest on his earnings.

Sorry to keep on about prisons but it gets to be on my mind. I guess I must have been twelve or thirteen when we went on this coach trip, not long before the war. And at this place in Scotland they took us to this little castle. Just me and Dad because Mam didn't care a lot for castles and she stayed back on the coach talking with some of the other women. Right in where the cellars would be in this castle, they had this great big stone pot to put prisoners in. It's hard to describe but it was shaped like a pot, like a sort of flower vase for only one or two flowers, so that it would be about a twelve-foot wide circle at the bottom, narrowing into a neck just wide enough to drop somebody through. The idea was, when they got a prisoner, they dropped him down the neck of this pot and he would fall about eight or ten feet and there he was in prison. I guess if they ever wanted to bring anybody out they would have to lower a rope down and pull him back up through the neck of the pot. I can remember being fascinated with this place. Maybe part of the horror of it was that I read lots of boys' adventure stories where brave, clever chaps were always escaping from prison. Judging by the stories, prisons were mainly places you escaped from. Yet, when you looked down into this pot you could not imagine how anybody could ever escape. I mean you couldn't climb up the side walls because they curved inwards to the neck. There was no door or way out, other than back up the narrow part where you'd been dropped through. So you would just stay down there in the dark in your own shit for years and years. You'd know you could never get out. Funny thing was, at the end, the guide pointed to a kind of little channel on the outside of the pot and said that sometimes people in the castle would put bits of warm food in that hole so the smell would waft through into the pot and torment the prisoners. The prisoners were more than half-starved. Yet that didn't seem all that horrible to me. True, they were tormenting the prisoners but I got to thinking that at least when it happened, when the prisoners smelt the food, it would mean that somebody knew they were there. They were important enough to be tormented. If people torment you it means they've remembered you. God knows how it was for real but to me the terror of that pot was that you would be dropped into it and utterly forgotten. Something like trying to torment you with the smell of food was not as frightening as that. It's funny, but lately, I've been back in my imagination to the visit with my Dad to that castle and I can remember it as clearly as if it were yesterday. I was so twisted up by it that I was quiet for a long time afterwards (very unusual for me) and Dad got worried.

You ask why I don't go to any of the evening classes here in the prison. You are right insofar as one or two of them might be interesting. I suppose, if I'm honest, I don't go because I'm in a kind of sulk. I'm not going to have something just because they provide it. I don't know if I can make you understand this. Did you know we have a pamphlet called Information for Male Prisoners. *I wonder if they have one called* Information for Female Prisoners *and if that's very different from ours. Just curious. Anyway we have this brochure like you have a brochure for everything these days. It tells you all the rules and regulations and facilities and it's sensible enough. But one of the key things is number nine on page seven, under the heading Change of Appearance. It says that if you wish to alter your appearance, for example growing or shaving off a beard, you must obtain the Governor's permission to do so. Now, rightly or wrongly, that does something to me. I don't know that I actually want to grow a beard but it's out of the question anyway, because of number nine, page seven. I'm not going to have a Governor's permission beard. I know the evening classes are not quite the same thing but it all has to do with what parts of your life belong to you and what parts belong to other people. I will brood about it though.*

Going back to that stone pot prison in Scotland. It seems a daft thing to say but I think it quite broke my heart.

Please, when you write, love, tell me all about what you are doing and how things are among the dreaming spires. I guess you will be starting on holiday about now. When you go away anywhere, please to send me picture postcards. Lots of them. I can put them up on the wall. How are your parents. Are they coming over to do their English country house squire bit. Wonder what they will think of your book when it's published. I'll bet that apart from disagreeing with just about everything it says, your Mam and Dad will be puffed up with pride about it. Not happy about this chest infection thing you wrote about. Never mind if it makes you sound like Marlene Dietrich. It seems to me you've had it too long and you ought to see your medic about it. I thought you Yanks were proper keen on medical check-ups and having your health attended to. See to it. No argument.

Arnold leaned against the safety fence that stretched along the landing and glanced back at the squat figure who stood guarding one of the cells, arms folded. The sobbing and wailing, muffled by the closed cell door, rose and fell.

'He's giving him some gyp, all right.'

Joe stared down at the men strolling about, two floors below.

'What's Bobbie done.'

Arnold did a slow push-up, on the fence bars, grunting with the effort.

'He's gamblin' daft, isn't he. Silly young bugger. Places his bets with Gilbert and hawks his bum around to pay off. Looks like this time he's come up short and Gilbert's havin' a word with him.'

'Where's Bobbie's mates.'

'They've buggered off, haven't they.'

'Why doesn't he ask the screws to help him.'

Arnold spat on his hands where the thin fence rail had cut into them.

'What good would that do.'

'They could have him put apart on a forty-three. Keep him safe.'

'Nah. They've both got loads of bird to do yet. Just take Gilbert longer to catch up with him and he'd add on more pain to make up for the time.'

Joe flinched at the sound of a long squeal from the cell.

'Somebody should stop it.'

'It's his own daft fault.'

'I'm goin' to ask him to stop it.'

Arnold's head jerked round.

'You've got to be jokin'.'

'No. I'm not.'

'What the hell can you do.'

191

'Not sure. I can ask him to stop.'

'You're fuckin' crazy.'

'Not necessarily.'

Arnold walked away a few steps, then came back.

'Listen, Joe. I know you're a kind-hearted old bugger but think a bit. Gilbert's a real Daddy. If you try interferin' with him, he'll have his mob work you over. The worst thing you can do is to get into his bad books.'

'He's got no right to treat Bobbie like that.'

'He's every fuckin' right. It's down to Bobbie owin' him money.'

'He's no right to torment him.'

'For fuck's sake, Joe. Show some sense.'

'I'm goin' to see what I can do.'

Arnold pushed Joe in the chest.

'If you go pokin' your nose in there, you needn't expect me to back you up.'

'I didn't say I expected you to.'

'I'm havin' nothing to do with it.'

'Please yourself.'

'You're on your own as far as I'm concerned.'

'OK.'

'I shall not change mi mind.'

'I shan't expect you to.'

'Well then.'

Arnold walked away, turned and shouted 'You're a fuckin' nutter.'

   Joe walked slowly back down the landing and stood in front of the man guarding the cell.

'I want to talk to Gilbert.'

'He's busy.'

'I know he's busy. That's what I want to talk to him about.'

'Fuck off.'

From the cell, Joe could hear someone crying and talking at the same time and realised he was hearing a babbled version of the Lord's prayer.

'Tell him I want to see him. Now.'

'Fuck off.'

'If I fuck off I'll be back in a minute with a screw.'

The man frowned.

192

'You're askin' for a lot of trouble, cunt.'

Joe put his hands on his hips.

'If I get a lot of trouble, I promise you I'll spread it around. We'll all get a share.'

'He'll half-kill you.'

'Do I go and fetch a screw or don't I.'

The man spat on Joe's shoes, opened the cell door and went in, closing it behind him. Joe hopped awkwardly from one leg to the other, wiping the toes of his shoes on the back of his trouser legs. The man came out a minute later and held the door half-open.

'You can go in, cunt.'

Joe heard the door close behind him. He leaned on it.

Gilbert was sitting on the single bed with Bobbie kneeling head down, on the floor, in front of him. Bobbie's trousers were draped round his knees and his buttocks were covered with wheals and bruises. Gilbert was resting his head on the wall and his feet on Bobbie's neck. Joe licked his lips and said 'I want you to stop hurting him.'

Gilbert smiled at him.

'Well, well. I didn't know you were that way inclined, Joseph Telford. You hear that, Bobbie. Mister Telford's come to save you, isn't that nice of him. I said isn't that nice of him.'

There was a mumbled 'Yes, Mister Gilbert' from under his feet.

'Little snag though, Telford. He doesn't want to be saved. He loves our little games. Don't you, Bobbie.'

There was another mumbled 'Yes, Mister Gilbert.'

'Show you.'

Sliding his feet off Bobbie's neck and locking a fist into his hair, Gilbert pulled the young man's head hard forward into his crotch and squeezed it tightly with his thighs, so that he was unable to breathe and made hooting noises. Joe straightened up and stood stiffly by the cell door. After a while, Gilbert opened his thighs and Bobbie hung, his head suspended by the grip on his hair, gasping noisily. Gilbert said 'You liked that, didn't you, Bobbie.'

Bobbie said 'Yes,' hoarsely.

'If you don't let him alone, I'll tell the screws what you're doing.'

Gilbert wedged the middle finger of his left hand against the thumb and flicked it sharply against Bobbie's nose, so that he cried out.

'You really don't know our rules, do you, Telford.'

'I don't give a fuck about your rules. I'll stir it up with the screws, the Governor, the bloody lot.'

Gilbert let go of Bobbie's hair and slapped his face.

'You know, I really think you might just do that. You're just stupid enough.'

He yawned.

'But what good would it do. Or what harm for that matter. Nobody will verify what you say. Not even this little nance here.'

He tapped Bobbie's face with the toe of the shoe.

'And after all the fuss I'd have to see to it that you were crippled, just to make the point.'

'What point is that.'

'That I'm an important man and creeps like you don't mess me about.'

Joe looked round the cell.

'I didn't know there were important men in this place.'

Gilbert fumbled a cigarette and lighter out of his breast pocket.

'And you're supposed to be some sort of a political, know how things work. You're a twat.'

He blew smoke at the man crouching at his feet.

'Ninety-nine per cent of the sods in here are like you and little Bobbie. Just numbers. Zombies. Fuckin' walkin' dead. Me, I've got a business. I've got an organisation. I've got power. Me and the Governor.' He waved his cigarette.

'I could stick this fag up Bobbie's arsehole and ask him if he liked it and when he'd finished yowling he'd say "Yes, Mister Gilbert". Like a demonstration.'

Joe shook his head.

'Now I'm a busy chap and I like my work. So you bugger off and I'll toil away at a simple lesson for Bobbie. How he expects me to pay up when he wins his bets so I expect him to pay up when I win. Goin' to teach him what fair is.'

'How much does he owe you.'

'What's it to you.'

'How much.'

'Thirty-four quid.'

'Suppose I pay it. I can let you have twelve quid tonight and I can get the rest in by the end of the month.'

194

'Why do you want to pay off for this queer little bastard.'

'What's it matter. It's money. It squares you up.'

Gilbert pulled Bobbie's head forward, resting the chin on his own knee. He patted the tear-stained face.

'So somebody loves you, you dirty little git. Who'd have thought it. Question is, do I want the money more than I want to teach you a lesson, little darling.'

Joe took a step forward.

'You're a practical man. So long as the debt's cleared.'

Gilbert looked up at him.

'Don't push it, Telford. You've stretched your luck a hell of a long way as it is.'

He wiped his hands on the front of his tunic and hummed to himself.

'Still, I suppose you're right. Fun's fun but I am a practical man.'

As he left the cell he said 'Pay the money to Harris on Two's and don't ever give me any more lip. Not ever.'

Joe looked down at Bobbie who was still crouched on the floor. 'You can get up now.'

Bobbie stayed where he was.

'No, he might come back. Thank you very much, Mister Telford.'

'OK. Main thing is don't put any more bets on with Gilbert. Or anybody else for that matter.'

'I'm grateful to you. I am grateful to you. I'll try and pay you back.'

'Fine. Heed what I say. I used to work for a bookie. Don't gamble. They're right when they say it's a mug's game.'

Still crouching on the floor, Bobbie repeated that he was grateful. Joe spoke gently.

'Get cleaned up and remember what I said.'

He backed out, leaving Bobbie still crouched on the floor.

It was late evening, as he was coming back to his cell with his mug of cocoa, that Joe was stopped by a grizzled little man, who looked carefully this way and that before he spoke.

'I've got a message from Bobbie. He appreciates what you done, no end. He's grateful. He says on Friday cinemas, you're to sit at the back right-hand side and he'll come and suck you off.'

Joe's hand trembled and he spilled cocoa on to the landing.

'Tell him. I won't. I mean tell him it's good of him but he's not to bother.'

195

The grizzled man stared at him.

'He doesn't expect you to pay. It's for free.'

'Just the same I'd rather not.'

'He's one of the best cocksuckers in this place. There's blokes pay a lot for him.'

'Tell him thank you but no.'

The man shrugged his shoulders, said 'Please yourself' and walked away. Joe stood trying to keep his mug of cocoa steady. He muttered 'Christ but this is a poorly sort of place.'

Joe fondled the book, running his fingers down the spine and brushing his palm over the cover. Jan watched him, cuddling her teacup.

'It's a good straight title.'

He traced his finger along the heavy type of THE WOBBLIES and beneath it, in smaller type, *The Story of the Industrial Workers of the World.*

'I like the picture.'

He angled the cover so that light from the canteen windows fell on the old sepia photograph of American strikers facing armed police, outside a factory gate.

'And this is the best bit.'

He pointed to the name, squarely printed at the bottom of the front cover. *Janis Bragg.*

'It was your idea, Joe.'

'It's your book and I'm bloody proud of you.'

'Look at the page after the title.'

Slowly he opened the book and stared at the dedication.

To Hector Otis Sealy and Joseph Telford, men of the people.

Twice he cleared his throat without speaking, looked vaguely round the room at the other prisoners and their visitors and said in a croaky voice 'I'll bet I'm the only one in here who's had a book dedicated to him.'

'I hope you don't mind being alongside Hector.'

'I'm honoured. I remember you telling me about him.'

'You've got a lot in common.'

'I'll bet the old man was as dotty about you as I am.'

196

For a long time Joe turned pages in the volume, reading a few lines here and there, darting to the index and finding a passage, checking through the list of chapter headings, studying the opening paragraphs, nodding his head, sipping his tea and eating squares of chocolate with great care, so as not to stain the book.

Finally, Jan put her hand on his.

'It's yours, Joe. You can read it whenever you want. Now tell me how you are.'

Reluctantly, he closed the book but kept his left hand resting on the cover.

'Not bad. About the half-way mark now so I guess it's easier. Like cycling downhill.'

'You given any thought to your own book.'

'Some.'

He patted her book.

'This should inspire me.'

'Do you get all the news in here.'

'Pretty well. Newspapers and telly.'

'What view do you take of the miners' strike.'

Joe raised his eyebrows.

'What view do I take.'

'Yes.'

'I reckon the poor sods are doomed.'

'Why so.'

He undid and refolded the flap of the dust jacket on the book.

'They don't realise how big a thing they've taken on. At least they don't seem to. This is a really significant bloody strike. It's not just about pay and conditions. It's about major management decisions, closing pits. The bloody government can't possibly let 'em win. It'd upset the whole flamin' apple cart, knock skittles of shit out of the power set-up. It's too important a strike for the miners to be allowed to win. It's a real political effort.'

'You can smell a workers' management smell, our Joe.'

'Just a bit.'

Jan's face darkened.

'I get sick just thinking about the Nottingham scabs. The sons of bitches are not just stacking up coal for the management, they're breaking the heart of the strike.'

He frowned.

'They could do with a bit more imagination, though. Scargill and company.'

'You've got a notion.'

He leaned forward.

'Look. All this bloody drift back to work campaigning the Coal Board are trying on. Pits are like a lot of industrial set-ups, they need a solid minimum number of men before they can work at all. So for Christ's sake, why don't the NUM branches at each pit instruct a set number of their men to return to work. But keep the number below what's needed to turn the pit. The Coal Board can't tell which men are genuinely returning to work and which are carrying out union tactics. The men back at work give their pay to hardship funds. The day the pit looks like turning some coal, half of them are instructed to go back on strike. So the Coal Board boasting about figures of men returning to work won't mean a fuckin' thing. They won't know how many are just there to get money out of the Board and into the union. Men who'll go back on strike if it looks like a few cobbles of coal might get shovelled.'

Joe had been speaking rapidly but his voice suddenly died away, discouraged. He pushed his empty teacup round and round in its saucer, listlessly.

'Listen to me. I'm a right bugger. Ranting away. In this place.'

'It's a fine idea, Joe.'

'I'll fetch us some more tea.'

He picked up their teacups and trudged to the canteen counter.

Daydreaming back from the library, Joe turned a corner and bumped hard into a prison officer who was standing in the centre of the corridor. The book he was carrying fell out of his hand and skidded along the floor, pages fluttering. Pushing Joe back a step, the officer brushed the front of his jacket and tugged it straight. He made an exaggerated sighing sound.

'Have you ever tried walking with your eyes open, Telford.'

Joe stood stiffly, mouth tightly closed, feet apart, hands clasped behind his back. The officer looked him slowly up and down.

'Not really a man of great vision, are we.'

198

Joe recognised the phrase as coming from one of Jan's letters and flushed. Pointing a finger in the direction of the book, the officer said 'Pick it up.'

'It was your fault.'

'How d'ye mean, my fault.'

'You were stuck still in the middle of the corridor.'

'And you came marching round not looking where you were goin'.'

'You don't expect to find somebody stuck like a statue, right in your way. When you come round a corner.'

'I wasn't stuck in your way.'

'You were.'

'You weren't looking where you were going.'

'You must have heard me coming. You could have stepped to one side.'

'Listen, your Lordship. I'm not here to step aside for you. Now you just smarten up your ideas. And get that book picked up.'

'It's your fault that I dropped it.'

'Pick that book up.'

'I shan't.'

'For the last time. Pick the book up.'

Joe looked down at his own feet and muttered 'Pick it up yourself.'

'I heard that.'

'So what.'

'I shan't tell you again. Pick the book up.'

'I won't.'

'Right. You pick it up or I'm putting you on a charge.'

'Please yourself.'

'I'm not joking. I'll have you straight onto a White Sheet under Rule Eighteen. Disobeys any lawful order.'

'Up to you.'

'Right. Go back to your cell and stay there.'

Joe stepped round the officer and marched back to his cell.

He stood, hands pressed against his trouser legs, in front of the Assistant Governor's large desk, the prison officer to his left. While his personal file was read through, he studied the array of potted plants along the office windowsill and tried to name them, the spider plant and the Christmas cactus he was certain of, the fourth along looked, he thought, like a Tradescantia but the one with thin, shiny upright leaves and the creeper were strange to him. He contemplated asking what they were but thought better of it. Without moving his head he switched his focus to the calendar on the wall to his left. He admired its picture of a handsome bridge, with angular buttresses. He strained his eyes but the print underneath was too small for him to read the name of the bridge. He had just moved his gaze to the labels on the grey cabinets to his right when the Assistant Governor looked up from the file and spoke.

'We'll begin by establishing the facts of the case. Though I must say they seem simple enough and not, I may add, open to any great diversity of interpretation. According to Officer Sharrow, you repeatedly refused to pick up a book, government property, which you had dropped in carelessly colliding with him. Instead, you argued, in a provocative manner, that Officer Sharrow should pick it up.'

'Yes, sir.'

'You admit this.'

'Yes, sir.'

'And as Officer Sharrow describes it, the whole thing amounted to wilful disobedience, the deliberate and repeated refusal of a direct order, properly given. Do you admit that.'

'Yes, sir.'

'Without equivocation.'

'Yes, sir.'

The Assistant Governor grunted and murmured 'I suppose that's something.' He looked again at the personal file. 'You know, Telford, I find this puzzling. Puzzling and disappointing. By all accounts you are not only a sensible man, you're an intelligent man. There is no record of your being intransigent before. Indeed you seem to have been something of a model prisoner, well aware of the necessary rules and regulations of an institution of this kind and apparently willing to play your part in maintaining them. Yet here we have you behaving in a way that is both childish and dangerously undisciplined. Refusing repeated opportunities given to you by Officer Sharrow to carry out his instruction and generally adopting, towards him, a manner that was recalcitrant and quite unacceptable. It amounts, in fact, to treating the simple requirements of good order with an attitude bordering on

200

contempt. I am willing to try but, I must confess, I cannot readily see your conduct as excusable.'

'No, sir.'

'Have you any kind of explanation to offer.'

Joe was again staring at the pots on the windowsill and, with a surge of pleasure, realised that he could identify the plant with the upright leaves. It was a young mother-in-law's tongue.

'I know it doesn't excuse it, sir, but I've been very depressed lately, not sleeping well, worrying a lot, painful headaches. It all seemed to mount up, sir, so all at once, I lost grip of myself. Couldn't seem to make sense of what was happening.'

'Have you seen the doctor about this.'

'No, sir. I was trying to pull myself through it.'

'Naturally, I'm sorry to hear you've been below par but it doesn't justify blatant indiscipline.'

Joe nodded his head, vigorously.

'Not at all, sir. I quite understand. No excuse. It's just that I'd like to apologise to Mister Sharrow for my misconduct. I just wasn't myself. I'm deeply sorry for any disrespect, sir.'

The Assistant Governor looked towards Sharrow.

'Any comment you'd like to make, Mister Sharrow.'

Sharrow stared up at a point on the cornice moulding. 'I did give the prisoner every opportunity to carry out the instruction, sir.'

'Yes, that's clear. However, it could have been worse. If other prisoners had been present, for instance.'

'Yes, sir. I did inform the prisoner that I would have to place him on a charge if he failed to comply with the instruction, sir. He knew what was bound to happen, sir.'

'True. That is clear from your report. On the other hand I take it you accept the apology. As an apology, that is.'

Sharrow's grip, on the clip board he was holding to his chest, tightened.

'Yes, sir.'

The Assistant Governor tugged at his earlobe, his eyes flickering between Joe and Sharrow, finally settling on Joe.

'Telford, I'm going to reserve judgement in this matter. Give myself time to ponder, see how things move along. Meanwhile, I would make two points where you are concerned. Firstly, if, as you say, you are suffering from some kind of malaise you should request medical attention. We provide medical facilities, it's up to you to have the good sense to make use of them. Secondly, think seriously about your conduct before you again jeopardise your remission of sentence for good behaviour. I am sure you have no wish to do that.'

'No, sir.'

'I would also stress that my taking no immediate action on this charge is not a comment on the charge as such. The charge was fully justified, fully. Particularly in view of the fact that Officer Sharrow had given you every opportunity to make amends for your initial intransigence. Do I make myself clear.'

'Yes, sir.'

'Very well. We must hope that this disgraceful exhibition turns out to be a freak occurrence and that you show your more customary self-discipline and sense of co-operation in future.'

'Yes, sir.'

On his way back to his cell, Joe giggled and mumbled several times, 'Sam, Sam, pick up thy musket.'

Stretched out across the front seat of the car, head resting on the passenger door, Jan stared at the gate of the prison. For a long time there was no sign of life, till a man in a peaked cap and blue raincoat stepped through the inset wicket gate and set off down the hill. Jan leaned forward, wanting to get out of the car and run after the man, to ask him if he knew Joe Telford and did he know how he was getting on. She settled down again and picked up the thread of her argument with herself.

You are a crazy kid. You are no nearer to Joe here than you are at home or at work or sitting in the Brighton Pavilion. With all these walls between you, you cannot see him, hear him or smell him. You are totally cut off from him. So why do you drive all the way to this spot to sit and look at all that monstrous bloody stonework. You just look at it. Being here is no kind of contact with Joe. It just shouts out loud that the two of you are separated.

True, yet I must be, at most, only a few hundred yards from Joe, maybe a lot less. Maybe he's just on the other side of that wall and if I shouted out loud, he could catch the echo of my voice.

202

Maybe he's going to look out of that poky little window up in the tower and he'll recognise my car and know I'm here, close to him. Whatever anybody says, he's just over there. Very close.

No. This is crappy self-indulgence. It does Joe no good at all. It's like when you visit a grave. You don't do it for the person buried there. No way can they benefit from it. You visit the grave so you can find an easy way in to your memories, so you can feel loving, so you can sit and comfort yourself. If you really wanted to reach out to Joe you would write him longer letters, be nicer to him on visiting days, you would not just sit here massaging yourself with your feelings about him.

If I knew what part of the prison he was in I could work out how far apart we are. Think about it. Joe's told you a lot about the routine, all the fixed times for things. So. It's just after five. They leave work for tea about four and about five they go back to their cells and stay there, locked up, till Association at six o'clock. So he must be in his cell. Now his wing is to the left of the visiting place and further back. So he must be over there, about two hundred and fifty yards away. Which is not all that far. He could be writing a letter to me at this very moment.

Saying you're close to him because you're here is just playing with words.

Joe squatted on his heels and read the same paragraph in his book for the third time, trying hard to ignore the rasping of the wire wool pad as Arnold scoured the table top. He closed his eyes and let his chin sink on his chest as Wiggsy came into the cell and Arnold started to recite his complaint again.

'You seen this, Wiggsy.'

Wiggsy flopped onto his bed and opened out his newspaper.

'Seen what.'

'This silly bugger an' his paintin' set. 'Stead of paintin' on his paper, like anybody else, he spreads it over half the table. Now I've got to get it off and it's stuck like glue. It's all in the cracks. Hell of a job to get out. You'd think he'd have more sense.'

Joe opened his eyes and tried to speak placatingly.

'I offered to clean it up, Arnie. I'd still like to.'

'I want a proper job made of it. You're bloody famous at spreadin'
paint but it's a different thing cleanin' it off.'
'It's only where it went a bit over the edge.'
'It's a bloody mess. What you reckon, Wiggsy.'
'Doesn't bother me.'
'Well it bloody well should. Place is bad enough as it is. We don't
have to make a pig sty out of it. Sloppin' bloody paint about. Can't
think why he got paints in the first place.'
'I thought I'd try somethin' new.'
'You know what thought did. Walked behind a muck cart and
thought it was a weddin'. That right, Wiggsy.'
Wiggsy held his newspaper up so that it shielded his face.
'Suppose so.'
'Are you intendin' to do any more of this bloody paintin'.'
Joe closed his book.
'If I do, I'll spread newspaper underneath so no paint can get on
the table.'
'Don't worry. I'll bet you manage to spread it about. One way or
another.'
Arnold spat on his wire wool pad.
'Which reminds me. Which one of you two buggers has been
usin' my soap.'
Joe yawned and mumbled 'Not me. I've got my own soap.'
Wiggsy said 'No.'
'I suppose we've got a soap thief on the landing. Specialises in
soap. Sneaks in here to nick a slice and allus off my bar.'
Joe picked at skin around the nail of his left forefinger which was
reddened and peeling.
'What makes you think somebody's using your soap.'
'Because I've got eyes. I know how fast it should go down and how
much should be left.'
'Your soap lathers a lot. It's bound to go down fast.'
'Do you think I can't tell when somebody's been at my own soap,
you spastic bugger.'
'Well, why should Wiggsy or me use it. We've got our own soap.'
Arnold straightened up and glared at him.
'Maybe the same reason you gave your soddin' extra blanket back
in, without askin' me if I wanted to use it.'
'Bloody hell, Arnie. That was months ago.'

204

'It still shows your attitude. Fuck you, Jack, I'm in the lifeboat.'
'I didn't know you wanted it. You already had an extra blanket of your own.'
'You never bloody asked. You just weren't bothered. So long as it suits you, that's all that matters. Like splashin' this bloody paint about.'

Joe opened his book and began again to read the same paragraph.

The curtains, hanging from the overhead rail, kept the bed in a deep shadowy pool, yet still it seemed to Jan that Charles Frederick's face glistened. She watched his fingers pick restlessly at the quilt. Sometimes he lay still for so long that she became convinced he was dead. Then, suddenly, he would say something in a sharp whisper.

She wriggled in her low, upholstered chair and held her wrist so that a gleam of moonlight, tracking through the narrow break in the curtains, fell on the face of her watch. It was after two and she was surprised to find the night so quickly running its course.

Outside a breeze stirred itself and a branch began tapping lightly on a window. She reached out and stroked his hand. It felt dry and warm and silky, reminding her of the skin of a live snake she had been given to pet when she visited a state park as a child.

His eyes opened and the words came, soft but clear.
'I've got the book.'
She leaned towards him.
'Yes, Charles. Which book, love.'
He moved his head from side to side.
'Your book. The one you put Joe's name in. You gev it to me.'
'That's right, Charles. You said you liked it. I'm happy you like it.'
He frowned.
'I've got it. In the cupboard. By the bed. Where I keep it.'
He stared around him, scratching at the bed cover. Jan stroked his arm but he still seemed agitated. She levered herself out of her chair and sat on the side of the bed looking at him. His eyes flickered to and fro. She leaned across, opened the door of the

205

bedside cupboard, pulled out the copy of her book and held it up for him to see. He nodded and muttered 'You wrote in it.'
'That's right. It says "To my very dear friend Charles Frederick".'
She put the book on the bed and rested his left hand on it. He closed his eyes and seemed to fall asleep.

After a while she slid quietly off the bed and rested in the chair. With her eyes at the level of his body she could just detect his shallow breathing. Sometimes she found herself short of breath because, unconsciously, she was imitating the slow, slight movements of his chest.

She dozed for a while, slipping into a confused dream in which she was lecturing to a bored class of students and Charles would stay alive only if she could make them feel an interest in him. She pointed out that he had joined in the Jarrow March but remembered that he was not from Jarrow and failed to work out what part he had played. The attention of the students was wandering and desperately she insisted that he was not to be judged by incidents. The hall was emptying and she shouted *incidents are not important*. She was trying to coin a slogan about him being loyal and faithful when his voice brought her fully awake.
'Closed in. Feel closed in.'
He lifted a hand, as if he was trying to push the darkness away from him. Jan stood for a moment, gathering her senses, before slowly drawing back the curtains on the window side of the bed and letting a pale wash of yellow moonlight flood over him. His hand fell back to the bed cover and he lay, eyes open, smiling. She leaned over him, kissed his forehead lightly and said 'How you making out, Charles.' He looked up at her but remained silent and, after a few moments, closed his eyes.

She tip-toed to the other end of the room and checked that the old man in the bed by the door was still sleeping, undisturbed. Back in her chair, she rested her head so that she could see the far side of the front lawn and the low-hedged field beyond, with its single gaunt beech tree in the middle. Somewhere to the left an owl hooted and was answered from close to the house.

It was after three before Charles spoke again.
'There was no reason to settle.'
Jan started and said 'Yes, love.'

206

'Sandblaster was never fixed right in the first place. So whose fault was it.'

He turned his head towards her and she put her hand on his arm.

'Spineless buggers. Want the union to settle for ha'pennies compo. I shall tell 'em.'

He was quiet for a while before saying 'Give 'em the rough side of mi tongue.'

She stroked his arm.

'That's right, sweetheart. You tell them.'

His face took on a pinched look.

'You wouldn't think a friendship would end. Not a real one. After all that time. Since we were kids. Bloody Christmas time.'

'What was Christmas time, Charles.'

'Too proud. Root on it.'

He was quiet again till he said, in a very calm voice, 'Hate movin' house. Allus a lot of fuss.'

Her doze was broken by the sound of a lavatory flushing on the floor below. She put her hand on the blankets and felt his heart fluttering. Pulling herself upright in the chair she sat primly, hands folded in her lap, feet pressed to the ground, determined to stay awake.

Sharp fragments of birdsong sounded from outside, merging into a babble before ebbing away. She scratched her head fiercely, stood up and opened a window for a few moments, savouring the contrast between the sharp wintry air and the musty steam heat of the room. Patches of cloud began to move across the moon, alternately obscuring and illuminating the figure on the bed. She wondered vaguely if she should say a prayer of some sort but decided that since neither she nor Charles believed in God, there was no point. Her mind moved to songs that might suit and she tried to remember past the opening line of 'There's a Long Long Trail A'windin to a Good Land Afar'.

Again he spoke with startling suddenness.

'Where's our Joe.'

She took his hand and winced as he gripped it tightly.

'He's in prison, Dad. He would be here if he could. He loves you.'

'That's right. Did you know he caught chicken pox. At Cleethorpes. When he was a lad. Had to hire a car and bring him back. Quarantine. Spoilt us holiday. Not his fault, mind you. But

207

did spoil us holiday.' He began to cough and it hurt Jan to feel how weakly his body jerked, as if there were not enough strength left, even for coughing. He half-turned so that his head lolled onto her arm. She caught some of the phrases he mumbled at intervals.

'Sort itself out in the long run. Bugger's bound to. Just watch what you're doing. Agree to differ.'

His head rolled back onto the pillow and his eyes closed. She stood, said 'Charles' and waited. She felt again at the soft, hurrying heartbeat and put his hand back down by his side.

Some time later, watching him from her chair, she began to wonder if he were dead. Cautiously, she slid her hand under the blankets and onto his chest. She could feel no heartbeat. She tried but failed to detect a pulse and put her palm on his forehead which felt cool. She felt strangely embarrassed, checking to see if Charles were dead, when he might not be dead. Trying to think of other tests she remembered about breath on glass and scrabbled a hand mirror from her handbag. She could detect no misting when she held it to his mouth and was still trying to think of other methods as she stared at the hard stillness of his face and knew that her tests were foolish and he was dead.

For a long time she sat stiffly in the chair unable to think what it meant that he was dead, her limbs curiously numb. Finally, she said 'I'm sorry, Charles' and immediately her body relaxed and she began to breathe more easily. She looked at her watch. It was nearly five and it seemed too early to go and tell Matron that he was dead. Nor did she want to go along the corridor to lie down on the bed in the side room that had been made up for her. She decided to sit with Charles till it was full morning.

Their table was next to the window that looked out onto the exercise yard. Joe watched snow drifting slowly down into the courtyard, sugaring the ground and the side walls and the turrets and the Gothic outlines of the chapel to a smooth roundness that made the place look more like a story book castle than a prison. He turned to face Jan, who had wedged herself against the radiator that ran under the window.

208

'Apart from who was there tell me what it was like.'
She warmed her hands round her thick tea cup.
'It was good. Well, I don't know how you figure funerals but I
thought it was good. The old minister feller must have talked to
people in the nursing home about Charles Frederick. I don't
think he knew him very well personally but he made up a nice little
speech about him. And it's a real lovely old churchyard. It's not
like American cemeteries where everybody's laid out in rows. All
the graves are here, there and everywhere and they're different
shapes and sizes and a lot of them are old and all green with moss.
It's real quaint.'
Joe rubbed condensation off the window.
'I've seen it. Dad took me there a couple of times when he was
able to walk better. I knew he always fancied finishing up there.'
He dipped a biscuit in his tea and nibbled at it.
'Whereabouts is he buried.'
'He's over by the long wall away from the church. The grave's
very close to one of those old trees with knotty trunks.'
'A yew tree.'
'I guess so.'
He carefully folded the wrapper around the remains of his bar of
chocolate and tucked it in his pocket.
'Funny thing that. Dad was a pacifist all his life and he winds up
buried next to a little armaments factory.'
She raised her eyebrows.
'Don't follow you, Joe.'
'The yew tree. The English long bow was mostly made of yew.
And some king, might have been Henry the Second, ordered
yews to be planted in all churchyards. So they'd have a good
supply of yew for long bows when he was raising new armies.'
She tapped the side of his head.
'That was a pretty roundabout bit of thinking, our Joe.'
'Suppose so. What's to be on the gravestone.'
'They'll make it plain. Just his name, the date he was born and the
date he died. Like he wanted.'
'Fine.'
He grinned and pointed his finger at her.
'We could have put an obituary on it from that old joke he used to
tell.'

'What was that.'

'Dad had a lot of these old-fashioned sort of jokes he used to tell. One was about these two blokes who lived in the same place and all their lives they hated each other and they competed in everything. They were always trying to be one up on each other and win out over the other one. Finally one of them dies and to show that he's still sort of winning he has put on his gravestone *Snug as a bug in a rug*. A while after the other bloke dies and is buried next to the first bloke and on his gravestone it says *A bloody sight snugger than that other bugger*.'

Jan touched his hand.

'It is an old-fashioned joke.'

'He was an old-fashioned sort of feller.'

Joe seemed to go into a sulk. After a long silence he said loudly 'I suppose you think I should have asked permission to go to Dad's funeral.' Jan avoided looking directly at him.

'They might have let you. I did enquire and they said sometimes prisoners were allowed out to attend funerals of close relatives.' He sipped at the remains of his tea and smacked the cup hard back into its saucer.

'Why do you think I didn't. Ask for permission.'

'I'm not sure, Joe. It was up to you.'

'Christ knows I wanted to be there.'

'I guess I thought you didn't want to ask any favours of the prison people. Something like that.'

'No. Nothing like that.'

'I'm sorry if I misunderstood. Tell me why.'

Joe sat with his hands clasped in his lap, staring at the table. When he finally spoke, his voice cracked. 'I suppose it's because I'm weak, really. There are some things I can't face. I wanted to go to Dad's funeral. I wanted it a lot. But when I go out of here it's got to be for good. I can't face the idea of going out of here for any reason and then coming back in. Sounds feeble, I know, but I think that would sort of finish me off. If I went outside and had to come back in. I'm sorry.'

Jan reached across and ruffled his hair.

'Don't be sorry, Joe. I sure as hell can understand you feeling like that. When you come out we'll go and see Dad's grave. We'll take him a big bunch of flowers. That won't be long. Time's moving on.'

210

Joe brightened suddenly.

'Yes. It won't be long now.'

Jan smiled.

'That's another old joke.'

'What is.'

'The phrase. It won't be long now. In an American joke that's what the Rabbi says at the ceremony of circumcision.'

Joe clapped his hands.

As they started to move from the table at the end of visiting time, a couple came across to them and the young man spoke nervously.

'Joe, I wonder if you'd let me introduce my wife to you.'

Joe patted his shoulder.

'Betty, this is Joe Telford. He's the one that I told you about, who helped me a lot.'

Joe shook hands with a schoolgirlish-looking woman and said 'Softy, this is my friend Janis Bragg. Jan, this is Betty Evans.'

There were more handshakes and Betty Evans murmured that she was very grateful to Joe for all he had done for her husband. Jan asked Betty where she came from and Betty said near Scarby and that she came in by bus. It was settled that Jan would give her a lift back home. They arranged to meet outside and as the couple parted, Jan turned to Joe and whispered 'You called him Softy.'

'Well, that's his name. What we call him in here.'

'Why.'

'Well he is a bit of a softie. He cries a lot and sometimes he just sits down and keeps saying I want to go home over and over again.'

'Isn't that a bit harsh. Calling him Softy.'

'I never thought. It's just what he's called.'

Jan kissed him and as she moved to the door, Joe shouted after her 'Be careful with your driving, with the snow' before joining the end of the line of prisoners who were disappearing through the door to the left of the counter.

Joe looked up from the letter he was writing, his attention caught by a swelling in the noise of talk in the corridor, outside the cell. It was as if everyone was suddenly speaking faster and louder. He

211

looked across at Wiggsy, who was squatted on his bed reading a newspaper.

'Lot of noise out there.'

'Summat must have stirred 'em up.'

He watched Wiggsy hold the newspaper close to his eyes then further away, canting it at an angle.

'Sure you don't need glasses, Wiggsy. You seem to have a bit of bother with the paper.'

Wiggsy clumsily refolded the paper to another page.

'Nah. Nothing to do with eyesight. I'm a poor reader. Have trouble making out the words.'

Joe broke off a square of chocolate from his bar and sucked on it.

'They've got reading classes. Why don't you go.'

'You feel daft. Like a little kid. Sittin' in rows learnin' your ABCs.'

'Be worth the bother.'

Wiggsy put his finger on the line he was reading and moved it along, from word to word.

Arnold trotted into the cell, levered himself onto the top bunk and sat cross-legged, looking down at them, breathing hard, eyes shining.

'You haven't heard.'

'Heard what.'

'Got it from Bertie Manners. Just how it happened. Everybody's talking about it.'

'Talking about what.'

'Randall. They got to him. Smashed his bollocks.'

Joe fiddled with his pen, put it down on the letter and clasped his hands behind his neck.

'I thought he was a forty-three. So they couldn't get at him.'

'He was but they were smart. Moultrie and two of his mates. They get this fake message to Randall that he was wanted in the hospital. He believes it and starts across. They jump him by the kitchen. Jam a flour bag over his head so he can't see who's got him and spread him out on the floor. Moultrie puts his boot into his balls half a dozen times and stamps on his prick for good measure. They say it's all just pulp now. So, how about that. Finished his child molestin' days for him. They reckon the medic might just as well chop it off for what good it is. Screws are rushin'

212

about pretending they want to find out who did it and they reckon some of the sex offenders won't come out of their cells, they're that frit.'

Arnold stopped speaking and stared at Joe.

'What's up with you.'

'Nothin'.'

'There fuckin' is. You look sour as hell. Aren't you pleased Randall got what he deserved.'

Joe shuffled paper and pen round the table.

'I'm not sure anybody deserves that.'

'Don't talk fuckin' soft. You heard what he did to them two little girls. Maulin' 'em about. One of 'em nearly died. And you want him bloody pampered.'

'It's not a question of pampering. He was sent to prison. That's his punishment.'

'And it's nothin' like enough. They should castrate buggers like him and if they won't do it, we'll attend to it. That's the ticket, isn't it Wiggsy.'

Wiggsy folded his newspaper and tucked it under his pillow.

'It was bound to happen. You could see it comin'.'

'And a bloody good thing too. You agree, soft-hearted Joe.'

'No.'

'Listen, Telford. There's lots of blokes in this nick with little kids. You think they want the likes of bloody Randall walkin' about out there. After their kids.'

'Mutilation stopped being a punishment in England a long time ago.'

'All right, clever bugger. But if I were you I'd keep your trap shut about being nice to molesters. Somebody might decide to sort you out.'

He lay back on his back, muttering to himself. Later, he chuckled and said 'Anyway, that message was true enough. He was wanted in the hospital.' Joe tried to go back to his unfinished letter but found he had nothing to write.

Delicately, the external examiner smoothed his forehead, leaned across to the internal examiner and spoke in a half-whisper. Jan sat cuddling the awkward bulk of the bound volume of her thesis in her lap and staring at the bristly pig in a coat of arms wrought in the wooden panelling of the wall facing her. She wondered if the owner liked having a bristly pig in his coat of arms.

She caught the phrase 'Very generous of you' muttered by the internal examiner. The external examiner clicked his teeth and said 'Miss Bragg, I stand by my contention that it is both customary and good scholarship to give page numbers in book references but since your supervisor did not, it seems, insist, we'll let the point rest there.' Jan ducked her head and said 'Thank you.'
'Now, let us return to our muttons.'
He consulted his notes, waving his pen above them, before underlining a point, heavily.
'If we could consider the section page two hundred and sixteen onwards.'
All three thumbed their copies of the thesis to page two hundred and sixteen.
'What we have here is a relatively lengthy examination of the writings of one Telford. I have some minor reservations about the commentary itself but I confess that I am primarily intrigued by the extended treatment. I have been able to trace only one or two passing references to Telford's work in the general literature of the area. Hence my puzzlement as to why you choose to make him something of a centrepiece.'
Slowly, Jan turned the pages of her thesis, scowling.
'I thought I had answered that question. In the thesis. In commenting on Telford's work. I imagined I was making a point by point case for taking it seriously. Paying attention to it.'
The external examiner furrowed his brow, pulled his copy of the thesis off the desk and balanced it on his knee.
'Certainly your commentary has points of interest. I'm not denying that. But the fact remains that Telford is hardly mainstream.'
Jan closed her copy of the thesis and hugged it to her.
'Maybe that's a fault in mainstream.'
'I'm not sure I take your point. What does it mean. A fault in mainstream.'
'I thought the whole point of research was to avoid repeating pat judgements. Go beyond standard and conventional sources.'

214

'Indeed it is. But we still have to distinguish between major and minor sources, do we not.'

'And in this section I examine the possibility that Telford is a major rather than a minor source. Particularly since, unlike academics such as us, who simply discourse on the topic from our armchairs, he has worked in democratic collectives and writes from gut-level experience.'

The external examiner sighed and peered again at his notes.

'Let me put another point to you. Your thesis explicitly deals with the syndicalist tradition in Britain. Yet Telford, although British, seems to be much more in the continental tradition. He sets syndicalism in the context of elaborate political and social theory, rather than seeing it as a purely industrial venture.'

Jan's voice sharpened.

'True. And maybe that makes him an important voice in a British tradition which has been starved of political thought and is shit scared of ideology.'

The external examiner looked towards the internal examiner who shrugged his shoulders. He flicked through the pages of the thesis and spoke without looking up.

'I seem to have run into something of a storm, though why escapes me. Shall we leave it that this section of your thesis provides a source for those who wish to explore the byways, as well as the highways, of syndicalist writing. Now, if we turn to page two hundred and forty we can address ourselves to the tangled web of co-operative financing.'

Tully hovered by the table, smiling nervously down at Joe. He started to put his hand out but took it back when Joe made no move. He shuffled his feet and said 'It's very good of you to see me. To let me visit you.'

Joe pointed to the chair on the other side of the table.

'You may as well sit down.'

Tully slipped onto the chair and sat with his hands clasped in his lap.

'I'm very grateful.'

'Yes.'

'It's my last chance, really. To speak to you. I've got a new job. In America. In California. I am going to work on computer language translation programs. There's a big future in it. In on the ground floor. I'm flying out next week. Long-term contract.'

'Aye.'

'I appreciate you letting me talk to you. All things considered. It's very generous of you.'

Joe nodded.

'Janis still won't talk to me. She shouted at me but she won't talk to me. She called me a Judas.'

'You surprised.'

'Not really. I had hoped but I suppose it's not surprising.'

Joe patted the empty table top.

'Visitors usually get tea and wads and so forth.'

Tully looked startled.

'I'm sorry. I didn't think. What shall I get.'

'You'll need a tray. Get whatever you want and for me you can get a milky tea, a bar of fruit and nut chocolate, the big one, twenty cigarettes any brand and I think I'll have a fruit pie. One of the ones in silver tinfoil.'

Tully started towards the counter. Joe called him back and made him repeat the order. When he returned with the loaded tray, Joe pocketed the cigarettes and put the fruit pie and the bar of chocolate next to his tea.

'You can sit down again.'

Tully fiddled with his teacup, spilled tea into the saucer and poured it back into the cup.

'I suppose I really came to say I'm sorry.'

'For shopping me.'

'Yes. I'd like to try and explain.'

Joe bit into his fruit pie.

'Go ahead.'

'I'm not sure I can. It might sound silly. It seemed to make sense at the time but looking back is different.' He cleared his throat. 'You see, when Evelyn told me about you and her going to Blackpool we had this row. It just went on and on. Got very nasty. No holds barred. Saying all sorts of things. I said she'd betrayed me and she kept on about how good you were. In bed. She compared us. How mature you were, compared with me. I told

216

her to shut up but she wouldn't stop. She kept giving details. I tried to get her to be quiet but it only seemed to make her think of more things to say. I slapped her and she humiliated me more. She called me this name.'

He picked up his teacup and held it, without drinking from it.

'What name was that.'

He licked his lips.

'She said I was a prickless little shit.'

'So.'

'I walked out of the house. I just wandered round the streets and more and more I got it into my head that it was you that humiliated me. On purpose. Deliberately. It was all twisted up in my mind. So I decided to get even with you. I went into a phone box and rang up the police and told them. I was in this sort of rage, so I didn't really think about what I was doing. If she hadn't gone on about how it was with you and her, I would never have done it. I suppose I was jealous.'

'Seems a bit like it.'

'I couldn't help myself.'

Joe pulled the last of the tinfoil away from the remains of his fruit pie.

'That's your explanation.'

'I knew it was wrong as soon as I'd done it. I just stood there frozen. I knew I shouldn't have done it. It was her saying about men and boys.'

Joe finished his fruit pie and peeled back the paper on his chocolate. Tully scratched viciously at his forehead.

'It was an impulse really. But I couldn't do anything to take it back.'

'Impulses are like that.'

'I felt frozen.'

'You said that.'

Tully flushed and looked down at the table.

'Of course, if I'm honest, I was a bit frozen with fear. I was sure when they got you, you'd tell them about me. To get your own back on me. I sort of went into hiding. I was terrified. Waiting for the police to come and pick me up. My career would have been finished.'

He looked up and stared at Joe, blinking.

'Why didn't you, Joe. Why didn't you tell them about me.'

'I wouldn't give 'em the satisfaction.'

'I see.'

'I'm not sure you do but it doesn't matter.'

'I am very grateful to you, Joe. For not telling them about me. After what I'd done to you.'

'It wasn't for you.'

'All the same.'

Their talk dwindled away and Joe pointed to his empty teacup. 'I could do with a refill.'

After he had fetched the tea, Tully wriggled in his chair and opened and closed his mouth several times, before saying 'Still, you did know Evelyn was my girl. You could have respected that. You didn't have to do what you did with her, behind my back. She wasn't naturally promiscuous, till you started. You must admit I had a right to be upset, at what you did. Very upset.'

'You reckon.'

'Yes, I do.'

Slowly, Joe tapped his spoon against cup and saucer. He seemed to be listening to the different tones given out by the pottery.

'Do you know what solidarity is.'

'Of course.'

'What is it.'

'It's acting together. In trade unions. The Poles took it as their name.'

'It's a bit more than that.'

'If you want a dictionary definition.'

'It's a kind of loyalty that working people try to have to each other. It doesn't depend on whether you like your mates or what they've done to you personally. It's just that if you're going to fight exploitation you have to stand by each other. Same as soldiers in a regiment. For the cause, if you like. If you don't do that, there's no hope for rebellion. If you let personal feelings divide you, the powers that be will roll right over you.'

'So why did you take Evelyn away from me.'

Joe went back to tapping his spoon on his cup and saucer. After a while he looked up at Tully and said 'We don't have to sit it out to the end of visiting time, you know. If there's nothing else you want to say.'

218

Tully looked towards the door he had come in by.

'Not really. I just wanted to say I was sorry for what happened.'

'OK.'

Tully stood up, hesitated and said 'Do you hold it against me.'

'What the actress said to the bishop when they were dancing.'

'What.'

'She said I know I'm making it hard for you but don't hold it against me.'

'Do you forgive me.'

Joe put his head on one side.

'How do you feel about yourself.'

'Myself.'

He looked down at his feet.

'I'm not sure. It was the wrong thing to do. I admit that. But I did have a grievance. I mean anybody could understand why I did it.'

'That's fine then.'

Tully looked vaguely round the room.

'It was a big effort to come here. To see you. In prison.'

'I reckon it would be.'

'I shan't see you again. With going to America. California.'

'I don't suppose you will.'

'I hope things go well for you.'

'Thanks.'

'Will you shake hands.'

Joe tilted his chair back, so that he could look up at Tully more easily.

'What would that mean.'

'I don't know. I'd like to.'

'You're a silly bugger.'

Tully held out his hand, Joe muttered 'If it please you' and shook it.

After Tully had left, Joe sat a while, sipping his tea, before pocketing his chocolate and signalling to a prison officer that he wanted to go back to his cell.

It turned out to be a false alarm when I got there. Some sort of polyp they can deal with easily. But it was great to see how my fond and doting (that's right for parents isn't it) cheered up when the threat to Dad was

lifted. I wandered round the old Virginia mansion and everything
seemed warm and familiar yet curiously remote, nothing to do with my
life. Kinda like a film you saw long ago and raved about but now it's a
distant image. Dad, god bless him, made a mighty fuss of me and even
got around to hinting that when you come out of prison he would (for my
sake, you understand) find you a job with HV International or some
other of his corporations. It was a helluva task trying to explain to him
why you were unlikely to settle down as a regular guy, forty-second
vice-president in charge of paper clips, with a button-down mind and a
Florida sun tan. Still, the offer's there, old son. Savour it. But it's nice to
be back in my own castle. Re-doing the hall in no mercy lime. How's that
grab you.

And you make me mad, child, feeling sorry for Tully. Never mind
how pathetic he looked. I know his kind of shitty little ratfink. He'll do
fine for himself. Not to worry. Ten-fifteen years from now he'll be living
high off the hog. Split-level ranchhouse with guitar-shaped swimming
pool, analyst, plastic blonde wife, barbecues famous throughout Silicon
Valley for their real radical talk. Yeah, man, far out. So don't you waste
your sympathy, sweet Joe. I'll tell you what I wish for Tully when I see
you – the censor lad would cross it out if I put it in a letter.

Joe, TIME IS A MOVING ON. To the day of Jubilo. I am making
preparations for us. Think you'll like. I've got the summer term off as a
sabbatical so if you like we could stay at my place Easter, through
summer term through summer vac. We could holiday at will with plenty
of time for you to ponder your book and me to work on some publication
from my PhD thesis. But also, it shall be sloth, self-indulgence, sin,
strolling, and all other good things beginning with S. I am going to make
up for all you have endured, I promise.

Pressing the envelope firmly to the table, Joe painstakingly traced
out the address in big block letters, beginning *Dr Janis Bragg*.
Gazing at it with satisfaction, he fancied underlining Jan's title
but reflected that it might embarrass her. He had just sealed the
envelope when Arnold slouched into the cell, squatted on his
bunk and shouted 'All right, you buggers, it's a strip search.'
Wiggsy, who was trying to buff a shine onto his shoes with a piece
of rag, muttered 'Oh shit.'

220

'Why the spin.'

'Two blokes on C wing tried to break out last night. They didn't get far but when they copped 'em they found they'd got all sorts of gear, rope, picklocks, cash, wirecutters, the lot. So big panic about what we've all got hidden away. Governor's frothing at the mouth an' he's ordered an ears to arsehole search, every peter, storerooms, workshops, kitchens, Association Hall, hospital, exercise yard, the lot. We've got to stay banged up till it's over. Fuckin' pain.'

Joe put his letter in plain view, on the centre of the table.

'How long before they get to us.'

'Not long. They've started on this landing. You can hear 'em.'

The three men sat quiet. Listening to the banging of cell doors, the scraping and thudding of shifted furniture and the shouts of prison officers, echoing from the end of the landing.

Wiggsy gave up on his shoes and lay on his back, eyes closed. Joe emptied his locker and arranged the contents on the lid. Arnold paced about, occasionally opening the cell door and peering into the corridor, whistling tunelessly between his teeth. He stopped pacing in the middle of the cell and said 'Wiggsy, you listening.'

'Yeah.'

'Both of you. Tek heed. When the screws get here it had better be three bags full, sir. All the way. They're bloody rattled. Melia on Two was a bit slow and the buggers bounced him off the wall and broke his nose. So no messin' about. Right.'

Wiggsy and Joe nodded agreement. The noises on the landing moved closer.

The cell door was kicked open and the senior of the three officers shouted 'Right, lovely lads, strip. Let's see those beautiful bodies.' Quickly the three prisoners undressed and stood facing the walls of the cell, arms above their heads. Two of the officers began a meticulous search of their clothing while the senior officer stood behind Joe.

'Come on, Telford, don't be coy. Spread your legs.'

Joe edged his feet farther apart. He felt a hand furrow through his hair and poke his ears. His buttocks were forced apart and a rubber-gloved finger was thrust up his arsehole.

'Turn round. Mouth open.'

He looked into Joe's mouth.

'Shut it. Now out on the landing, stand still by the door, no talking. Got it.'

'Yes, sir.'

The officer moved over to Wiggsy. Joe walked gingerly out onto the landing. Soon the other two joined him and they stood naked, side by side, arms folded, facing down into the well of the block, listening to the sound of their cell being ransacked.

When the prison officers came out of the cell the senior man stood in front of them as if he were reviewing a parade.

'Right, my lucky lads. Work is cancelled, exercise is cancelled, Association is cancelled. You stay in your cell till you're called for meals. Got it.'

The prisoners chorussed 'Yes, sir.'

'Back inside.'

They trooped into the cell and the door was locked behind them. Silently, they surveyed the mess. Clothes, personal possessions and bedding were scattered about the floor, postcards and pictures pulled from the walls, mattresses, bunks, tables and chairs upended. Joe hunted through the jumble and found his letter to Janis. It had been slit open. He looked round and murmured 'Searching's all right but they sure do wreck the happy home.' Arnold swung to face him and shouted 'What the fuckin' hell do you care. You're buggering off anyway.'

After checking the time on her wristwatch, Jan looked up and was amazed that, exactly on time, the little door, inset in the huge arched gate of the prison, opened and Joe stepped through it. He was clutching a brown paper parcel and facing the door, speaking to someone she could not see. The door closed and he turned to face the road. She walked unsteadily across to him and they stood, a little apart, regarding each other. Joe dropped his parcel onto the cobblestones, they grabbed hold of each other and hugged fiercely. Jan repeated his name many times and Joe said in a choked voice 'Doctor Bragg, I presume.' They kissed clumsily and finally drew apart and stood facing each other, holding hands, breathless. Jan stammered 'Welcome home, Joe' and Joe said 'It's good of you to meet me.'

'That's a stupid thing to say.'
'Yes, it is.'
'Have you had breakfast.'
'Last of my porridge.'
'Good.'
'That was a pun.'
'Fine.'
'You're very beautiful.'
'You're beautiful too. And don't argue with me. You are beautiful.'
'If you say so.'
'It's a true fact.'
'Have you been waiting long.'
'I love you.'
'Yes.'
Joe picked up his parcel.
'It feels different from visiting days.'
'It is different.'
'Yes. That was a daft thing to say.'
'The car's just across the road.'
Joe looked carefully left and right at the kerb edge and they crossed the road. Jan unlocked the car on the passenger side, tossed his parcel into the back and stood holding the door open, chauffeur-style.
'Like you used to say. Home James and don't spare the horses.'
'It's an old song.'
'Shall we.'
He looked up and down the road and pulled at his ear, as if he were trying to remember something.
'Jan.'
'Yes, Joe.'
'Would you mind, for a minute. There's a little park down the hill. It's not far. If we could go and sit in it. Not for long.'
She kissed him.
'Sure, pet. Let's go.'
   A few yards down the hill, he stopped and gazed back at the prison.
'It's funny. All that time and I've hardly ever seen it from this side.'

223

'Does seem strange.'

'Do you think all the people who walk past it and look up at it really understand what it's about.'

'In what way, Joe.'

'Inside there you've got to be exactly where they put you. It's like you're being held still. So you can't go anywhere. However much you want to. You can't take a little walk when you want to.'

'I guess they don't know what it feels like.'

'That's it. That's it exactly. Everybody's so used to walking about. They can take a day trip to Scarborough if they want to. They don't understand what it's like when you're locked up all the time. They couldn't know. Not while they can move about when they want.'

They walked on down the hill and turned right into the park. She followed him as he wandered about, looking at the flower beds with their scatter of daffodils and crocuses, examining an empty paddling pool, reading the bye-laws inside a glass case, closely observing a cat stalking birds along a privet hedge and shouting 'Scat' when it was about to spring. Finally, he settled on a bench, facing an asphalted space with slide, swings, round-about, see-saw and climbing frame. Intently he gazed at a little girl who, in her turn, was watching boys coming down the slide head first, lying face down. When the slide was clear, she clambered slowly up the steps, cautiously rested her chest and head on the smooth brass and gazed down the slope. Pulling herself up she sat down, face forward, and slid to the bottom. Again she watched little boys seeming to dive down the slide and once more she climbed up the steps. She stood at the top, holding the curved side rails, frowning. Twice boys pushed past her and swanned away down the slope. Tongue sticking out, she lowered herself head first, face down on the slide, gripping the iron sides tightly. Carefully, she inched down until she could jam her feet firmly against the rims. Easing her grip just enough to allow her body to move, she slid very slowly down and stood up grinning. Joe murmured 'Now there's courage for you.' Jan pointed to where a gang of boys had pushed themselves onto each end of the see-saw and were shrieking as they were lifted clear of their seats by each violent bump up and down.

'They do go to town on the teeter-totter.'

'See-saw.'

'Right.'

One of the boys playing football on the neighbouring grass skyed the ball and it bounced towards Joe. He stood, trapped it and sidefooted it back.

'We don't see kids in nick.'

They walked slowly back to the park gates. He stopped, gazed down the hill and said 'I just fancied a short walk round town. Not for long.' She linked arms with him.

'Sure. Saturday morning outing.'

As she turned to face down the hill, he hesitated and she found herself tugging him.

'OK.'

'I wondered if you'd mind if I went on my own. For a little while.'

She kissed him.

'Course not, pet. I've got a book in the car. You take your time and join me when you're ready.'

'Thanks.'

'Have a fine promenade.'

In the town square, Joe found a bench, noted it was donated by Edith Swanson, 1902–1973, and sat on it, absorbed by the flow of traffic and people.

His heart lifted when three buskers, trumpet, accordion and tambourine, shuffled along the gutter opposite, noisily beating out 'When the Saints Go Marching In'. He scurried over and put a coin in the tambourine man's hat and followed them, till his attention was caught by a self-service café. He walked back along the road to a newsagent, bought a paper and settled to read it over a cup of tea in the café. He was studying a map-illustrated article on local country walks when a big tear splashed down onto the newspaper. He smiled, left the paper on the table for someone else to read and set off back to the car.

Jan cuddled the breakfast crockery into the kitchen and stacked it next to the supper plates of the night before. Back in the living room she contemplated Joe, who was sitting in a basket chair, gazing out of the French windows, books and bits of notepaper scattered at his feet.

'Want another cuppercorfee.'

He grunted.

'Is that a yes grunt or a no grunt.'

'A no grunt.'

'OK.'

She settled at the large dining table, books, notepad and coloured pens laid out, the heavy-bound volume of her PhD thesis propped up in front of her. For an hour she wrote steadily, sometimes humming or muttering to herself. Joe dozed, the basket chair creaking from time to time as he changed position. Once she said 'You working, Joe' and he murmured 'Thinking great thoughts.' Occasionally, she crossed to the bookcase to rummage around for a text.

She rose and did a few stretching exercises, groaning dramatically. Walking to the fruit bowl, she said 'Apple, orange or banana.' Joe said 'Apple' and she threw one across, took one for herself and went and sat down next to him, propping her feet up on his lap.

'How's my favourite ex-con.'

He bit into his apple and considered the question.

'Fair to middlin'.'

She smiled to herself.

'Going to fish for a compliment, sonny boy.'

'Fish away.'

'How does it feel to be in bed with a beautiful lady every night, after all that celibate time in the lousy old jailhouse.'

He patted her ankles and stared up at the ceiling.

'It's like the difference between living in a cold house and living in a warm house.'

'That'll do. You fancy a compliment.'

'Like what.'

'The other night. It never happened to me before. When I woke to find you already inside me. Waking up to find I was being made love to. It was . . .'

'Was what.'

'I dunno. Wonderful.'

'I'm glad. I thought you might feel I'd been a bit sneaky.'

226

'No. Just very loving.'

They watched blackbirds bullying their way to first pickings in the breadcrumbs that a neighbour was scattering over her lawn. Jan complained at him for eating the core of his apple and he said it was the best part.

'How's carving up the thesis going.'

'Mighty fine. I've finished the first draft of the Worker Management article. Like to see the conclusion.'

'Would.'

She fetched two sheets of manuscript from the table. He read them, plucking at his bottom lip and nodding.

'Bloody good. Ideas are packed in a bit tight, though.'

'The journal has a five thousand word limit on articles. Can't afford to spread out.'

'Take a bit out of the middle and lengthen this part. Conclusions are about the only thing people take any notice of.'

'Think about it. Ready for coffee yet.'

'Sure.'

Over coffee they talked about the reviews of Jan's book on the Wobblies, till she pointed to the scatter of notepaper on the floor.

'How's the life and times of Joe Telford coming along.'

'Bit slow.'

'Gotta speed you up, old son. Month gone by. Time the great work was taking shape.'

'I've done bits and bobs.'

'Can I see.'

He picked up one of the books, fiddled through loose sheets of paper tucked into the back and handed her a scribbled page. She turned to the window light to read it.

When I was a boy, in the village, we used to play a game called Rally Can Coe. I can only guess at the spelling since I never saw the words written down. We played it in late autumn and winter evenings because it needed shadows and darkness to hide in. We would split into two equal sides, maybe seven or eight in each, one hunters and the other quarry. A tin can was put in the middle of the road opposite a street lamp. We always chose a place with lots of walls, ginnels and open backs for dodging and hiding. The quarry gang were given a minute to scatter and hide. The hunters left one boy, as guard, by the can and the rest went off to capture the quarry. If they spotted, chased and tigged one of the quarry

227

*he was a prisoner. He was taken back to the can and by the rules he must
stay in prison – within ten paces of the can – until he was freed. He could
be freed if another member of his gang crept up to the prison, rushed in
and touched him. Then they both ran off straight away, before they could
be touched by the lad who was guarding the prison. If one of the quarry
managed to kick over the can, all the prisoners were immediately free
and could run off. The game could go on a long time with lads being
captured, freed and recaptured till the hunters had got everyone in. My
memories of the game are to do with terror and excitement. Crawling
through the darkness, alongside a garden wall, trying to reach a point
near enough to the can to make a sudden dash at it. And all the time my
heart thudding for fear the guard would catch me.*

Jan pulled a strand of hair down and chewed it.

'What's a ginnel.'

'Sort of a tunnel between terraced houses. So you can get
through to the back without having to go round to the end of the
terrace.'

Joe raised his eyebrows.

'Any good.'

'It's fascinating.'

'Thanks.'

She held out the page.

'Only I was wondering when you'd get into the political life and
times of Joe.'

He took it back from her and looked at it.

'I suppose I have got a bit buried in my childhood. Not sure why.
It's just where my mind turns to. I start to think and I think of
when I was a lad.'

'Maybe you have to work through it. Before you can take up the
main theme.'

'Could be.'

He tucked the sheet of paper back inside the book.

The phone rang and to Joe it sounded like talk of university
matters, full of phrases like 'admission system' and 'reserve list'.
Jan put down the phone and stood in the middle of the room,
hands on hips. She announced loudly 'I have an idea. I have a
great idea.'

'Such as.'

'Keeping it secret till I come back. Be a surprise. It needs some

228

shopping. I'll be gone about an hour and I'll come back like Father Christmas. You be all right.'

'Fine.'

She scurried round collecting coat, car keys, handbag and carrier bag, kissed Joe several times and repeated the instruction that he was to make himself a sandwich if he got hungry.

After she had gone Joe took the page of manuscript out of the book, read it through and added a note about how you often planned with another lad for one of you to distract the guard, while the other freed the prisoners and the one who distracted the guard often got caught. Later, he put on a tape of Lionel Hampton, followed by one of Jack Buchanan, and was listening to Fats Waller when he heard the car pull into the drive. Hastily he switched off the hi-fi and when Jan came in he was sitting in the basket chair sorting out bits of notepaper.

From the hall she shouted hello, took off her coat and appeared clutching a bulging carrier bag. She brought it across to him, patted his head and tipped a cascade of glossy brochures onto the floor. 'There you are, sweetheart, the world at your feet.' She flopped into the chair across from him. 'France, Germany, Italy, Greece, Yugoslavia, you name it. Even Andorra. They've got a wine festival. Continental canal trips, luxury coach trips round nine capitals in eleven days, back to nature in a falling-down farmhouse in the Dordogne, sun-baked beaches on Greek islands, old battlefields in Belgium, museums everyplace. Yer takes yer pick. Eat and drink our way round Europe. What you think. Down the Rhine on a steamboat. Your wish is my command. Speak oh great wise chief.'

She stopped, a little out of breath.

'A holiday.'

'We started into this writing lark too soon, love. Much too soon. It was my fault. I should have thought. You come out of prison and I lock you up here. Not fair atall atall.'

'We've been out a lot. For jaunts.'

'Yes but we need a real break. Lots of time in a completely new place, exploring, pleasing ourselves. Lap of luxury. Sightseeing. You telling me all the history.'

He picked up a brochure and smoothed his hand over a cover picture of the Piazza del Campo in Siena.

'There's a lot to choose from.'

'Don't be intimidated by all the glossy package travel, pet. If we want to, we can take the car across to France and drift around, anywhere we fancy. If we find a place that appeals we lie up for a while. Be free as a bird.'

'Be expensive.'

'Be worth it. Anyway, my birthday's coming up soon. Pop can make it a present.'

He picked up another brochure and studied an aerial view of Amsterdam. She watched him, intently.

'We don't have to settle on anything now. We can cuddle up with our fantasies and sort something out in the next week or so. Whatever you feel like.'

'You want to go soon.'

'Sooner the better.'

He held a brochure in each hand, looking vaguely at each in turn before dropping both of them back on the pile. He rubbed his palms on his trousers and sat upright in his chair.

'As it happens, I was thinking of going home for a bit.'

'Home.'

'Yes.'

'Back to Scarby. Hannover Street.'

'Yes.'

Jan smiled uncertainly and said 'If that's what you want' then added 'Do I get to come.'

He flapped his hands.

'If you specially want to. I thought, perhaps, on my own, just for a bit.'

'How long is a bit.'

'Not sure. Month or two. We could see.'

She stood up, pushed the chair away from her and walked slowly round the room before sitting down again, at the dining table.

'How long have you had this idea.'

'Not long.'

'For God's sake why.'

'Sort things out. Might get some of the book written.'

'That'll be the day.'

'You never know.'

'It's what you want.'

230

'I think so.'

'You're not happy here.'

'It's been grand here. You know it has. It's just that I'd like to be home for a while.'

She chewed at her thumbnail.

'If it's what you want. We'd better sort out some housekeeping money. So you can manage.'

'I'll be all right.'

'How.'

'Pritchard will give me my old job back.'

'You can't be sure.'

'I think he will.'

'He might have got somebody else.'

'I don't think so. I talked to him on the telephone.'

Jan got to her feet, her face flushed.

'When. When did you talk to him.'

'Not long ago.'

'When.'

'A week or so back. More or less.'

'Damn it, Joe. You've been planning this all along. You never intended to live with me. Did you. You've been conning me all the time.'

Joe's voice trembled and he held his hands out palms outwards.

'It's not like that. I love you.'

'I'll bet.'

'I do.'

'In your fashion, I suppose.'

'You don't understand.'

'You're damn right, I don't. What the hell have you got up there that you haven't got here.'

'It's just that I haven't been alone for a long time.'

Jan sat down and fumbled with the papers on the table, squaring them off, closing the thesis and piling it with the other books. She rested her head on her arms and stared at the wall opposite. When she spoke, she sounded weary.

'Shall I drive you over.'

'I can get the bus.'

'Are your things packed.'

'No.'

231

'Amazing. You'd better pack them.'

Joe hesitated, mumbled something inaudible and went into the kitchen. He came back with a sheet of brown paper and a ball of string and put them on the end of the dining table. Jan leaned across and swept them onto the floor.

'For Christ's sake. Do you have to carry things round in parcels.' She stamped upstairs and returned with a big canvas holdall. 'Use that.'

In silence Joe moved from living room, to bathroom, to bedroom, collecting his belongings and stuffing them into the holdall. As he finished collecting his clothing from the bedroom, Jan shouted from below.

'There's two new shirts I bought for you, on top of the wardrobe. Pack them.'

Standing by the hallway, in his raincoat, the holdall clutched in his hand, he said 'I'll be going then.'

'You've got everything.'

'I think so.'

'The shirts are drip dry. They don't need ironing.'

'Right.'

He started to turn, hesitated and said 'I'm sorry, Jan.'

'Are you.'

'Yes. I do love you.'

'You said that.'

'It's true.'

'But you don't want to live with me. That's too much of a trial.' She stared at him, crossed the room, kissed him and turned him towards the hall.

'You'd better get your show on the road.'

He mumbled 'Yes' and left the house.

Jan stood back from the front bay window so that she could see out but not be seen from the outside. She watched Joe walk slowly down the estate road. Twice he turned and half-raised his hand but she stood unmoving, until he had disappeared from sight.

Briskly she walked into the kitchen, ran hot water into the sink and pushed the pile of dirty crockery into it. Overusing the washing up liquid she scrubbed savagely, jamming soapy plates into the rubber rack on the draining board. She winced each time

232

she plunged her hands into the water, which was too hot. Jabbing viciously at a streak of hardened egg yolk, she banged the plate against the side of the sink and broke it in two. She shouted 'Shit' and tears streamed down her face. Blindly, holding onto a towel rail, she raged in a choked voice. 'You bastard, Joe Telford. You're trying to bugger up both our lives. You stupid son of a bitch. What's the point. What's the bloody point. Going to hide away in your pig of a shack. Makes no sense. Not even a proper goddamn road to it. Well you just wait, you bugger. You don't get rid of me like that. I'll sort you out. You bloody moron. We belong together. You hear me.'

Dabbing her face with a tea towel she shuffled out of the kitchen and stood hiccuping in the middle of the living room. She caught sight of the pile of travel brochures on the floor and moved to pick them up. Then she kicked at them, stumbled to the far side of the room and dropped down onto the settee, her head on the cushions, her feet resting on the arm. She sniffed, wiped her arm across her nose and waited for the hiccuping to stop. After a while she said aloud 'It can't end like this, Joe. There's too much between us.'

Later she turned onto her side and fell into a light sleep.

As he crossed the plank bridge over the ditch, Joe looked up the hill, at Hannover Street, and began to think of names for it. *Dead End Dump. Mouldy Mews.* How about *Piffling Place.* As he reached the top of the hill, he murmured *Truncated Terrace.*

His knock at the Hursts' door was answered by Nelly. Her face lit up and she pulled him through into the living room, squeaking 'Albert, Joe's back. He's back.'

Albert said 'Evenin'' but did not look up from the newspaper he was reading. Joe touched his shoulder and said 'Evening Albert.' Nelly fussed over him, patting his arms, pulling his holdall onto the floor, pushing him into an armchair and asking him if he was well, without giving him time to answer. Several times he had to refuse supper on the grounds that he had eaten in Scarby, saying he just wanted to borrow tea, milk and sugar. Nelly scolded him for being in such a rush and vanished into the kitchen.

233

Joe looked towards Albert who raised the newspaper so that it covered his face.

'How are things, Albert.'

'Not bad.'

'You'll have had plenty of water for your reservoir. Just lately. All the rain.'

'Enough.'

'Better than last year. Tricky time that. For a while.'

'Yes.'

Albert turned the page of his newspaper.

'Anything much happening. News. In the paper.'

'Not a lot.'

Joe rested his head on the chair back and studied the picture of Roman gladiators, assembling for combat, that occupied the wall above the mantelpiece.

Nelly came out of the kitchen carrying a large cardboard box which she set down in Joe's lap.

'That'll get you started, lad. There's tea, milk and sugar. I don't think it's the tea you use but it's not bad. And some powdered coffee. There's bread, marge, two eggs and a rasher for your breakfast. Bit of fruit cake. It's shop cake but it's all right. Soap. I've wrapped it so it doesn't taint. A big pasty you can have later, if you fancy, just needs heatin'. Some toilet roll, dust cloths and soap powder. Did some cleanin' on the house a while back but it'll need a little going over. We had your chimney done in March, when ours was seen to. Thought you'd want. Now you give us a shout if there's anything you need.'

Joe stood up, tucked the cardboard box under his arm, picked up the holdall and kissed the top of Nelly's head. He said 'Bless you, love, that's a real help.'

She followed him out of the front door and spoke in a half-whisper.

'You'll not have to mind Albert, love. He was upset about the prison business. Took funny about it. Being prison. But he'll get over it, now you're back. I'll see he does. It's only a mood.'

'Hope so. Thanks again for the stuff.'

'Say if you need owt else.'

Inside his own house, he dropped the holdall at the bottom of the stairs and dumped the box on the kitchen table, sniffing at the smell of dust. He lit the fire, which was set, hung his raincoat in the hall and jacket on a chairback. Standing for a while, arms folded, he looked out of the front window at dusk settling on the narrow valley. He sighed, wound up and set the alarm clock on the mantelpiece, crossed to the kitchen and put away the contents of the cardboard box. He heard the faint sound of voices and putting his ear to the wall he caught the sharp tones of Nelly Hurst saying something, at length, about poor Joe Telford, only occasionally halted by a brief rumble from Albert. Ear pressed to the wall, he found himself looking at his rack of home made bottles of red wine. He picked one out and checked the label, which dated it back over two years. Carefully he uncorked the bottle, poured a glass and let it stand for a few minutes while he took the holdall upstairs and stowed the contents away in bedroom and bathroom. Back in the kitchen, he sipped slowly at the wine and smacked his lips. Carrying glass and bottle back into the living room he reflected that going to prison had the advantage of allowing your wine to mature properly.

He was standing, back to the fire, pouring a third glass of wine, when the end of a stick appeared above the front windowsill and tapped on the glass. He put his glass and bottle down by the armchair, slid the bottom window up and looked out. Albert Hurst was leaning over the wall that separated the two gardens, the stick in his left hand.

'What can I do for you, Albert.'

Albert picked at his nose.

'I remembered how keen you were on the Liverpool football club. Thought they were the best.'

'Still think so.'

'So I thought you might not know they're on telly, tonight. Just started. They're playing some London team.'

'I didn't know, Albert. It's very good of you to tell me. I'll want to watch it.'

'Thought you might.'

'Thanks a lot.'

'It just crossed my mind.'

As Albert turned away, Joe shouted 'Just a second, I've got something you might like to try.'

He hurried through to the kitchen and came back with a bottle of the red wine. Stretching as far to the left of the window as he could he just managed to pass it to Albert, who laid himself across the top of the wall.

'It's turned out very well. Smooth. See what you and Nelly think. It's a bit better than usual.'

Albert brushed dust from the top of the wall off his shirt front and peered at the label on the bottle.

'That's nice of you, Joe. I'll look forward to it.'

'Let me know what you think.'

'I will.'

'See you then.'

'Right.'

Joe shut the window, steered his television stand to a position opposite the armchair, pushed the plug into its socket and switched the set on. He moved behind it to put a few lumps of coal on the fire and brushed his hands on his trousers. From the kitchen, he fetched the slice of fruit cake that Nelly had given him. Lowering himself into the armchair, he picked up his glass of wine and checked that the screen showed football. Propping his feet on the stretchers of the stand, he sipped at his wine and smiled as the Liverpool back line shook itself straight and began to flow forward.